THE BLUE FLOWERS

Also by Raymond Queneau

THE
BLUE FLOWERS

BY RAYMOND QUENEAU

Translated by Barbara Wright

With an afterword by Vivian Kogan

A New Directions Book

This edition published by arrangement with Editions Gallimard, Paris.

This translation of *Les Fleurs Bleues* was originally published clothbound in
1967, by The Bodley Head in the United Kingdom (under the title *Between
Blue and Blue*) and by Atheneum Publishers in the United States. First pub-
lished as New Directions Paperbook 595 in 1985.

Manufactured in the United States of America
Published simultaneously in Canada by Penguin Books Canada Limited

Library of Congress Cataloging in Publication Data

Queneau, Raymond, 1903-1976.
  The blue flowers.
  (New Directions paperbook; 595)
  Translation of: Les fleurs bleues.
  I. Title.
PQ2633.U43F513 1985   843'.912   84-25544
ISBN 0-8112-0945-8 (pbk.)

New Directions books are published for James Laughlin
by New Directions Publishing Corporation,
80 Eighth Avenue, New York 10011

ὄναρ ἀντὶ ὀνείρατος

PLATO

I

On the twenty-fifth of September, twelve hundred and sixty-four, at break of day, the Duke of Auge appeared at the summit of the keep of his castle, there to consider, be it ever so little, the historical situation. It was somewhat confused. A few odd remnants of the past were still lying around here and there, rather messily. On the banks of a nearby gully two Huns were camping; quite near them a Gaul, a Haeduan, perhaps, was boldly immersing his feet in the fresh, running water. On the horizon were outlined the flabby silhouettes of tired Romans, nether Norsemen, old Francs and Christmas Carolingians. A few Normans were drinking calvados.

The Duke of Auge sighed, but nevertheless continued his careful examination of these antiquated phenomena.

The Huns were preparing some steak tartare, the Gaul oise smoking a gitane, the Romans were drawing the Greeks, the Norsemen were snoring, the Francs were looking for their sooterkins, and the Carolingians were waiting to see whether anyone was concealing any Ossetians. The Normans were drinking calvados.

'So much history,' said the Duke of Auge to the Duke of Auge, 'so much history, just for a few puns and a few anachronisms. I think it's pathetic. Shan't we ever get away from it?'

Fascinated, it was some hours before he stopped watching these rejects refusing to disintegrate; then, for no apparent outward reason, he left his look-out post for the lower levels of the castle, indulging, as he went, his mood, which was bellicose.

He didn't beat his wife, because she was defunct, but he beat

[7]

his daughters, who numbered three; he beat some men-servants, some maid-servants, some carpets, he struck some irons while they were hot, camp, some money, and finally he cudgelled his brains. Immediately afterwards he decided to take a short trip, and go to the capital city, without undue pageantry, accompanied only by his page, Mouscaillot.

He chose from among his palfreys his favourite percheron whose name was Demosthenes, because he talked, even with the bit between his teeth.

'Ah, my good Demo,' said the Duke in a plaintive voice, 'I am right sad and right merancholic.'

'Is it still History?' asked Sthenes.

'It withers all my joy,' replied the Duke.

'Courage, my Lord, courage! Come on up and we'll go for a blow.'

'That was indeed my intention, and something more, besides.'

'What was that?'

'To go away for a few days.'

'I hear thee and rejoice. Where, my Lord, do you wish me to take you?'

'Far, far from here. Here, the mud is made from our flowers.'

'. . . our blue flowers, I know. But more precisely?'

'*You* choose.'

Sthenes, when the Duke of Auge had got up on to his back, made the following proposition:

'What would you say to going and seeing how the work on the church of Notre-Dame is getting on?'

'What!' exclaimed the Duke. 'Haven't they finished it yet?'

'That's what we shall ascertain.'

'If they go on working to rule like that they'll end up by building a mahometory.'

'Why not a buddhoir? A confucianal? A sanct-lao-tsuary? You mustn't get so depressed, my Lord! En route! and at the same time we'll present our feudal homage to the saintly King Louis, the ninth of that name.'

Without waiting for his master's reply, Sthenes started trotting off towards the drawbridge which lowered itself in a functional sort of way. Mouscaillot, who wasn't saying a word, for fear of getting a swipe round the chops with a gauntlet, followed, mounted on Stefan, so named because he was not very chatty. While the Duke was brooding over his resentment and Mouscaillot, following his prudent policy, was persevering in his silence, Sthenes alone went on chatting gaily, and tossing merry quips at the people he saw going by, the Celts with a gallican air, the Romans with a caesarian air, the Norsemen with a nauseating air, the Huns with a honeyed air, the Carolingians with a nartish air and the Francs with a sui generis air. The Normans were drinking calvados.

As they were bowing very low to their beloved suzerain, the yokels were muttering fearsome threats which they knew to be inefficacious and which therefore didn't outstrip the limits of their moustaches, that's if they were wearing them.

Sthenes was going along the highroad at a good pace, and finally held his tongue, as he couldn't find anyone to talk to any more, since the traffic was non-existent; he didn't want to disturb his cavalier, who he felt was dozing off; as Stef and Mouscaillot shared this reserve the Duke of Auge finally fell asleep.

He lived on a barge moored near a big town and his name was Cidrolin. He was served a not very fresh crayfish with glaucous mayonnaise. While he was decorticating the animal's legs with nutcrackers, Cidrolin said to Cidrolin:

'Pretty lousy, this stuff, pretty lousy; Lamélie will never learn to cook.'

He added, still addressing his remarks to himself:

'But where on earth was I going like that, riding a horse? I can't remember. Anyway, that's typical of dreams; I've never ridden a horse in my life. I've never ridden a bicycle in my life, either, but I never ride a bicycle in my dreams and yet I do ride a horse. There must be some explanation, that's obvious. This crayfish certainly is lousy and this mayonnaise is even worse and why don't I learn to ride a horse? In the Bois de Boulogne, for instance. Or even a bicycle?'

'You wouldn't need a driving licence, either,' he is told.

'All right, all right.'

Then the cheese is brought.

Made of plaster.

Some fruit.

Where vilest worms do dwell.

Cidrolin wipes his mug and mutters:

'Another fucking fiasco.'

'Doesn't stop you having your siesta' he is told.

He doesn't answer; his chaise-longue is waiting for him on deck. He covers his face with a handkerchief and he's soon within sight of the walls of the capital city, without bothering about how many days' journey it had been.

'Great,' exclaimed Sthenes, 'we're there.'

The Duke of Auge woke up, with the impression that he'd had a bad meal. This was when Stef, who hadn't said a word since they'd left, felt the need of addressing the company in these terms:

'Alme and inclyte city . . .'

'Silence!' said Sthenes, 'If anyone heard us talking, our good master would be accused of sorcery.'

'Brrr,' said the Duke.

Ditto his page.

'Brrr,' said Mouscaillot.

And to show the proper way for a horse to express himself, Sthenes neighed.

The Duke of Auge dismounted at the Crooked Siren, which a passing troubadour had once recommended to him.

[10]

'Name, Christian names, rank?' asked Martin the hostiler.

'Duke of Auge,' replied the Duke of Auge. 'Joachim yclept and am accompanied by my devoted page Mouscaillot, son of Count d'Empoigne. My horse ys nempned Sthenes, and the other one ys nempned Stef.'

'Residing . . .?'

'Thiarch, near the bridge.'

'Archi-respectable, then, I'd say,' said Martin.

'So I should hope,' said the Duke, 'because I'm beginning to get pissed off with your rotten little questions.'

'Forgive me, my Lord, it is by order of the King.'

'Aren't you going to ask me what I've come to the capital city for, though?'

'No need! My Lord has come to see our whores, who are the most beautiful in the whole of christendom. Our saintly King hates them greatly, but they are ardent participants in the finances of the forthcoming crusade.'

'Thou art in vicius errour, hostiler. I have come to see how the work on the church of Notre-Dame is getting on.'

'The south tower is growing apace, and they are about to start the north one and the gallery connecting them. They are also altering the higher parts to give more light.'

'That's enough!' roared the Duke. 'If you tell me all about it there'll be nothing left for me to do but go back home, and that I woll not.'

'Me neither, so I'll bring your supper incontinent.'

The Duke ate copiously, then he went to bed and slept with a very good appetite.

He hadn't finished his siesta when he was awoken by two nomads calling him from the top of the bank. Cidrolin answered them by signs, but they couldn't have understood that language because they went down the bank to the gang-plank and boarded the barge. There were a male camper and a female camper.

[11]

'Anteheksi,' said the male camper, 'ma nosotros sind eksyk-sissä.'

'A good beginning,' Cidrolin rejoins.

'Capito? Lostes . . . exyxissä . . .'

'A sad fate.'

'The campink site? Lontano? Ons . . . kauaksi . . .'

'He talks well,' murmured Cidrolin, 'but is he speaking vernacular European or neo-Babelian?'

'Aha,' said the male camper, manifesting all the signs of lively satisfaction. 'Do you fairshtayer European?'

'Un poco,' replied Cidrolin, 'but put down your packs, noble strangers, and have a drink before you go.'

'Aha, capito: drink.'

So the noble stranger, beaming with joy, put down his pack and then, disdaining those articles of furniture destined for that usage, squatted on the floor, supplely crossing his legs beneath him. The young lady who was accompanying him did the same.

'Could they be Japanese?' Cidrolin wondered under his breath. 'Their hairs are blonde, though. Maybe they're Aïnos.'

So, turning to the boy:

'Are you by any chance an Aïno?'

'I? No. Me: boy friend of whole world.'

'I see: a pacifist?'

'Jawohl. And what about that drink?'

'Keeps his mind on the essentials, this European.'

Cidrolin clapped his hands and called:

'Lamélie! Lamélie!'

An entrance.

'Lamélie, something to drink for these noble strangers.'

'What?'

'Some essence of fennel, for instance, with some still water.'

An exit.

Cidrolin leant over towards the nomads.

[12]

'Well, my little fledglings, so you're egarrirtes, are you?'

'Lost,' said the girl. 'In the shit.'

'Could you be French, my pet?'

'Not yet: Canadian.'

'And what about that drink?' asked the squatting figure. 'Schnell, let's have one!'

'He's a bit of a bore,' said Cidrolin.

'Oh, he's not a bad guy.'

'And naturally what you're doing you're both going to the camping camp for campers.'

'We're looking for it.'

'You're as good as there. It's along the river, not five hundred yards up-stream from here.'

'Wir sind arrivati?' exclaimed the boy, getting back on to his feet in a single movement. 'Trwah song maytr? Andiamo!'

He put his kit-bag back on his back, a kit-bag which could easily have weighed a ton.

'We're waiting for the essence of fennel,' said the girl, not budging.

'Ouell, ouell.'

He removed his ton of baggage and sat down again as naturally as if the deck had been a lotus.

Cidrolin smiled at the girl and said, as if he were complimenting her.

'Well-trained.'

'Well-trained? Don't get you.'

'Well, yes; just raise a finger or give him a look and he obeys.'

She shrugged her shoulders.

'You're a bit short on the grey matter,' she said. 'He's staying because he's free, not because he's well-trained. If he were well-trained he'd already be on his way to the camping camp for campers. He's staying because he's free.'

'There're even some ideas in a little head like that,' murmured

Cidrolin, looking with greater care at the Canadian, and in particular at the blonde down on her thighs, and at the soles of her shoes. 'Well, yes, some ideas . . .'

Whereupon the essence of fennel and the still water got brought. They drank.

'And how do you go nomading?' asked Cidrolin. 'On foot, on horseback, by car? By helicostrike, by bike, by hike?'

'We hitch,' replied the girl.

'You hitch-hike?'

'Of course we hitch-hike.'

'Personally I sometimes travel by hitch-taxi. It's less economical.'

'Pooff, money.'

'How right you are. What d'you think of my essence of fennel?'

'Not bad. Me prefer pure water.'

'It never *is* pure here. The river's the sewer and the tap's chlorine.'

'Wouldn't you like him to sing you something?'

'What for?'

'To thank you.'

'For the essence of fennel?'

'For the welcome.'

'That's nice of you. Thank you.'

The girl turned to the boy and said:

'Sing.'

He fumbled in his equipment and brings out a banjo of minimal proportions whose strings he immediately started to scratch. After a few preliminary chords he opened his mouth and they heard these words:

'I love Paimpol and its cliff, its belfry and its old pilgrimage . . .'

'Where did he learn that?' asked Cidrolin when it was over and he'd thanked the virtuoso.

'In Paimpol, of course,' replied the Canadian.

'How stupid I am,' said Cidrolin, hitting himself on the fore-head. 'I hadn't thought of that.'

The minibanjo returned to the rucksack, the boy readopted a standing position and held out his hand to Cidrolin.

'Gin-couillon Panoo,' he said, 'and ah rivadairchi.'

And to the girl:

'Schnell! Are we going oder aren't we going?'

The girl gets up gracefully and harnesses herself presto.

'Well-trained,' said Cidrolin under his breath.

The nomad protested:

'Nein! Nein! Not drained: free. Sie es libre. Anda al campus omdat sie es libre to andare al campum.'

'I know, I know.'

'Adieu' said the girl, and now it was her turn to hold a hand out to Cidrolin. 'Thanks again and maybe we'll come back and see you if we have time.'

'That's right,' said Cidrolin.

He watched them climb up the bank with all their luggage.

'Got to be tough, for that job,' he murmured.

'Will they come back?' asked Lamélie.

'I don't think so. No, they'll never come back. What'd I have done with them? They've only just gone and I can hardly remember them. They exist, though, and they probably deserve to exist. They'll never come back to get lost in the labyrinth of my memory. It's an unimportant incident. Some dreams seem to be made up of unimportant incidents, you wouldn't remember things of that sort in your waking life, and yet they interest you when you catch them in the morning chaotically shoving them-selves up against the door of your eyelids. Maybe I was dreaming?'

Lamélie didn't have to say yes or no to him; in any case she hadn't waited for the end of this speech.

Cidrolin consulted the clock in the cabin and observed, not without satisfaction, that the episode of the nomads had been only a fairly short interlude in the time he allotted to his siesta and that he could decently resume it for a few more minutes. So he stretched himself out on his chaise-longue and managed to fall asleep again.

II

'What do I behold?' exclaimed the King, who was sitting under his oak tree, 'is not that my well-beloved Auge advancing towards me?'

'The same, Sire,' replied the squireen, bowing very low. 'My respects,' he added.

'I am happy to see you in flourishing health,' said the King. 'How is your little family?'

'My wife is dead, Sire.'

'You didn't kill her, at least? One never knows, with you.'

The King, out of his benevolent indulgence, smiled and the throng that surrounded him only admired him the more.

'Still no heir?' asked the King.

'Alas!' said the Duke. 'I have only my triplets, which, I assure you, is my cross.'

'Talking of crosses,' said the King, 'I'm very glad to see you. We're preparing a new crusade and we're naturally counting on your joining us.'

'Doesn't appeal to me much.'

'Ttt ttt. You mustn't make your mind up until you've heard the thing in detail. In the first place, we shall not be going to Egypt this time (that would be an asserlute waste of time) but we shall set sail for Carthage.'

'That has no greater appeal for me.'

'Carthage? Come come, my well-beloved Auge, even if only for its historic memories . . . Saint Augustine . . . Jugurtha . . . Scipio . . . Hannibal . . . Salammbô . . . don't they mean something to you?'

'Nothing at all, Sire. Me not be an intellectual.'

'Ah Auge, my well-beloved Auge, you really will have to come with me to disembowel some infidels.'

'Nenni, Sire. This time I'll have none of it.'

'You no longer wish to discomfit the worshippers of Mahom?'

'Look, Sire, I have retired to my little castle in the country, there I am bringing up the daughters with which the good Lord has afflicted me, there I nurse, though without sodewynge them, the marsh fevers I brought back from Damietta and other distant colonies, that saintly man my chaplain, the Abbé Onesiphore Biroton, is leading me towards the paths of sanctification, why, Sire, yes, why should I leave my little province in order to be brought back to it the year after salted in a pickling-jar?'

The saintly King sighed.

'In short,' he said, 'you don't want to go and cleave el Mostanser Billah in twain?'

'Let him cleave himself in twain all by himself, Sire, such is my last word.'

'Ah! I can see I'm going to have a great deal of trouble organising this eighth crusade.'

This made the good saint and King quite sad.

'Oh, come,' said the Duke of Auge, 'you'll always be able to find a good fourth part of a hundred nodcocks to accompany you to those distant shores.'

'Indeed I hope so,' said the King with melancholy.

'May I take my leave?'

The King gave his acord.

As he was withdrawing, the corner of the Duke's face became the recipient of a whole shipload of rotten eggs and withered tomatoes; the throng listening to the saintly King holding forth under his oak tree considered that the said saintly King was showing himself to be of culpable weakness in relation to this cowardly vassal who preferred the comfort of his little castle to the hazards of a Christian expedition somewhere around Bizerta; and this all the more as they themselves, borgeis, artisans or vileyns, ran not the slightest risk of seeing themselves despatched to what were formerly Cathaginian shores there to suffer scimitar blows or catch unsodewable diseases.

'Boo, boo, the trollop,' they cried, 'oh the rotten chicken-heart, the shite-a-bed scoundrel, the porcine looby, the whoreson shirker, the lousy patriot, the wicious wild-boar, the rotten ring-worm, the brazen false-heart, the caitiff Paulician, the verminous Jemmy-Jessamy, the lily-livered mange-pot, the ord'rous poltroon, the false-hearted sneaksby who wants to leave the tomb of Lord Jesus in the hands of the pagans and who answers his King back. Long live Louis of Poissy! Boo, boo, the trollop!'

And they went on chucking bleeding cow-pats and truffled turds at the Duke, who finally got annoyed. Drawing his braque-mard he flourished it with such sweeping gestures that he put to flight vileyns, artisans and borgeis, all of whom dispersed rapidly around and about but not without a good deal of trampling on one another, which caused to be slawe a few dozen of them for the repose of whose souls the saintly King later prayed with efficacy.

Nauseated, the Duke made his way towards a bathery to cleanse himself from the residua of the public hostility.

'Ah! the swine,' he muttered, 'there's no freedom any more if the homagers start interfering. He, Louis, hasn't forgotten the services I rendered him at Damietta and Mansura. He knows what a colonial war is, he understands me. He, Louis, he wants to go back: that's his business. He, Louis, he isn't like me, he's a saintly man, we'll end up by seeing his name on the calendar; whereas these homagers booing me, what do they actually want?

To liberate the holy sepulchre? They're not the slightest bit interested. What they want is to see all the noble lords like me disembowelled by the Wogs so that they can invade our castles, drink the claret wine in our cellars and, who knows? Violate our mothers, our wives, our daughters, our maid-servants and our lambs.'

'And our mares,' said Sthenes.

A passer-by started.

'And our mares,' said the Duke out loud.

He leant over in the direction of the individual:

'It was I who said: "and our mares." It was I, d'you hear, homager?'

As the Duke was rolling ferocious eyes, the other replied very politely:

'That dought I not, yf yt please your grace.'

Then he disappeared, scarcely reassured.

'It's high time we left this town,' said the Duke. 'We have seen the work on Notre-Dame, admired the Sainte Chapelle, that gem of gothic art, done the necessary homage to our saintly King, all this is well and good, but I feel that things are going to deteriorate with the population; so, after we have bathed, we shall go and dine in a first-class tavern to cheer ourselves up, and leave immediately afterwards.'

While his clothes were being cleaned and he was simmering in the hot water, the Duke fell asleep.

After shutting the gate behind him, Cidrolin looked to see if there were any inscriptions defiling the fence that separated the sloping ground adjoining the barge from the boulevard. There were none. Having done so he decided to cross the road and go and see how they were getting on with the work in progress opposite. They were supposed to be building a block of flats; for the moment there was only a hole.

Having taken the necessary precautions, Cidrolin found him-

[19]

self safe and sound on the other side of the road. He cautiously approaches the hoarding, on which was stated Danger – Lorry – Exit. At the far end of the site a mechanical shovel is collecting debris from the cellars to fill one of the lorries whose exit is advertised as being so dangerous. White-helmeted men are coming and going. Things are being discharged in a corner. All this must be intelligible to a builder.

A passer-by has come up to Cidrolin; they both watch the lorry getting filled up. When it was full, the lorry climbed up the ramp which took it out of the hole. Cidrolin prudently got out of its way. The moment it was on the level the lorry drove like mad at the boulevard; the passer-by jumped back, to a squealing of brakes.

'Did you see that?' the passer-by, who had gone quite pale, said to Cidrolin. 'That son of a bastard nearly ran me over.'

'He didn't actually do anything of the sort,' replied Cidrolin objectively.

'He did the best he could.'

'You'd been warned. It was written up there: 'Danger – Lorry – Exit.' When I was at school I used to wonder why we learnt to read, now I know: to get out of the way of lorries.'

'Could be, but just suppose that I'd learnt to read too, but a different language from yours. Must I inevitably be run over, then?'

A gentleman riding a mobylette braked suddenly, dismounted, and, leading his vehicle by one ear, came up to them. He was dressed in a long black gown and wearing a sombrero of the same colour with turned-up edges.

'Ad majorem Dei gloriam,' said he, holding out his hand.

'Monsieur doesn't know French,' said Cidrolin.

'Sed tu?'

'I can just about understand it.'

'Good, good.'

He got back into the saddle, rode a short way along the pavement contrary to the regulations, and rejoined the road a little further on, disappearing in the flow of cars.

'As conciliatory as a Father of the Council,' said the passer-by.

Cidrolin yawned.

'Are you sleepy?' asked the passer-by.

'No, I'm hungry. The lunch-hour approaches. I must ask you to excuse me, I'm going to continue my anteprandial walk, the circuit of which I haven't yet completed.'

'I,' continued the passer-by, raising his voice, 'was telling you, you may remember, that I was a foreigner. Do you remember the lorry?'

'Are you one of those nomads?' asked Cidrolin politely.

'I? Far from it. I live in an hotel . . .'

'and I live in that barge . . .'

'a luxury hotel, even . . .'

'a house-boat . . .'

'there's a toilet in the bathroom . . .'

'it's moored . . .'

'a lift . . .'

'I could even have a telephone . . .'

'a telephone in the bedrooms . . .'

'it has a blue number with figures on just like a house . . .'

'you can dial direct to foreign countries . . .'

'it's number twenty-one . . .'

'and on the ground floor there's a bar . . .'

'I could fish, from my bedroom . . .'

'an American bar . . .'

'I could fish, if I fished, but I don't like fishing.'

'You're quite right,' said the passer-by, suddenly becoming interested in what his interlocutor was saying: 'fishing is just as cruel as bull-fighting . . .'

'I'd never made the comparison,' said Cidrolin modestly.

'Just think for five minutes. They're sadistic maniacs, anglers.

They've usurped the reputation of good philosophers. Frankly, don't you think the hook is slyer and more viciously barbaric than the espadrille?'

'The espadrille?'

'Those things they stick in the brute's neck.'

'Are you sure that's what they're called?'

'That's what I'm calling them for the moment, so that's what they're called, and as it's me you're talking to for the moment and nobody else you'll just have to take my words at their face value.'

'The fact is that I understand you perfectly.'

'You see! Well, let's terminate our conversation at this point and content ourselves with these premises of mutual and unescal understanding between peoples and of future peace. May I be allowed to continue my walk? Delighted to have met you.'

The passer-by withdrew just as the foreman was whistling to signal the non-tea break. Cidrolin embarked on the business of crossing the boulevard, which he did with extra prudence, since it was the hour when the horseless carriages go for their libations. Arriving safe and sound on the other side of the road he was able to observe that both fence and gate were innocent of graffiti.

The essence of fennel and the still water, the litre of red wine and the mustard pot were awaiting Cidrolin. He was served some anchovies and butter, some black pudding cooked according to a country recipe with earth-apples and sky apples, some roquefort and three babas. The anchovies are pluvious herrings, the black pudding and its apples turn out to be inconsistent, the roquefort creaks under the knife, and the liquid in the flabby babas could never have claimed to be anything rummier than water.

Cidrolin sighs and murmurs:

'Another fucking fiasco.'

'What is there to eat in your first-class tavern?' asks the Duke of Auge.

The taverner replies.

[22]

'There's borshch, that's shoup made from schlavonic beech-root, and tripe à la viducasse, the whole washed down with wine from the slopes of Suresnes.'

'Hardly enough to get round to your back teeth,' said the Duke scornfully.

'Has your Lordship ever eaten any borshch?' retorted the taverner, provoked to insolence.

'My word!' exclaimed the Duke to Mouscaillot, 'he takes me for a gaby! I've known it since the days of Queen Anne!'

Impressed, the taverner bowed low.

'I can see from your mien,' continued the Duke, 'that you're wondering who Queen Anne is.'

'Well um . . . your Lordship . . .'

It was quite clear that the taverner had in fact no idea.

'Ah, Mouscaillot,' said the Duke, 'our good Kings and gentle Queens are soon forgotten by the people. Two hundred years have barely passed and this taverner no longer knows who Anne Vladimirovitch was, but that doesn't stop him serving borshch. Ah well!'

Taking advantage of this point scored, the Duke continues in these terms:

'Beforehand, taverner, I'll have a little glass of some ecphractic liquor, essence of fennel, for instance. Can you serve me a little glass of essence of fennel?'

'Ah, my Lord!' exclaimed the taverner, on the verge of tears, 'I most humbly entreat you not to blot the escutcheon of my three stars.'

Whereupon he did quite a bit of bowing and scraping.

'That,' said the Duke, 'reminds me of the salaams of the worshippers of Mahom.'

'Can I serve you some essence of fennel?' went on the taverner in a heartbreaking voice. 'I even have several different brands, my Lord.'

'Give me the best, then! And get them to feed my horses with good hay, good straw and good oats.'

This was done with alacrity. The Duke whiffed up several little glasses of essence of fennel with a drop of still water. Two dapferous and muscular menservants were bringing in a big olla of borshch when there suddenly appeared a person who was uttering cries of terrorstrickenness. He was trembling, and his yellow and vermilion mottled-green face was tending to become as white as chalk.

'Oo la la,' he was saying, dancing up and down on the spot. 'Oo la la.'

'Hector,' said the taverner, 'aren't you ashamed and abashed at coming and disturbing my refectory in this way? I shall give you the stick. This serving-man is my palfrenier,' he added, for the Duke's benefit.

'Oo la la, sweet Jesus,' the serving-man who was a palfrenier continued to wail. 'Oo la la, I was so frightened, I was more frightened than I've ever been in the whole of my poor and humble life as a serving-man who is a palfrenier. Oo la la, how frightened I was!'

'Tell us what happened, for goodness' sake!'

'Couldn't I have a little glass of essence of fennel to fortify me?'

Hector held out his hand towards the bottle on the Duke's table, but the Duke rapped him sharply over the knuckles.

'Owch,' said Hector.

'But what happened, what happened?'

The taverner was getting annoyed.

'May I not enjoy my borshch?' asked the Duke, with formidable irony. 'Tell those dapferous and muscular serving-men to put that olla on the table and . . .'

'His horse talks!' Hector started bawling. 'His Lordship's horse,' he added, pointing most impolitely at the Duke, 'he talks like you and me! Oo la la!'

[24]

'What a dolt,' said the Duke.

'Ah,' said the taverner, with a threatening air, 'if you're lying . . .'

'I swear it's true! I swear it's true! His Lordship's horse talks! He speaks! he jabbers!'

'But this is the devil's work!' exclaimed the taverner.

At these words the dapferous and muscular serving-men dropped the great olla whose contents ran all over the floor. The whole household fell on its knees in the shoup, burning the said knees and making muchel signs of the cross; paternosters could be heard deflagrating all over the place.

'In default of borshch,' said the Duke calmly, 'we might have some tripe.'

But the cook, overcome by the ambient emotion, had just dropped the dish into the fire.

'Another fucking fiasco!' yelled the Duke.

In the meantime the rumour was starting to spread through the surrounding streets that there was a talking horse at the Three Star Tavern, which the good people took advantage of to indulge their loquacity and comment on the event in these terms:

'Out of the abundance of the devil the horse speaketh.'

'If the cockadoodle coo, the beans will rot in the stew.'

'To boisterous crab, oyster is drab.'

'When the fish start to talk then the pig turns to chalk.'

'When she's got bells on her bubs, she's Beelzebub's.'

And other extremely salty prouverbs issuing from the magnificent false bottom of the folkloric sapience of the eel de France.

'My Lord,' said Mouscaillot, 'things are beginning to deteriorate, as you foresaw. Don't you think we should go home?'

'Without our dinner?'

Outside, people were starting to shout:

'To the stake with the nigromancer! to the stake with the dowser!'

'You're right,' the Duke went on, 'we are far from popular in the neighbourhood.'

He got up; followed by Mouscaillot he went out to the stables, which instigated flight, scuffling and yapping.

'Ah, my good Demo,' said the Duke, 'what made you demonstrate your gifts to that palfrenier? Now we're really in the cack with that bawling mass dying to abernen us alive.'

'Well, my Lord,' replied Sthenes, 'the knave was doing a bit of graft, he didn't give me my oats. Would it have been your pleasure that I let myself be cheated thus?'

'No, no, my good Demo, you were right. The wicked palfrenier will die of the evil eye, and serve him right. En route!'

A considerable throng was already waiting for them outside.

'Oh, oh,' exclaimed several parishioners, 'there's that rotten squireen who refuses to cross himself! That Albigensian must be a worshipper of Mahom and his palfrey's undoubtedly called Satan.'

Shards and stones started raining on the Duke and Mouscaillot; then it was blazing logs, larding-needles, step-ladders and parpens. Everything about the Duke was displeasing and the good people were getting highly annoyed with this heretic, aristocrat and provincial, but you don't take the Bastille every day of the week, especially in the thirteenth century.

Drawing his braquemard for the second time that day, Joachim d'Auge darted into the fray and slew two hundred and sixteen persons, men, women, children and others, of whom twenty-seven were licensed borgeis and twenty-six on the point of becoming so.

In order to make their way out of the town they also had to discomfit some archers.

III

'Oo-oo', someone called.

Cidrolin doesn't budge, at regular little intervals his breathing raises the handkerchief he's covered his face with.

'Oo-oo,' someone called, more loudly.

'Another Canadian with her banjo-player,' murmured Cidrolin under his handkerchief.

'Oo-oo.'

It's an oo-oo that's coming nearer.

'She's by herself. She's got a nerve.'

Cidrolin makes up his mind to emerge from his siesta. He yawns and gets up. On the other side of the gang-plank there was in fact a damsel equipped as a camperess.

'Excuse me, Monsieur,' says she. 'The camping camp for campers, please?'

He replies to this question with another question.

'You wouldn't be Canadian by any chance, would you?'

Sure enough, she is indeed Canadian and not by chance but by necessity seeing that she was born that way and isn't married to a foreigner (she doesn't state that she is a virgin) and hasn't had herself naturalised Roubaisian or Zanzibian. Looking at her more carefully Cidrolin realised that he hadn't so far looked at her really carefully and that, not being a racialist, he hadn't seen that she was a red indian.

'Me surprise you, no?' she murmured.

'Not in the least,' replied Cidrolin.

'Me Wyandot,' she said, 'and me proud of it.'

[27]

'Dot's as it should be.'

'Why? Are you being funny?'

'No, no. Don't make me dot my whys.'

'Me woke you up, yes?'

'I'd be telling a lie if I said no.'

'Then you're cross with me?'

'Beloved, be not coy.'

'And this camping site? Are you finally going to tell me where it hangs out?'

Cidrolin executed some gestures which determined the situation of that place to within some four inches.

'Me thank you,' said the Canadian Wyandot, 'and me do beg you to excuse me for having disturbed your siesta, but they say that the French are so obliging. . . . so helpful. . . .'

'That's just a saying.'

'So I took the liberty . . .'

'Liberty! Do you still believe in liberty? As you do in the obligingness and helpfulness of my compatriots? Might you possibly be over-credulous, Mademoiselle?'

'What? Isn't one allowed to believe in liberty any more in France?. . . . or equality?. . . . or fraternity?'

'Pull yourself together, Mademoiselle, there's no need to get so emotional about such trifles. Look, what d'you say to coming and having a little glass of essence of fennel on my barge, would that make you feel better?'

'Here we go! a sex-maniac! That's another thing they all told me. Every Frenchman . . .'

'Mademoiselle . . . please believe me . . .'

'If you think, Monsieur, that you are likely to attain your blagatory and lubricious ends by proferring philanderous utterances designed to lure me into your perverse lair, me, a poor defenceless bird, a poor Wyandotte, even, you've got another think coming, Monsieur, you've got another think coming!'

[28]

Turning on her heel forthwith, the young lady climbed up the bank again, manifesting, in so doing, the harmonious musculature of her posterior.

'There's another female Canadian I shall never see again,' murmured Cidrolin. 'I certainly shall have seen some female Canadians, though, bags of 'em, even, bags of female Canadians, with or without bags, at that; with, or rather without, those charming sheepskin chackets they actually call female Canadians and flog over here as the fine efflorescence of Canadian haute couture; without, natch, because the only female Canadians I see, it's in the summer. Or the spring. Or the autumn. Huh, I ought to have drawn her attention to the fact that it's a fine autumn day today: maybe she wouldn't have taken that the wrong way.'

He went into the cabin to look at the time and, as a consequence of this examination, he lay down on his chaise-longue once more to complete his interrupted siesta.

When he opened his eyes again he perceived all around him everything that he usually saw; the walls of his bedroom, the narrow window that let a bit of light into it and, lying on a bundle of straw at his feet, the faithful page Mouscaillot, surrounded by a few dogs, all of whom had names: T'Ali Hoh, Talihoe, Tallyho, Mohrt & Cetera. A familiar spectacle which did much to reassure the Duke, who got up and started kicking this little family awake, which provoked some snivelling and barking.

Having said his prayers and relieved his bladder down the stairs, he made his way to the chapel to hear Mass said by his chaplain, Onésiphore Biroton. Onésiphore Biroton was a priest who believed in shock-tactics; for every kick the Duke gave him he gave him back two, so the Duke was highly fond of him, and on this particular day he couldn't wait to discuss several important points with him. Hardly had the Abbé Biroton itemissaested than the Duke led him out on to the bailey and said:

'Now listen, Onésiphore, I have muchel anxieties which I'm going to pour into your ears.'

'Did you have some trouble in the capital city?'

'That's not the point,' said the Duke, irritated. 'And anyway, do you know I did or do you imagine I did?'

'Hm, hm,' said Onésiphore. 'While you were away your daughters were as good as gold-capped weaver birds.'

'Ouais. We'll come to that later. For the moment I've got three questions to ask you, which are: primo what you think about dreams, secundo what you think about the language of animals, and tertio what you think about world history in general and general history in particular. I'm listening.'

'Hm, hm,' said Onésiphore. 'Distinguo . . .'

'No distinguos!' yelled the Duke, stamping his foot. 'D'you hear? No distinguos, no dialectics, none of that sort of thing. I want something solid. I'm listening.'

'Hm, hm,' said Onésiphore. 'I can't answer three questions simultaneously: my speech is linear, like all human speech.'

'What are you getting at?'

'At this: I shall have to answer one question first, then another, and finally the last. Which one do you wish me to start with?'

'With the second.'

'Optime. And which was the second?'

'Stupid ass, have you already forgotten my questions? And do you really want me to repeat them? Eh, do you, old pious-face?'

The Duke caused a good clout behind the right ear to follow these words. The Abbé retorted with a well-placed crack on the nut and a well-placed push in the mush.

'Well,' said the Duke of Auge, spitting out an incisor, 'start where you like. With the first one, for instance.'

'I haven't forgotten your questions, just their order.'

'Well, start where you like.'

'I'll start with the dreams.'

'Good. Tell me what you think about dreams.'

'Some come from God and others from the Devil.'

'You wouldn't be an Albigensian, by any chance?'

'Nay, my Lord, and it's good Catholic doctrine to say: there are two sorts of dream; some come from God and the others from the Devil.'

'How can you tell the difference?'

'Oh, that's immediately obvious.'

'How? Buffoon, how do *you* tell the difference? *I* can't tell the difference.'

'It's simple, though. If you see the sky, or angels, or even simply birds, on condition that they aren't night-birds, the dream comes from God; if you see flames, demons, or even simply rampant animals and more especially snakes, then the dream comes from the Devil.'

'I never dream of anything like that.'

'And what do you dream of, your Lordship?'

'I often dream that I'm on a barge, I'm sitting in a chaise-longue, I put a handkerchief over my face and I have a little siesta.'

'Siesta . . . handkerchief . . . barge . . . what sort of words are those? I cannot comprehend them.'

'They're words I've invented to designate the things I see in my dreams.'

'So you practise neologism, my Lord?'

'Don't *you* start neologising, now; that's a privilege that's reserved for Dukes. Well, from the Italian barca, a regular phonetic descendant from the Latin barca, I get barge; from the Latin sexta hora I get the Spanish siesta, which I don't bother to change, and from curchef and kerchef, syncopated forms of coverchef and keverchef respectively, I get coverchief, a cloth used to cover the head, and hence kerchief. I add hand, I take my kerchief in my hand, and I then re-cover my head with it.'

'We've come a long way from sapiential and christian

[31]

oneirology. Your semantic science, my Lord, stinks of heresy.'

'In what way might it be heretical to dream of a barge?'

'I'll agree that it is far from common to see angels and saints in one's dreams. Most often, if I can judge from my own experience, dreams are only concerned with the petty incidents of everyday life.'

'What about them then, buffoon, do they come from the Devil or from God?'

'Neither from the one nor from the other. They are immaterial. Positively immaterial. Ad primam respondi.'

'Huh, huh! You don't get out of it so easily as that, my dear Abbé. I don't need *you* if I'm only going to get feeble observations like that, I'd be quite capable of inventing them all by myself. Do you really think I'll go on giving you your daily swill if you content yourself with such banalities? I demand another answer.'

And he aimed a smart kick at the Abbé's right tibia, which target it reached. Onésiphore tried to reply by an onslaught on the epigastrium but it was dodged, and he measured his length. The Duke immediately jumps on him and starts trampling on him, shouting:

'Answer me pi-face! Answer me!'

The Abbé indicates that he will.

'Well then,' says the Duke getting down off his victim.

'Well then,' says the Abbé getting up on to his feet again, 'dreams of that sort come from the intermediary world inhabited by goblins, fairies, gnomes, brownies, elves, leprechauns, imps, undines and melusines, beings who come neither from God nor from the Devil, and who are dedicated neither to evil nor to good.'

'Well, haven't you become benevolent. What would the Holy Inquisition think of that?'

'Optime. And that's how I answer your question. Ad secundum, which is about animal language . . .'

[32]

'You're getting a move on, now.'

'. . . I say that it is not universally agreed that Adam's sin involved the animal world in the Fall. The most eminent theologians dispute that. On the other hand, as it stands to reason that they didn't take part in the construction of the tower of Babel, there's nothing to prevent them making themselves understood amongst themselves.'

'Theologians?'

'No, my Lord, animals.'

'Trivial! I was talking not about animals who talk to each other, which is a commonplace, but of animals who talk the language of men; and as for you, you talk through your hat.'

The Duke raises his hand to give a backhander, but the Abbé beats him to it and sloshes him a straight to the chin, which causes his interlocutor to vacillate.

'Ad tertiam, respondeo . . .' the chaplain hastened to say.

'Ttt, ttt,' said the Duke, putting his jaw back into place. 'Not so fast. I should now like to hear you talk about animals who talk in dreams. Do they come from God or from the Devil?'

'Not the slightest importance. Completely immaterial. Ad tertiam . . .'

'Ttt, ttt. You told me just now that rampant animals in dreams came from the Devil.'

'Dixi.'

'And if they talk?'

'Bis diabolici.'

'And if you talk to them?'

'Ter diabolici.'

'And if they answer you?'

'Quater.'

'Good. I find that highly satisfying, because I've never had a conversation with a snake in a dream; not like our mother Eve.'

'She didn't dream.'

[33]

'What did Adam dream of when God put him to sleep so that he could take out his rib?'

'That's a fourth question that we can put off till tomorrow. Ad tertiam, respondeo.'

'Ttt, ttt. I haven't finished with the talking animals yet. And what about cars? Do they come from God or from the Devil?'

'Cars? I know not what they are.'

'They're living, squealing beasties that run about in every direction on their round paws. They don't eat anything solid and they only drink petroleum. Their eyes light up at nightfall.'

'Nevere seyn oon.'

'I see them in my dreams. Thousands, myriads, legions. I see them invading the streets and the roads. They go by along the embankment, they're the things that make the continuous rumbling noise I hear from my barge . . .'

As the Abbé Biroton wasn't interested in hearing people's dreams, he fell asleep.

'For the greater glory of God.'

Cidrolin turned round.

'Oh, sorry,' said a man dressed in an elegantly-cut iron-grey suit. 'I know you, I didn't mean to bother you. You live around here.'

'I live on the barge over the road,' said Cidrolin, 'and . . .'

'Senough. 'bout ship! Adieu.'

The quasi-clergyman got back on to his mobylette and went off towards the camping camp for campers. Cidrolin, who was watching the building workers at their labours, also continued his walk in that direction. Behind some barbed wire Goddams, Brabantines, Netherlanders, Suomiphones, Picts, Gauls, Cimbrians and Norlanders were going about their business, which consisted of wending their way from their caravan or their tent to the lavatories, from the lavatories to the showers, from the showers to the canteen and from the canteen to their caravan or their tent,

[34]

while they were waiting to take the return road to Elsinore, Salzburg, Uppsala or Aberdeen. Various kinds of music accompanied these different activities and the piercing song of multiple transistors was occasionally drowned by choruses in foreign tongues accompanied by bagpipes, bugles or ocarinas. Some particularly optimistic characters were uttering loud cries of satisfaction whilst beating their breasts with their fists in order to evoke the rolling of a drum.

Other sight-seers were examining the situation with Cidrolin; one of them said:

'We're looking at them as if they were exotic animals; this isn't the zoo, though.'

'Almost,' said Cidrolin.

'All the same, you're not going to tell me they're animals and not men.'

'Prove it,' said Cidrolin.

'They talk.'

'What about parrots,' said Cidrolin, 'don't they talk?'

'They don't understand what they're saying.'

'Prove it,' said Cidrolin.

'Bloody bore you are! It's impossible to have a conversation with a bloody bore like you.'

'We've just had one, though, and an extremely interesting one. It isn't every day that the sight of a camping camp for campers gives rise to observations that would almost be worth recording on tape.'

'Tape recording my nostrils,' said the nauseated sight-seer as he withdrew, muttering.

From afar the quasi-clergyman gave Cidrolin a cordial little wave. Cidrolin answered him extremely politely, and then went home. Some insulting inscriptions had been daubed on the fence and gate. Cidrolin went to fetch a paint pot and a brush to cause these graffiti to disappear.

[35]

IV

On the café terrace some couples were practising the French kiss and the saliva was dribbling down their amorous chins; among the most desperately leech-like were Lamélie and an omnibudsman, particularly Lamélie, because the omnibudsman didn't forget to look at his watch from time to time in view of his professional duties. Lamélie shut her eyes and devoted herself religiously to the science of tongues.

Came the moment of separation; the omnibudsman slowly started ungluing operations and, when he had attained his object, there was a plop. He wiped himself with the back of his hand and said:

'Gotta blow.'

And he distributed a little beer over his desiccated mucous membranes.

Lean and languid, Lamélie gives him a look.

He pulls some francs out of his pocket and taps on the table with them. He says in a fairly loud voice:

'Waiter.'

Lamélie, lean and languid, gives him a look.

The waiter comes up for the pay-off. At this moment Lamélie throws herself on her omnibudsman and starts all over again. Her partner finds it necessary to express himself by signs, which, however, are easy to understand. The waiter picks up the change. The spectacle doesn't excite him in the least. He moves off.

The omnibudsman embarks on a new ungluing process. He

manages it by easy stages and there is another plop. He wipes his lips with the back of his hand and says:

'This time I really gotta blow.'

He drains his half pint and gets up nimbly.

Lamélie gives him a look, lean and languid. She follows her leader, and says:

'I'm not in any hurry, I'll come for a ride with you.'

'Za lot of traffic at this time of day, you know, we always run late, shan't have time to talk to you.'

'I'll watch you turn your little handle on the machine on your stomach, I'll hear your voice when you call out the fare stages, I'll be quite happy.'

'You can't be sure of getting on. Going to be a lot of people.'

There were. Two hundred and seventeen people were cooling their heels in a queue constituted in accordance with the official regulations. Lamélie waited, people got in, the bus filled up and she was still a good long way away in the mass of postulants when her loved one, with a graceful flourish, swung down the sign that said full up and tugged at his little bell. The whole lot drove off. The omnibudsman made a gesture with his hand which may perhaps have been addressed to someone lost in the waiting file, which was getting longer and longer. Lamélie turned on her heel and tried to carve a clearway through the queuing crowd. As she was trying to stem the current, people remarked:

'Make your mind up, ducks.'

'Another one who thinks we aren't buggered about enough as it is.'

'Silly bitches that change their minds, they're the end.'

'They queue the wrong way round and then they're surprised you grumble.'

A lady yelled:

'Stop pushing, will you? Can't you see my stomach!'

'If you're pregnant,' retorted Lamélie cantankerously, 'better get in the priority queue.'

A citizen, who hadn't understood a word of this dialogue, exploded.

'Make way!' he yelled, 'make way! a pregnant woman isn't feeling well!'

'Make way! for Christ's sake, don't you understand? A pregnant woman!'

'Out of the way! Let's have some respect for pregnant women, and pride in maternity!'

'Make way! Make way!'

'Out of the way!'

Lamélie found herself cast out from the crowd of waiters like a tuft of sea-wrack on a Norman shore. She walked away. She passed the café again; various couples on the terrace were still pretending they were leeches. Feeling quite melancholick, Lamélie reached the embankment.

Little by little she found herself in front of the Ark.

Cidrolin was resting on the after-deck; he was very comfortable but he wasn't snoozing, he was looking into the middle distance. Lamélie's arrival didn't change his lack of behaviour in the slightest. It was only when the essence of fennel and the still water were brought that he modified his attitude and at the same time took the floor in one sense and went half-way to taking it in another. Sitting up, he said:

'The inspector of corbitary contributions has been.'

'I came back by bus.'

'He inspected everything.'

'The conductor was a giggle.'

'I came in for some compliments.'

'He said something funny to every passenger.'

'He decided the Ark was entitled to two anchors in category A.'

'He talked to me, too.'

'Not three anchors yet. Two isn't at all bad though.'

' "You certainly have got more shape than a season ticket," '
he said, ' "and you've got a hell of a lot more curves than a book
of tickets." '

'Obviously I shall have to pay more taxes, but think of the
status.'

' "Huh you, well Ida know, huh you," that's what I re-
torted.'

'There's one thing he pointed out.'

'But I couldn't help laughing.'

' "You call it the Ark?" he said, "there aren't any animals on
board, it's paradoxical." "Yes, that's true," I answered, "it *is*
paradoxical, but that's the way it is." "Fine, fine," he added: "it
was just a remark, you know." "Well, so was mine," that's what
I added. And so he went. He was pleased with himself and I was
pleased with myself. Up to now, apart from the grub, this has
been rather a good day – but it isn't over yet. Anything can still
happen.'

'That chap – I like him.'

'What chap?'

'The conductor on the 421.'

'There isn't only one, I presume.'

'The one I know.'

'*I* don't know him.'

'I've just been telling you.'

'Then you're not interested in the fact that the Ark has been
promoted to two anchors in category A?'

'Pathetic. Why not three? I work hard enough I should have
thought.'

'We'll have to wait a bit. We'll have them one day, our three
anchors.'

'And why not four?'

[39]

'I know, I know.'

He stretched out his hand for the bottle of essence of fennel to pour himself out a new dollop.

'You drink too much,' he is told.

He shrugged his shoulders and helped himself liberally.

'Well,' he asked, 'what about your conductor?'

'Essence of fennel, it drives you mad, it's in all the papers.'

Cidrolin frowned, ceased to frown in order to empty his glass, and then frowned again with some intensity. Four deep lines dug into his glabella. He grumbled:

'You've spoilt my pleasure. Another fucking fiasco.'

The bottle, the still water and the glasses are taken away.

'Tell me about your conductor.'

'I've got work to do.'

'Shall I get the paint pot?'

'No, there's nothing there.'

This being the case he lay down once more on his chaise-longue and started looking into the middle distance again.

A detachment of royal security companies appeared on the horizon; the look-out man came to advise the Duke of Auge of its approach, and the Duke made such a row yelling the necessary orders that the Abbé Biroton woke up.

'The securicorpses are coming,' said the Duke, rubbing his hands. 'We'll atomise them.'

'What's going on? Why the securicorpses?'

'Ah yes! I hadn't told you. I slew a few bourgeois who were bugging me.'

'Wrath is a bad counsellor. You'll have to do penitence.'

'As much as anyone likes, but these fellows certainly have more sinister intentions.'

'Our saintly king doesn't take the indiscretions of his noblemen lightly.'

'He takes us seriously,' said the Duke with satisfaction.

There were now several detachments approaching the castle, coming from different points of the horizon.

'Things are deteriorating,' murmured the Abbé, 'things are deteriorating.'

'Don't worry, if they get nasty I've already told you: I'll atomise them!'

'Good God, are you going to become a rebel, into the bargain?'

The securicorpses were now surrounding the castle, the most heroaldic of them came up to the drawbridge and, by signs as sonorous as they were heraldic, intimated that he wished to transmit a message to the Lord of these parts.

The Abbé lamented:

'What a business! What a business! And I find it highly questionable . . .'

'Ah yes, you haven't answered my third question yet, the one about world history in general and general history in particular.'

But the herald was ushered in, and he started to explain to the Duke that the saintly King wasn't at all pleased, that to slay the bourgeois for slender reasons wasn't done any more, and that the nobility ought to take it for granted that one just doesn't disembrain people without rhyme or reason, by conseyquence of the whiche Joachim Duke of Auge would have to extract from his treasury one hundred refined pure and unalloyed gold écus (minted at Tours) per head per stiff, which without the slightest doubt would add up to a considerable sum, all the more so as there were some people with split heads who hadn't quite finished dying yet, and that Joachim Duke of Auge should get it firmly into his head that this sum would be but partially utilised to indemnify the widowers, widows or orphans and would in the main serve substantially to subsidise the crusade now in course of preparation.

What was more, Joachim Duke of Auge would have to recite six thousand six hundred and fifty-seven paters, as many aves and three times less confiteors and have as many masses said as there were slain, whyche masses he would attend with bare feet, in his shirt, and with his head covered with ashes, cold or hot as he pleased.

And that Joachim of Auge should further get it well into his head that the saintly King would have had him hanged by his two ears until death did then ensue if the saintly King had not kept some remembrance of the services rendered by Joachim of Auge to the Christian cause at Damietta as well as at Mansura.

Finally, that Joachim of Auge could keep his refined pure and unalloyed gold écus (minted at Tours) and reduce by half the number of his paters and the number of his aves even though that number was an odd number and by a quarter the number of his confiteors, even though four was an aliquant part of two thousand two hundred and nineteen, nothing being changed with regard to the masses with however permission for the Duke to attend them shod and dressed as he wished, all this on the simple, benign, blessed and pardoning condition that he join the saintly King and go and eviscerate some Saracens on the next Crusade.

'Never,' replied the Duke of Auge. 'I've already explained to him that I never want to set foot in those impossible dumps again. One crusade is a lot; two is too much.'

'Then, my Lord,' said the herald, 'you have no desire to seize the Holy Sepulchre from the hands of the Infidel?'

'But we've had it, you poor nodcock! He's only going to get more cold-jellied Bouillons out of it. Our Holy Father himself doesn't believe in it any more. We've been sweating our guts out for nearly two hundred years now trying to get it back, but there it still is, in the hands of the Infidel, the sepulchre.'

Horrified by these utterances, the herald crossed himself.

'And,' went on the Duke of Auge, 'do you really think that by going to Tunisia we shall seize it from the hands of the Infidel, the sepulchre? Tunisia! Why not the country of the Amaurots or the Hamaxobians? While he's about it, our saintly King, why doesn't he go as far as the countries where the Indians live, or the Seres? Why doesn't he set sail on the Oceanic sea until he gets beyond the isle of Thule, maybe he'd find an unknown land around those parts with some extra infidels to atomise.'

'Moderate your ardour, my Lord,' murmured the Abbé Biroton. The herald went on crossing himself non-stop.

'No, no and no,' concluded the Duke of Auge. 'Me no go crusade. I'll say all those concatenations of patravefiteors, I'll go to all those ashy masses and I'll relinquish my beautiful refined pure and unalloyed gold écus (minted at Tours), but as for going and messing about in the vicinity of the Boggie Syrtes, I can only repeat: no, no and no. Such is my answer, and having said that I should like to point out that our saintly King has forbidden those of us who have the right to coin our own money to allow our sols and our écus to circulate outside our own domains, but that he nevertheless wants to see the colour of them. In conclusion, herald, I enjoin you to disembarrass our territories of your displeasing presence and of that of your acolytes, which is no less displeasing. I have spoken.'

'I shall hasten to do so, but I cannot leave until I have received a preliminary instalment of the pecunial penitence by which you have been penalised, my Lord, an instalment which amounts to um, let's have a think, seven thousand two hundred refined pure and unalloyed gold écus (minted at Tours) plus twelve sols (minted at Paris) for the registration fees and four half-farthings for the stamp.'

'Don't I get a reduction for having been a member of the seventh crusade?' asked the Duke with a pale grimace, the pale grimace he was in the habit of making the moment anyone had designs on his sous.

The herald replied firmly:

'No. The calculations is correct.'

[43]

He added:

'It is only possible for it to increase, never for it to diminish.'

Joachim of Auge held his peace and composed his features to look as if he were thinking.

The chaplain guessed that the Duke was considering proceeding to open rebellion. The herald guessed the same thing. The Duke guessed that the other two had guessed. The chaplain guessed that the Duke had guessed that he had guessed, but didn't guess whether the herald had also guessed that the Duke had guessed that he'd guessed. The herald, for his part, couldn't guess whether the chaplain had guessed that the Duke had guessed that he'd guessed, but he did guess that the Duke had guessed that he'd guessed.

This terrible tension tended to lead to silence, which enabled every which one of them to hear Bélusine and Pigranelle singing sewing-songs, some horses neighing, some dogs barking, some securicorpses marking time and Phélise bleating.

'By my figgins,' the Duke finally exclaimed, 'my decision is taken; never will the saintly King see the colour of my refined pure and unalloyed gold écus (minted in Tours), never will I listen to ashy masses, never will I say concatenations of patravefiteors and never will I crusade. Avaunt, nodcock of a securicorpse! Retire from my high fortified walls with your fellows, for I am about to regale them with boiling oil and molten lead, an excellent culinary recipe to use up the left-overs of the royal security companies who would do better to go off to the crusade than to come and jum up good and noble lords like me. If the Capets start treating us like this we'll soon be seeing the aristocrats hanging from the lamp-posts. Didn't you hear what I said, herald? I said avaunt from here and avaunt from my territories, and if you don't make up your mind a bit quicker than that I'll rip open your belly with my teeth, so there.'

The horrified terrified herald, having crossed himself innumerable times, retrogressed the number of paces necessary to disappear from the sight of the Duke of Auge. The drawbridge was lowered to allow him to leave, and was then immediately raised again.

'Tell them to heat the oil!' yelled the Duke. 'Tell them to melt the lead, and to get a jerk on! Jump to it!'

'You may perhaps be overdoing it a bit,' said the chaplain timidly. 'After all, they're not so terrible, masses and prayers.'

'Yes, but it's my gold he's got designs on, that Capet.'

'Come come, my Lord, you don't really think you can give vent to your mad and headstrong humor on good borgeis and unfortunate vileyns without paying some small emolument to their widows and orphans, do you?'

'A small emolument, yes, I'm quite willing. All they have to do is come and get it, here. Don't need to make the King their agent so's he can collect his rake-off.'

'You calumniate your sovereign, my Lord.'

'I'm not talking about him. The poor man, *he*'s okay. It'd be his bailiffs and the officers of his privy purse who'd improve the shining hour with my beautiful shiny refined pure and unalloyed gold écus (minted at Tours). Who're you kidding? Come on, get cracking! Get the frying fat fomenting and the metallurgical matter melting!'

He rubbed his hands with satisfaction, while the royal security companies, a good distance away from the castle walls, started to lay hands on the foodstuffs destined for the revictualling of the Duke, his dependants and his beasts.

As the Abbé Biroton was drawing his attention to this unprincipled action, the Duke slapped his thighs in derision.

'I've taken my precautions. My reserves will allow me to hold out for as long as it will take the very Christian King to go off on his crusade and come back, if he does come back.'

'God preserve him!' said the Abbé automatically.

[45]

'If we have to, we'll eat some human flesh! Cooked, naturally; they say it has its charms. When we want something raw we'll make a sortie and pulverise those wicked securicorpses. I'm already rejoicing at the thought of their fulfilling their destiny here, and their remains manuring my radish fields, the radish being a plant to which I am extremely partial. And now, my Abbé, you're going to answer the third of my questions, id est, what you think of world history in general and general history in particular. The moment seems to me to be well chosen; I'm listening.'

V

'Coming then?' says Bertrande.

'What a bore,' says Yoland. 'What a chore.'

'You didn't only marry me for pleasure. Come on, get going!'

'Your sister, I don't mind seeing her, but your father, you know . . .'

'What do I know?'

'Nothing. Snuff.'

'So I should hope.'

'I know what I mean.'

'You're the only one who does, I hope. And come here and let me fix your tie. You'll never learn to tie a tie properly.'

'What you have to put up with.'

They have a date with Sigismonde and Lucet.

'Hm,' says Sigismonde, 'got a new car, have you?'

'Hardly worth mentioning,' says Lucet, 'it's obvious.'

'Coming with us?' says Yoland.

'We'll take ours,' says Lucet.

'Hm,' says Bertrande, 'you've got a new car too, have you?'

'Nothing extraordinary about that,' says Yoland. 'Everyone's always got new cars.'

'Whatever you do, don't start racing each other,' says Sigismonde.

No, they don't race each other, but they arrive at more or less the same time at the Ark. Cidrolin is repainting the fence along the embankment. Lamélie's waiting on the barge; she's got out the essence of fennel, the still water and the glasses. The women walk down the bank. The two men stay and watch Cidrolin making the last few brush strokes; they watch him like connoisseurs, in silence.

'Good work,' Lucet finally says.

'Beautifully done,' says Yoland.

'What about the barge,' Lucet asks Cidrolin, 'are you going to paint it too?'

'Next year,' replies Cidrolin. 'Every other year. It was painted last year. There, that's it.'

He picks up the paint pot and goes down the bank.

'Don't break your necks,' he advises them.

On the gang-plank he says:

'Mind you don't fall in the drink.'

Their glass of essence of fennel is waiting for them; the women are talking about the telly.

'You ought to get him to buy you one,' Bertrande says to Lamélie. 'What on earth can you find to do in the evenings? You must be hellish bored.'

'I'm biding my time,' says Lamélie. 'I shan't be here for ever.'

'What are you going to do?'

'Get married, of course!'

'Have you got someone in mind?'

'That'd be telling.'

She simpers.

[47]

'You'll be bored when she's not here any more,' Lucet says to Cidrolin.

'Oh, you know me. Takes a lot for me to be bored.'

'He always finds something not to do,' says Lamélie. 'He's very good at keeping himself unoccupied.'

'We know him just as well as you do,' say Sigismonde and Bertrande in chorus.

'Naturally,' says Cidrolin, 'I'd rather she stayed, but she's got to have a life of her own, this child, it's only natural.'

'It's only natural,' says Bertrande.

'It's only natural,' says Sigismonde.

'Then you've got someone in mind?' says Bertrande.

'That'd be telling,' says Lamélie.

She simpers.

'That's true,' says Lucet suddenly, 'why haven't you got the telly? It's an entertainment.'

'It's even educational,' says Yoland.

'Well, Lamélie,' says Cidrolin, 'while you're waiting to get married, do you want to be entertained or educated?'

'No, Dad, what I want to do is to fuck.'

'They don't fuck very much on the telly,' observed Lucet.

'They even don't fuck at all,' says Yoland.

'Stupids,' says Bertrande, 'that's because there's kids watching.'

'Your kids,' asks Sigismonde, 'would you let them watch as much as they liked?'

'Only when it's educational,' answers Yoland. 'Especially the news. That'll teach them French history – world history, even.'

'How come?' says Lucet.

'Well, yes, today's news is tomorrow's history. That's one thing less they'll have to learn at school, seeing that they'll already know it.'

'You're talking through the back of your neck,' says Lucet.

[48]

'History's never been what's in the news, and the news isn't history. Mustn't mix them up.'

'But that's just what you must do! it's just the opposite!! Gotta mix them up!!! Just have a bit of a think. Suppose you're watching telly, you see – and I mean, and I repeat: you see – Lucien Bonaparte ringing his bell, his brother in a corner, the deputies yelling, the grenadiers arriving, well, hell, you're watching the nineteenth Brumaire. After that you go to bed, you sleep for a hundred years and then you wake up; well, at that moment the nineteenth Brumaire's become history and you don't need to look it up in any books to know whatitiz.'

'That's daft,' says Sigismonde, 'there wasn't any telly in those days.'

'Granted,' says Yoland, 'but just take the news reels in the cinema, sometimes they put on old ones. Then you see the Tsar Nicholas shaking hands with Poincaré, the Marne taxis, Wilhelm II, the Crown Prince, Verdun: isn't that history? And yet it was news once.'

'It stays news,' says Lucet. 'Stands to reason; you see it in a cinema and they tell you: this is news.'

'That's daft,' says Yoland, 'then what *is* history for you?'

'It's when it's written down.'

'Yes, that's true,' says Bertrande.

'He's right,' says Sigismonde.

'He's a hundred times right,' says Lamélie.

Yoland bangs on the table.

'Mind you don't knock the essence of fennel over,' says Cidrolin.

Yoland bangs on the table minding he doesn't knock the essence of fennel over. He suits the words to the action:

'You must be silly dopes, all the same, not to understand what I mean.'

'We understand perfectly,' says Bertrande, 'but it's daft.'

[49]

'Just think for five minutes, for goodness' sake. One day some people signed an armistice, in nineteen eighteen, for instance . . .'

'Granted.'

'. . . and it was filmed. That day it was news and then, afterwards, now for instance, it became history. That's obvious, isn't it?'

'No,' says Lucet. 'It doesn't make sense. Because what you're calling news, you don't see it at the same time as the thing happens. Sometimes you see it a week or a fortnight after. You even find some local cinemas showing you the Tour de France in November. Given all this, then, at which moment does it become history?'

'At once! Illico presto subito! the telly is news that's congealing into history. No sooner done than said.'

'And when there wasn't any telly,' says Sigismonde, 'then there wasn't any history?'

'You see,' says Lucet, 'you haven't got an answer to that one.'

'Have a little more of this essence of fennel, go on,' says Cidrolin.

'What about you, Dad,' says Lamélie, 'what do you think?'

'I haven't got the telly.'

'We know, we know,' says Bertrande, 'considering that we're telling Lamélie that you ought to get her one so's she shouldn't get so bored.'

'Yes, but,' says Cidrolin, 'seeing that all she thinks about is fucking.'

'They don't fuck very much,' says Lucet 'on the telly.'

'They even don't fuck at all,' says Yoland.

'Stupids,' says Bertrande, 'that's because there's kids watching.'

'Your kids,' asks Sigismonde, 'would you let them watch as much as they liked?'

[50]

'Only when it's educational,' says Yoland, 'especially the news. That'll teach them French history – world history, even.'

'How come?' says Lucet.

'Well, yes, today's news is tomorrow's history. That's one thing less they'll have to learn at school, seeing that they'll already know it.'

'It's funny,' says Cidrolin. 'It seems to me that it's starting all over again, that I've already heard all this somewhere else.'

'And yet,' says Lucet, 'what we're saying isn't said so often. It can't have happened to you so frequently to hear remarks of so high a philosophical and moral tone.'

'Especially in the circles you've just been living in,' says Yoland.

Bertrande fetches him a kick in the tibias.

'Owch,' says Yoland.

'Did you suffer?' asks Cidrolin.

'The brute,' says Yoland.

'Well, anyhow,' says Cidrolin, 'I'm very glad to have seen you. You're very kind to me.'

'Are you throwing us out?' says Bertrande.

'Looks mighty like it,' says Sigismonde.

'Not at all,' says Cidrolin, 'only, well, when things start going round in circles, when I start wondering where I'm going to land, it's better to cut it short at once, I'd lose my sense of direction, I might find myself in the old days, or in the future, who knows, or even somewhere that doesn't exist, things that scare the pants off you.'

'What,' says Yoland to Lucet, 'if we got together and gave him a telly for his birthday, that'd stop his brain ruminating.'

'We'll see,' says Lamélie. 'For the moment the best thing is to let him have his siesta: that's still his best cinema.'

Of the securicorpses, all that remained were some ruined, moss-eaten graves; they'd been well and truly forgotten, the securicorpses who died in combat in the time of King Louis the ninth of that name.

The Duke of Auge opened one eye and remembered that the Abbé Biroton had been supposed to answer a certain third question and that he had done nothing of the sort. Opening his second and last eye, the Duke of Auge didn't observe any Abbé Biroton in his field of vision.

'Ah the shitty soul-shepherd, the gallows-bird, the drowsy nod-cock', groaned the Duke. 'I'll bet he's gone off to the Council of Basle, unless it's the one in Ferrara or Florence, you don't know where you are any more. In any case, I'm really fed up, now.'

He gets up and appears on the platform of the keep of his castle, there to consider, be it ever so little, the historical situation.

There were no Goddams in sight, nor men of arms of any party or nation whatsoever. It was even somewhat deserted. A few vileyns, here and there, were scratching the miserable soil, but they counted for little in the landscape, being scarcely perceptible.

The Duke looked at this sight with a dismal eye and then went down to the kitchens, intending to devour a lark stew as he went by, just to whet his teeth. A few scullions who hadn't noticed him came in for some hefty buskin-battering which sent them flying right and left. The cook, knowing the seigneur's tastes, hastened to bring him the coveted stew. The Duke regales himself, pulverises the bones, licks the terminal members of his mitts, and whiffs up a few quarts. He beams, he smiles.

'It's all very delicious,' he declares, 'but it's nothing like so good as a little five year-old child roasted on a spit.'

He roars with laughter.

'My Lord, my Lord,' says the cook 'I most humbly beg you not to jest about such horrors.'

'I'm not jesting, I'm being serious.'

'Then, my Lord, rather jest.'

'Make your mind up, Master Cook. Do you want me to jest or to be serious?'

'My Lord, I think it would be better if we were to exclude this topic from our conversation: ogres have anything but a fair name at the nonce.'

'But you know very well that this topic is meat and drink to me! He sighed and pined and ogred and his passions boiled and bubbled – but I don't intend that the seventh Charles or anyone else shall cause the noble Lord you call an ogre to have his far from silly brains blown out.'

'My Lord, no one is unaware of the fact that you permit yourself a certain culpable indulgence . . .'

'Eh? What! Would you reproach me for my fidelity to my good old comrade in arms, the noble seigneur Gilles de Rais?'

'Well . . . er . . .'

'Eh? What? after the two of us, under the command of Jehanne the Maid, had cloven all those Goddams in twain in the King's cause, you think I should drop him now he's in the mud? No, no, and no! That would be far from noble.'

'They say he's a very great criminal.'

'Old wives' tales! People make up these stories to vilify noble seigneurs like him and me. This Charles, the seventh of that name, now that he's more or less won the Hundred Years' War, and it's even been going on a bit longer than a hundred years, and you may observe, while we're on the subject, that our good Kings, however fly they may be, they take their time to win their wars, never mind, where was I? Oh yes, now that the discomfiture of the Goddams is accelerating, what with the clang of the hurrying feet of these Capetians, they may only need another fifteen years or so, yes, now that our King doesn't need us so very much any more to finish off the expulsion of the English I'm just waiting till he starts taking some anti-feudal measures designed to cut our claws and put us in our places. I mistrust him like the devil.'

[53]

'Oo oo, my Lord, don't invoke that villainous beast.'

'The trial of our good friend Gilles is a prelude to some cunning anti-feudal measures designed to cut our claws and put us in our places.'

'My Lord, you are repeating yourself.'

'In the first place, that isn't quite true: I added an adjective, and then, let me tell you, you thick creature, that repetition is one of the most odoriferous flowers of rhetoric.'

'I should be only too willing to doubt it, my Lord, were I not in mortal dread of your blows.'

Thus provoked, the Duke gets up, picks up a step-ladder and breaks it over the cook's back.

'My Lord, my Lord,' says the master cook, 'I humbly beg you to have the supreme goodness not to converse by hits and smarts.'

'Huh, you disgust me and you make me hungry. Bring me some dried fruit-drops to ungrease my teeth.'

The Duke devours his suckets, and then returns to his muttons:

'Well, Master Cook, do *you* approve of dragging a maréchal de France through a court of law?'

'My Lord, it is quite certainly very bad and very wicked.'

'They're simply picking on my poor friend. Say he did violate a dozen little boys and liquidate three or four, even so that's no justification for court-martialling the Marshal instead of courting him, especially when he was a companion in arms of our good Maid of Lorraine that the English burnt at Rouen.'

'My Lord, they say there were a thousand and three.'

'A thousand and three what?'

'Little children who were tortured, had their throats cut or were eaten by that wicked villain of a marshal. It's frightful, all the same, it's frightful.'

The cook was crying like a baby. Less furious than astonished, the Duke observed him.

'You haven't been reading stories about the Round Table by any chance, have you?' he asked him kindly.

'My Lord, I cannot read.'

'Then perhaps some minstrel of base extraction has insinuated some complaint of his own invention into the channels of your ears?'

'That's it, my Lord, that's it: it was a minstrel who corrupted my soul with a vengeful song asking the most Christian King for justice for the poor parents of the brats that blackguard of a marshal slew.'

'What an age!' said the Duke of Auge with a sigh. 'What an age! Well, I, whom you see before you, I am going hot-foot, on the feet of my horse, that is, my good Demo, I am going, I say, to see our wise King Charles, the seventh of that name, to ask him for the great and entire liberty of Gilles, Marshal of Rais, for his immediate deliverance and, what is more, for the punishment of all the legalists, latinising jurists and nawt-head followers of Roman law who take it into their heads to cack up a good soldier like shitty flies do a noble courser, and a victorious soldier, even, which is rare. Ho there! Where is my squire Mouscaillot? Let him prepare and saddle my good Demo!'

Saddled therefore was Sthenes by Mouscaillot, and see now the Duke on his way to the capital city, accompanied by the lordling mounted on Stef. The Duke felt in a chatty mood.

'Come a bit nearer, then, Mouscaillot, and I'll tell you the reason for our journey.'

Mouscaillot trotted his horse up to the same level as that of his seigneur, but tried to maintain between them the distance he judged necessary to avoid a sudden boff.

'Come on, come nearer,' said the Duke.

'I am coming nearer, my Lord, I am.'

'Come on nearer then, nigmenog,' said Sthenes, 'you can see perfectly well that our Duke is benevolently inclined at the moment.'

[55]

'How true,' said the Duke. 'Come nearer, then.'

So Mouscaillot had to ride spur to spur.

'Do you know, my friend,' the Duke asked him, 'why I am thus journeying to the capital city?'

'I know not.'

'Guess!'

'To have a bath?'

'I might, while I'm about it. Guess again.'

'To visit the whores and jezebels?'

'I might, while I'm about it. Guess again.'

'To go and admire the beautiful flamboyant porch of Saint-Germain l'Auxerrois, the porch that master Jehan Gaussel has just finished?'

'I might, while I'm about it. Guess again.'

'It's hopeless,' said Sthenes, 'he'll never guess, and you'll end up by beating him. And anyway, didn't you want to give him a surprise?'

'You're a wise gee-gee. Now listen, Mouscaillot. I'm going to see the King of France and ask him for justice for my comrade in arms Gilles de Rais, Marshal of France.'

'What! That rotten bastard?'

Mouscaillot goes rolling in the dust.

Stef stops.

Sthenes asks the Duke:

'Do I stop, too?'

'Carry on! he'll soon catch us up. That young man disappoints me and I don't feel like making conversation any more.'

'May I sing, then?'

'If you like, my good Demo.'

So Sthenes started bawling out his repertory at the top of his voice. He'd got to a rondeau that Charles of Orleans was just about to write: 'Wynter, thou art but a vileyn,' when they arrived within sight of the gate of a fortified city that some armed borgeis were guarding. Prudently, Sthenes shut his big mouth, and the last lap of the journey was accomplished in silence.

VI

While Mouscaillot was getting his wounds and bruises looked after by a local leche, the Duke of Auge was waiting for his supper in the inn at Mont-à-Lambert by devouring some eel brawn, each mouthful of which he washed down with a generous draught of claret wine. This put him in a better mood, and all the more so as each instant brought him nearer to the moment when the meal was really going to begin. Hence he welcomed with some benevolence a personage who seemed to be of quality and who came up and greeted him with such well-turned and gracious civilities that the Duke invited him to his table. The young seigneur accepts without beating about the bush and gives his name: Adolf, Viscount de Péchiney.

As Mouscaillot, bandaged by the leche, has just arrived, they start on the supper which opens with three soups of different colours: macaroon soup, pear soup and tripe soup. Next they get outside a roast with bud sauce and nutmeg sauce. They whiff up some quarts. After that they attack the second, well-spiced roast, they whiff up some more quarts, they finish with dried suckets and sweetmeats. Famine still reigned in the neighbouring streets, but they had to finish somehow.

'My young friend,' said the Duke then to the Viscount de Péchiney, 'have you not heard tell of the noble seigneur Gilles de Rais, Marshal of France?'

'Indeed I have, my Lord.'

[57]

'He was my comrade in arms! Marshal of France at twenty-five, what d'you say to that?'

'I say that that's a fine age for a marshal.'

'It is, isn't it? And do you know what's happening to him?'

'I heard he'd been put in prison.'

'They even want to behead him.'

'That makes me passing sad.'

'Well, my young friend, do you know why I have left my castle and come to spend a few days in the capital city?'

'That I wot not.'

'Well, my young friend, I am going to ask the King for a pardon for the marshal. I consider that a liberator of France cannot be treated thus. The fact that he may have roasted a few brats is no reason to forget the services he has rendered to his country.'

'Do not speak so loudly, my Lord, public opinion is extremely unfavourable to the marshal.'

'Don't give a damn. Going to see the King just the same.'

'And where?'

'What d'you mean: and where? Why, in Paris, of course.'

'He is not there.'

'What? The King isn't in his palace? Not in the Louvre? at the gates of which, watch his anxious servants do keep? where is he, then?'

'On the banks of the Loire.'

'Fat lot of use it was us delivering his fine capital city from the Goddams if it was just for him not to set foot in it.'

'My Lord, I should never allow myself to criticize our King Charles, seventh of that name.'

'Well, personally, I do allow myself to. I'm a Duke, and I'm entitled to eight stakes on my gallows-tree. I'm a direct descendant of Merovaeus, which is to tell you that for me the Capets are extremely small beer. What doesn't he think he is, this particular Capet: without us and the little shepherdess, we mustn't forget

[58]

the little shepherdess, without us, I say, the English would still be on the throne. And thus I consider it particularly unseemly that the King should not be in the capital city when I come to see him in it.'

'My Lord, you are not alone in thinking thus.'

'You amaze me. I'm usually quite alone in thinking what I think.'

'So far as the King of France is concerned, you would find friends.'

'So I should hope! Every noble seigneur would resent as I do such an affront.'

'And would wreak his vengeance for it!'

'Indeed he would, but that would be more difficult. With all that regular army, those franc-archers, those ordnance companies, and the Bureau brothers' artillery, just try and have a go now!'

'Apropos of the Bureau brothers, do you not consider that our King is surrounding himself a little too much by lowborn creatures such as the said brothers, and Jacques Coeur, and that Etienne Chevalier. . . .'

'My word,' said the Duke of Auge, 'you talk like a book.'

'I have a feeling I've read it in a book,' says Cidrolin, 'mendicant monks, they date back to the middle ages.'

'What about nuns,' says the passer-by, 'they never stop mendicating. I don't know if it's the middle ages or what.'

'And yet we're out of the middle ages,' says Cidrolin. 'At least. . . . it seems . . .'

'That quasi-clergyman with his mobylette,' says the passer-by, 'after all, he may be a con man.'

'He's never conned me,' says Cidrolin, 'I don't give him anything.'

'You might think about the others,' says the passer-by, 'the ones he may have conned.'

'I don't wish anybody any harm,' says Cidrolin.

'That's what you say.'

Cidrolin looks at the passer-by, whose face expresses nothing, and just then someone hails them.

'You're the one she's addressing her remarks to,' the passer-by says to Cidrolin.

'Hallo, Mademoiselle,' says Cidrolin.

'You, Monsieur, are the one I'm addressing my remarks to,' says the damsel to the passer-by.

'If I understand aright, Mademoiselle,' says the passer-by, 'you are hitch-hiking.'

'Me camperess and Canadian and . . .'

The passer-by signals, a huge car comes and draws up along the pavement, there's always room for huge cars, a chauffeur in livery gets out, opens the door, the damsel gets in, the passer-by says to Cidrolin:

'Did you see how the child smelt there was a huge car somewhere?'

He gets in after her and the whole lot disappears. Cidrolin says to Cidrolin:

'How many passers-by are there? The fact is there're a lot more passers-by than there need be, or else it's the same passer-by who reverberates from day to day. And the quasi-clergyman on his mobylette, he really is the same one . . . so far as you can judge; but the Canadian girls? all different, no doubt, seeing that there're Wyandots and Babelians. There may perhaps be some who're more on the mauve side, or garnet-red, and who speak unknown languages. This one was turning slightly ebony; after all perhaps they're all identical. Like the passers-by. This one isn't a real passer-by, he's got a uniform. Can I help you, Monsieur?'

'Could you tell me where Mademoiselle Lamélie Cidrolin barges?'

'Right here,' replies Cidrolin.

'Have *you* got something to do with that young person?' asks the newcomer suspiciously.

'I should hope so,' says Cidrolin. 'I'm her father.'

'That's very convenient then,' exclaims the other with lively satisfaction. 'As it so happens, I've come to ask him for her hand.'

'You certainly a lucky bugger: first person you meet is the one who answers your purpose.'

'Is it yes, or is it no? Oh, you know, it's not that I'm all that keen on it, but, all things considered, why not, after all, and then she's insinuated that she's got a bun in the oven, as my grandfather used to say, he was very much that way inclined too, it's obvious, because I've got at least seventy-two cousins who are either illegitimate or the issue of adulterous unions, and as I'm a man of honour, and you must realise that for us, in our job, there's nothing easier than to sow children right and left all along the route, I've even got a colleague who begat one in between the rue des Petits-Champs and the Opera, that's just to show you how well I know what I'm talking about, and if I didn't want to put things right it wouldn't be at all surprising, but there you are, that's the way it is, I feel like putting things right, so I'm inviting you to take advantage of this opportunity. And anyway I wouldn't mind living on a barge.'

'Don't count on it,' says Cidrolin.

'Zplenty of room on your vessel, though.'

'My daughters,' says Cidrolin, 'when they get married, they go and live somewhere else. That's the way it is.'

'Then you'd condemn us to an awful housing development?'

'My dear fellow,' says Cidrolin, 'that's your business. And anyway, there's not only awful housing developments, there's suburban detacheds, there's little flats on the fourth floor without a lift, there's stationary caravans and I'll spare you the rest.'

'Even so, there's bags of room.'

[61]

'Which d'you want to marry?' asks Cidrolin. 'Lamélie or the barge?'

'Well I haven't seen the barge yet.'

'It must be admitted,' says Cidrolin, 'that it certainly is a nice barge, and I will even go so far as to add that you might possibly consider it the barge to end all barges. Want to have a look?'

'It'll make me sad, if I think I'll never live in it.'

'Have to make the best of it,' says Cidrolin. 'You can always come and drink a glass of essence of fennel on it. In fact, I'll offer you one now.'

Cidrolin shows him the way, they go down the bank, step on to the gang-plank, the omnibudsman nearly falls into the filthy fluvial flow.

'I can see you've never worked on a river-bus,' Cidrolin says to him in friendly fashion.

Then he calls:

'Here's your boy-friend!'

It is to Lamélie that these words are addressed and she appears forthwith.

'Who is this gentleman?' Lamélie asks Cidrolin.

'Your intended, so it seems.'

'Don't know him,' says Lamélie, 'but if he wants a glass of essence of fennel we could offer him one.'

'I already have. All you have to do now is bring us that refreshment.'

Lamélie scarpers to realise this project.

'Well, my dear fellow,' says Cidrolin to the omnibudsman, 'what d'you think of my barge?'

'She's great,' replies the omnibudsman absent-mindedly. 'Is she really called Lamélie?'

'No, she's called the Ark.'

'Your daughter's called the Ark?'

'My daughter's called Lamélie.'

'Are you sure?'

'Don't you recognise her?'

The omnibudsman scratches his head rather obviously.

'Now . . . mjust wondering if . . . mjust wondering . . . Well, Ida know, is she really called Lamélie?'

'It's a fact.'

'It'd be pretty astonishing if another Lamélie, my one, lived on another barge round these parts too.'

'Why not?'

'Er um . . . the theory of probability . . .'

'Just an excuse for riddles and paradoxes. All the girls on all the barges all along the river may perhaps be called Lamélie.'

The omnibudsman looked as if he doubted it.

'On the barges that don't move,' Cidrolin added.

The Omnibudsman looked almost convinced. He would have made a great mistake if he'd been completely so because Lamélie, bringing in the essence of fennel, said to him:

'Well, pet, did I give you a fright?'

'It *is* her!' cried the pet gleefully.

'Have you spoken to Dad?'

'Yes,' says the pet.

'Does he say yes?'

'You ask him.'

'Can I marry the omnibudsman, Dad?'

'Yes,' says Cidrolin, and adds, not without melancholy: 'That's a good thing done.'

They drink toasts. They chat. They talk about the future ménage, since there's no question of living here, and in any case the omnibudsman wouldn't be all that keen, humidity, it's well known, it gives you rheumatism, and he's dead scared of rheumatism, is the omnibudsman. And then the brat, since it's a question of having a brat, he might take a header into the infamous sewerish ooze that stagnates round the barge, so they'll go and

[63]

look for a little detached in the suburbs, but with what for money, they wonder. Cidrolin wonders that too.

The omnibudsman doesn't dare ask him.

They might have to wait for the little detached in the suburbs. No harm in asking, though.

'How much will it be, what you give her?' asked the omnibudsman.

'How much what? Who's her?' says Cidrolin. 'Me and money matters, you know . . .'

'Um,' says the omnibudsman, 'um, the dowry, I mean, what they used to call the dowry, the little sum that's kind of the key to the marriage, I mean.'

'It isn't quite clear what you're trying to say,' says Cidrolin.

'Well, I mean, Lamélie, for her marriage, aren't you going to give her anything?'

'Nothing,' says Cidrolin.

'Really nothing?'

'Really nothing.'

'All the same, you must have a bit of money tucked away.'

'No doubt, but I'm going to have some expenses.'

'What sort of expenses?'

'Expenses in getting a replacement. You don't expect me to do without a woman, do you? To polish my shoes, make the grub and all the rest? 'll have to get myself another; another woman. And that can cost me a lot of money.'

'But,' says the omnibudsman, somewhat worried, 'Lamélie, she isn't your missis, she really is your daughter, isn't she?'

'Have no fear on that score,' declares Cidrolin, with authority, 'Lamélie is the third of the triplets of whom my deceased spouse was delivered as she expired.'

'Dno idea,' says the omnibudsman, overwhelmed.

'Don't take it that way, it's rather picturesque to marry a triplet. You'll amaze your buddies when they find out.'

'Yes, that's true.'

'And coming back to money matters, just can't be helped, I need someone to swab down the deck and dress ship over all on high days and holidays. You don't really expect *me* to do all that, do you, so I'll need some ready to find that rare bird, so it follows that you, well you've had it.'

'If that's how it is,' says the omnibudsman, 'I wonder whether . . . I wonder whether . . .'

'Remember our kisses,' Lamélie tells him.

'Come, come,' adds Cidrolin, 'you surely aren't going to pretend that money matters all that much to you, are you?'

'No, course not, and then, a triplet, all the same, a triplet, there might even be a chance of me getting my photo in the papers or being on the news on the telly, don't you think?'

'Without the shadow of a doubt,' says Cidrolin gravely.

'Well then,' exclaims the omnibudsman, 'come hell or high water, I'll have Lamélie, lolly or no lolly.'

'Good boy,' says Cidrolin. 'Well what did you think of my essence of fennel?'

'First class,' says the omnibudsman. 'First class.'

There is a silence.

'Well er,' the omnibudsman finally says, 'that's a good thing done. With your permission, I'll go home and tell my mum.'

'I warn you here and now,' says Cidrolin, 'that if it's to replace Lamélie, to sluice down the deck and do the brightwork, I don't want any of your mum.'

'But I had no intention of suggesting her.'

'I should hope not.'

Cidrolin gets up, the omnibudsman does ditto. Cidrolin says to Lamélie:

'I'll go with him; he gets giddy on the gangplank.'

He holds his hand because he's afraid he might take a header into the sludge; then they climb up the bank.

[65]

'Goodbye,' says Cidrolin to the omnibudsman.

He looks at the fence and the gate; they're covered in inscriptions. The omnibudsman says:

'I can't understand people who feel the urge to write. Is that about you?'

'Goodbye,' Cidrolin says to him.

While the omnibudsman walks slowly off, Cidrolin goes and fetches the pot of paint and, with a careful brush, spreads some beautiful green coats over the letter A; he concentrates; he overdoes it and the said letter reappears because it's got too much paint on, then he goes on to the letter S and his fervour does not diminish. He no longer hears the passing of the passing passer-by, nor the passage on the boulevard of thousands and thousands of cars. The Viscount de Péchiney is talking softly to the Duke of Auge. La Trémoille, Dunois and the Duke of Alençon are going to bring the Capetian to heel somewhat and remind him of the respect he ought to show for the well-born. Someone still more important has even joined them. The Duke of Auge wonders who that may well be, he adds that he hasn't the slightest idea. After a bit of persuading, the young seigneur admits that that someone is none other than the Dauphin.

'What!' exclaims the Duke of Auge. 'The famous eleventh Louis?'

'Himself,' replies the Viscount de Péchiney, 'but eleventh, he isn't yet, you know.'

'And would he conspire against his papa?'

'We are by no means conspiring, we are defending our legitimate rights.'

'I realise that; and what about my good friend Gilles de Rais, what will become of him in all this?'

'We shall go and deliver him.'

'I'll give you a hundred cloves of wool or cheese if events befall thus. In the meantime, let us drincan!'

And they drenk.

[66]

VII

The look-out man spotted two individuals mounted on mules coming towards the castle. The Duke of Auge was immediately advised. Then they recognised the Abbé Biroton, followed by the Deacon Riphinte.

'We'll play a trick on them,' said the Duke of Auge. 'We'll fire the bombard at them, and a few rounds of the culverin. You can go and get the shot back afterwards.'

The novice artillerymen didn't feel too sanguine about this, for it was the first time they would be using the Duke of Auge's new acquisitions. The bombard functioned in satisfactory fashion and a bullet went and dug itself in less than three hundred yards away from Onésiphore, who didn't understand any more than the Deacon Riphinte what was going on.

When the culverin balls came and landed in his immediate neighbourhood the chaplain threw himself off his mule to implore divine protection, and was forthwith imitated by the Deacon Riphinte. One of the culverin tubes burst, which stopped the firing, as the Duke didn't wish to risk blowing up, just for a little joke, a piece of material that had cost him a great deal of money.

While the surviving artillerymen were recovering the cannon-balls, the Abbé Biroton, followed by the Deacon Riphinte, went to report to the Duke.

'What a welcome, my Lord,' said the Abbé Biroton. 'I know you didn't mean any harm, but we had a narrow escape.'

'The result was more satisfying than I thought.'

'Then, my Lord, do you also possess the diabolical bomb?'

'I have to defend myself, my dear fellow. I'm expecting the

royal security companies from one day to the next and, as I've no wish to get trampled on, I've taken my precautions and put in a provision of modern inventions and the latest novelties.'

'Are you still having some differences of opinion with the King?'

'Non-stop. This time it's because of my good friend Gilles de Rais . . .'

'Oo! that rotten bastard!'

'Be quiet, turbulent priest. Would you be lacking in christian charity? My good friend Gilles de Rais has been well and truly executed, just like a vileyn, he, a noble seigneur and valiant warrior, when the Hundred Years' War isn't even over yet. As that did not please me, I joined with some other noble seigneurs and valiant warriors to teach the King a lesson; and do you know who was on our side?'

'That can y not devyne.'

'The Dauphin.'

'What! the famous eleventh Louis?'

'Eleventh – not yet. I won't tell you everything that has happened; what it comes down to is that the noble seigneurs behaved like nits and the Dauphin has let us down, to such good purpose that I am now the only one left face to face with the King of France in a state of open rebellion. Luckily I have my little cannons. Huh, since you're here, no fussing, now, you can bless them for me.'

The Abbé Biroton does so there and then, without arguing. This out of the way, the Duke pats him cordially on the back, enquires after his health, and asks:

'Well, what about that Council?'

'It deposed Eugenius IV and put Amadeus in his place, and the King of France is going to promulgate the Pragmatic Sanction which defends the liberties of the Gallican Church.'

'If I understand aright, you're taking the King's side.'

'Don't get carried away, my Lord, I was there merely as a

[68]

simple observer.'

'Hm! you look like the stuff traitors are made of, to me.'

'My Lord! A traitor! I? a simple observer, I repeat.'

'You may well repeat it, but I'm going to keep my eye on you and I'm wondering whether it wasn't my guardian angel who advised me to embellish your return with a little cannon fire. Personally I'm a Guelph and I'm feudal. If my chaplain starts getting modern ideas into his head I'll have no alternative but to tie him to the muzzle of a bombard and send him up to the heavens in little bits.'

The Abbé Biroton refrained from comment on this remark and, in the ensuing silence, the voices of Pigranelle and Bélusine were heard singing a rondeau that Charles of Orleans was just about to write: 'Wynter, thou art but a vileyn.' In the stables, Sthenes and Stef hummed an accompaniment to them.

'Your daughters seem to be feeling gay,' said the chaplain, in order to talk about something other than himself.

'Yes,' replied the Duke. 'I'm marrying them off.'

'All three of them?'

'Yes.'

'Even Phélise?'

'Even Phélise. You see, Onésiphore, since I became a widower the girls haven't met a soul. Thanks to the intrigues I've been getting mixed up in I've made some friends and allies, nits, as I told you, and, among the most nit-witted of all these nits I've got hold of three young dolts on whom I'm fobbing off my little treble: Pigranelle to Lord de Ciry, Bélusine to Count de Torves and Phélise to the Vidame de Malplaquet. And that's a good thing done. I hope we'll be able to celebrate these nuptials before the King's archers arrive.'

'Whom you hope to discomfit?'

'With my little cannons, I'm not afraid of anyone any more.'

The Duke of Auge rubbed his hands and manifested all the

[69]

signs of the most lively satisfaction, then, suddenly, he began to look anxious.

'And that world history I was asking you about, quite some time ago, now, I'm still waiting for your answer.'

'What do you want to know, exactly?'

'What you think of world history in general and of general history in particular.'

'I'm really very tired,' said the Chaplain.

'You can have a rest later. Tell me, this Council of Basle, is that world history?'

'Yes indeed. World history in general.'

'And my little cannons?'

'General history in particular.'

'And the marriage of my daughters?'

'Hardly even factual history. It's microhistory at the very most.'

'It's what?' yells the Duke of Auge. 'What the devil sort of language is that? Is today your Pentecost, or what?'

'Be so good as to excuse me, my Lord. It is, as you see, fatigue. And nerves. Those cannon-balls are terrible: a diabolic invention!'

'But you blessed them, sluggard!'

'The cannons, not their balls.'

'Oh! what a wicked hypocrite! Out of my sight, or I'll massacre you.'

Onésiphore disappears.

The Duke makes the tour of his ramparts, examines the horizon, which is devoid of any archers, caresses his bombard and culverins and congratulates his myrmidons. He even pronounces a little allocution:

'And if the chaplain comes and tells you that this is a diabolical invention, you can reply that if we'd had some artillery at the time of the Crusades the Holy Sepulchre would still be in Christian hands.'

Having said this he goes down by way of the kitchens to see if he can't scrounge something good, and then, suddenly changing his mind, he has his daughters summoned to his presence.

These three young persons immediately present themselves. They start by thanking their papa warmly for the mirth-provoking spectacle he offered them in bombarding and culverining the Abbé Biroton and the Deacon Riphinte, then they make respectful inquiries about the paternal intentions as regards the date of their nuptials. The Duke answers by asking them first of all whether they are finally going to allow him to get a word in edgewise. They should have no fear, he continues, everything is prepared, the seigneurs are coming hot horse-foot; as for the King's archers, the little cannons are there to receive them and, if they take it into their heads to appear before the castle walls, their atomisation will only, after all, be a pretext for additional mirth. This speech then appearing to him to be terminated the Duke's mood changes once again and he invites the triplets to relieve him forthwith of their presence, and if not, let them watch out. While he is climbing up to the summit of his keep to see if the King's archers have appeared in the neighbourhood, his daughters hasten to find the chaplain, whom they discover in the process of partaking of good cheer in the kitchens where he has retired in order to decorticate a few sour herrings which he moistens with claret wine. They interview him, but he can only avow that he knows precious little of the question that interests them and he invites them to recommend their souls to God by means of pious prayers.

'Baa, baa,' says Phélise.

She approves.

When the girls have gone, the chef suggests that the chaplain might reinvigorate himself a little more by eating a raised pie he is cooking, one made of mutton-suint and cinnamon.

'Gramercy,' says Onésiphore. 'Brrr, those cannonballs flying round my tonsure like flies, they were a terrible ordeal for such a peaceable priest as I.'

[71]

'And yet, chaplain,' says the master cook, 'you have no fear of blows, so far as I am aware.'

'You think so? Then I must have changed . . .'

'In any case, methinks the culverinade you underwent is only a very modest beginning. There's going to be a hell of a rumpus around these parts, and sooner rather than later. The moment our very Christian King, the seventh Charles, has liquidated the Goddams, and even before, he'll come and show the Duke where he gets off when he tries to be funny; and the business of defending that vile ogre, Gilles de Rais, that won't have made him so very popular, our Duke. Not in my eyes, at any rate; personally, I'm not in favour of cannibalism, even considered as a joke. Neither am I in favour of fi.earms, the scourge of our times. We are forced to kill, eviscerate and disembowel animals, that's true enough: we have to live; and then, they have no souls, isn't that so, my lord chaplain?'

'That is a question that could only occur to the mind of an Albigensian and, thank God, there are none left.'

'Then I'll bring you my mutton-suint and cinnamon pie.'

Onésiphore tastes it.

'Well,' says he, 'this is one consolation for my having landed up in this castle again, when I could have hooked myself a bishopric by a bit of intrigue at the Council, but I'm not an intriguer. All the same, here, we're more or less caught like rats in a trap. And what about these marriages; do *you* believe in these marriages?'

'Not in the slightest,' replies the master cook, 'nothing's ready, the tradesmen haven't been advised, and the reserves at my disposal wouldn't be enough for me to feed thirty noble persons, let alone to withstand a siege.'

'And our Duke is labouring under quite some illusions about his artillery. They fall every which way, his cannon-balls, in short, any old where; we haven't got the complete weapon yet;

and anyway, the King has some, too. A few well-directed cannon-balls on the drawbridge and the King's archers will have free access to the castle.'

'So the litel clergeon's going in for strategy, now!' exclaimed the Duke, who'd come in on the sly. 'And defeatist strategy, what's more! I don't know what's stopping me hanging him by his external glands.'

In the meantime, he can't stop himself pulling one of his ears. The indignant Abbé Biroton starts bawling like mad and, as this doesn't stop the other continuing, he takes a larding-needle from the fire and starts to grill the tractive hand. The Duke utters an appalling yell and lets go, shaking his combusted appendix. Thus liberated, Onésiphore enunciates his complaints in a limpid voice:

'To do that to me! A representative of God on earth! An observer at the Council of Basle! A member of the Apostolic, Roman and Gallican Church! On your knees, Joachim, Duke of Auge! Implore forgiveness, or I'll have you excommunicated; and then no more marriages, no more sacraments, no more anything! On your knees, Joachim, Duke of Auge!'

'And they rebel, what's more,' says the Duke in a mutter as he smears some fresh butter over his burn. 'I've been seeing this coming for quite some time; the clergy want to control everything.'

'On your knees, Joachim, Duke of Auge!' the Abbé Biroton goes on bawling. 'Implore forgiveness for your disrespect to your Holy Mother the Church. On your knees, and more quickly than that! I'm beginning to see some little baby devils galloping round you; they're only waiting for the right moment to carry your soul off to Hell.'

'And he has visions, on top of everything else.'

'And think well on these things; no more anything! no more sacraments! no more marriages!'

[73]

The Duke shrugs his shoulders, sighs, and kneels.

'Forgive me,' he says.

'That lacks warmth,' says the chaplain. 'Come now, a little more compunction . . . a little more faith . . .'

The Duke decides to give it the proper dose.

'I implore the forgiveness of my Holy Mother the Church, and that of the no less holy Abbé Onésiphore Biroton.'

He is forgiven.

'All the same,' he explained a little later to Mouscaillot. 'I wasn't going to risk going to Hell for a chaplain's ear. I might say that those little baby devils, I don't believe in them. Does he believe in them himself? Still, I can't set everybody against me, you've got to be artful in this world. I know, to take my mind off all that I'll go big-game hunting, the aurochs or the urus, for example. Saddle the horses and tell the hunt to get ready . . . I'll take a culverin, too . . . obviously if I score a direct hit there won't be much left of the game, though, there won't be much left . . .'

When Cidrolin opens his eyes again an orange sun is moving down towards the housing blocks in the sub-urban zone. He gets up, drinks a stiff glass of essence of fennel, brushes his nattiest suit and puts it on. First of all he goes and makes sure that the fence and gate are innocent of all graffiti, then he locks up behind him and here he is, walking off to the buses. He chooses one which takes him towards the centre of the capital city, and there he takes another for a secondary centre of the same city. The twilight continues, but cafés and shops are already lit up as if it were the middle of the night; it's true that in this secondary centre it's always the middle of the night, from dawn even unto dusk.

Cidrolin looks to the right and to the left in all the cafés as if he were looking for someone or simply for a place or a table that meets with his requirements. He dithers a bit, but finally goes into the Bar Biture, a bar that takes pains to look as if it looks like every other bar. Cidrolin sits down. Its only clients are two chaps who are standing at the counter and talking about the treble forecast. The boss is behind the counter, doing nothing, and listening to their comments on the forecasts; he is wearing a square semi-round oval cloth cap adorned with white polka dots. Its background is black. The dots are of a slightly elliptical shape; the major axis of each one is five millimetres long and the minor axis four, an area of slightly less than sixty-three square millimetres, say. The peak is made of an analogous material, but the polka dots are appreciably smaller and of a quasi-circular shape. Their area is not more than thirty-two square millimetres. There is a stain on the third spot from the left, counting from a position facing the wearer of the cap and starting from the edge. It's a stain made by essence of fennel. It is minute, but, notwithstanding its reduced dimensions, it retains the natural colour of the original substance, a somewhat pisslike colour, half-way between infra-red and ultra-violet. On careful examination of the adjoining spot, still continuing to count from the left when facing the wearer of the cap and keeping as near as possible to the edge, one can distinguish an infinitesimal blemish which likewise originated in the projection of a drop of essence of fennel, but its dimensions are such that one might take it simply for a thread of the surrounding black cloth that could have strayed in that direction and there taken on a yellowish hue owing to the effect of the neon lighting which falls on it as best it can from a tubular tube; in fact there are indeed some sudden stoppages in the functioning of this appliance and, at times, one might imagine that it is emitting signals in the alphabet invented by the famous American painter who was born in Charleston (Mass.) in 1791 and died in Poughkeepsie in 1872. By a remarkable coincidence, just above Cidrolin's head is hanging a reproduction of the dying Hercules, by Samuel Finley Breese Morse, a work which in 1813 won the gold medal of the Royal Society of Arts, London, England.

As it is hanging just above his head Cidrolin cannot directly see this reproduction which is in any case reflected in the vast mirror covering the whole of the opposite wall, but Cidrolin cannot see it indirectly, either, for one of the two customers is exceedingly tall and completely conceals the representation of the dying Hercules by Samuel Finley Breese Morse. The other customer, who is appreciably less tall than his interlocutor since he does not measure more than four feet eight, raises his eyes from time to time to this engraving of which he has a direct view, for he is leaning against the counter and has his back almost entirely turned to the boss who suddenly seems to perceive the presence of a new customer and, from a distance, without moving from the spot, without even making a gesture and even less removing his cap, asks Cidrolin what he wishes to consume.

This question doesn't in the least disconcert Cidrolin for he had been foreseeing it for some moments and preparing himself to answer it; thus his answer is not slow in making itself heard. It consists in a series of words forming a grammatically well-formed phrase and of whose meaning there can be no doubt, even in the mind of a bistro boss as thick as the one who keeps the Bar Biture. The bistro boss goes on listening for a moment to the considerations of the two customers concerning the treble, then he brings Cidrolin the desired drink, which is slightly tepid essence of fennel with a drop of still water. Cidrolin fabricates a manifest smile to demonstrate his indescribable, immense and perpetual gratitude for so much kindness and so much exactitude, and the man with the black cloth cap sprinkled with white polka dots, still solemn, retires majestically behind his counter.

A few minutes then pass during which the two customers try to solve the mysterious problems posed by the following Sunday's treble, one of the customers is exceedingly tall, the other is in semi-profile, with his back leaning against the zinc counter, which enables him to glance, from time to time, at the reproduction of

[76]

the work of Samuel Finley Breese Morse. He also now and then looks at the other man who is sitting there apparently drinking his essence of fennel. He can't find him of any interest, for his glance never lingers longer than three or four seconds on this individual who has no special peculiarities. He seems very definitely to prefer the dying Hercules of Samuel Finley Breese Morse. As his interlocutor declares that he has exhausted all the combinations that can reasonably be envisaged, he makes a slight pivotal movement, brings some small change out of his pocket and pays for the two desiccated glasses which are still encumbering the counter. Next he shakes the boss's hand and goes out, followed by his companion, the man who is exceedingly tall. The door shuts behind them.

The man with the cap washes the glasses. He doesn't say anything to Cidrolin.

Cidrolin doesn't say anything to him.

It is at this point that Albert comes in.

VIII

Albert abstains from any sort of extravagant display of surprise, recognition or joy at the sight of Cidrolin. He sits down calmly, he shakes his mitt, he asks the boss for a glass of champagne. When the glass is full, the man with the black cloth cap with white polka dots beats a retreat behind his counter and manages to make himself very small there.

Albert and Cidrolin speak in an undertone.

'Everything okay with you?' asks Albert.

'More or less.'

'Finding your way around in civvy life again?'

'All right. You get used to it.'

'You still living on the barge?'

'Yes.'

'You must be nice and quiet there.'

'More or less. Except that, for some time now, some silly dope's been amusing himself writing a lot of muck on the fence along the boulevard. I spend my time repainting it. The fence.'

'You're just making a fuss about nothing. Graffiti, what are graffiti? Simply literature.'

'Of course, but I prefer to paint them out.'

'And what else is wrong?'

'Apart from that, everything's fine. My daughter's getting married. The last one.'

'Bravo. Then you must be pleased. They're all off your hands.'

'I must admit I never thought she'd make it.'

'You see: never despair.'

'Oh, I wasn't despairing. It was more for her sake.'

'Of course.'

'Right. And now I'm going to be all alone on my barge.'

'I ought to come and see you one day, but you know, what with my business.'

'That's precisely why I wanted to talk to you.'

'I can't imagine what you can have to say to me about my business.'

'Oh but I have; you'll see.'

'There's nothing I'd like better.'

'Well, it's like this, I'm going to be all alone on my barge, now. I'll have to do the cooking, do my washing, mend my socks, swab down the deck, all of which are activities which bug me and which in any case are exclusively feminine. You see what I'm getting at?'

'I'd like to see from a bit closer to.'

'You wouldn't happen to know a young person, would you, not too young, all the same, who could take care of all that, do the

[78]

cooking, do my washing, mend my socks, swab down the deck?
I might say I don't necessarily insist on plowing her, not at all,
even, oh no, it'd just be for that, for what I've mentioned, to cook
the nosh, iron my shirts, mend my pants and keep the barge neat
and tidy. In the navy, you know, your day is never done.'

'Why don't you go to an employment agency?'

'With the reputation they've given me . . .?'

'Do you really imagine they're still thinking about you? They've
forgotten you.'

'They can't have, seeing that there's the chap who mucks up
my gate.'

'That's just your imagination.'

'It's not my imagination. It's written.'

'Personally I'd advise an employment agency.'

'I'd have thought that amongst all the girls you know there'd
have been loads who'd prefer my barge to an Argentinian brothel
or an oil harem.'

'Well, there I can assure you that you're wrong. There's no
future in what you're offering them; work nauseates them,
believe me.'

'All the same. All the same. It's not so terrible, what I'm
asking: sluicing down the fo'c'sle and the quarter-deck, knitting
a sweater, boiling the washing and buying the spuds in the
supermarket, that's not so terrible. I'd have thought that'd have
seemed much better than getting yourself knocked by hordes of
gauchos or a polygamous, belching sheikh.'

'How wrong you are. The girls who pass through my hands,
I'd be only too pleased to keep some of them here, I find them
real sinecures . . .'

'This is one.'

'. . . but *they*'re the ones who beg me to let them go to far-off
countries. They're unbelievable colonisers.'

'They're idiotic, your birds, You chat 'em up, you shoot 'em a line. Just for once, find one and make her believe the truth, to wit, that my barge is a chaste and pure abode which is better than stripteasing in a filthy tropical hole.'

'Sta minute. Personally I don't go in for the lousy hole. The joints I cater for leave nothing to be desired in re status.'

'My barge has got status, too. The inspector of corbitary contributions came the other day and he gave me some some hope that the Ark would soon go up into the three anchors class in category A.'

'Congratulations,' said Albert, impressed.

'You're a pal, aren't you?' said Cidrolin.

'Do you doubt it?' said Albert, indignant.

'Find me what I'm looking for, then.'

'It'll be difficult.'

'Course it won't. You station yourself in the Avenue du Maine . . .'

'You're not going to teach me my job.'

'. . . you see a girl who's just got off the train from Avranches, you say to her: Mademoiselle, I know of a barge, I don't need to tell you any more, all you'll have to do is just a bit of housework and the hash to get and you'll be able to sun-bathe, and at the same time watch the boat club rowing by, very good-looking boys. And it'll be true: she won't find herself on board a Liberian cargo boat destined for the remotest dumps in the whole world.'

'It's rather against my principles, what you're asking me.'

'Would you hesitate between your principles and friendship?'

'All right, all right. But I wouldn't do it for anyone but you. Onésiphore!'

The man in the black cloth cap with the white polka dots very slowly rotates thirty-seven degrees.

'Give us,' says Albert, 'a bottle of champagne. My special *cuvée*. 'It's,' he tells Cidrolin, 'the same as the Rothschilds, Onassis, and people like that have.'

[80]

Onésiphore opens a little trap-door and disappears.

'Look here, though,' adds Albert, embarrassed, 'There's still one question we haven't raised.'

'I don't want you to be out of pocket,' says Cidrolin. 'I'll pay, cache on delivery, exactly what you'd have got in the export trade.'

'I'll give you twenty per cent off.'

'You're a pal.'

Onésiphore brings the special *cuvée*.

They take a swig.

Onésiphore is entitled to a glass too, but he doesn't intervene in the debris of the conversation which is now coming to an end.

'Try,' says Cidrolin, 'and see that she's neither hideous nor too bloody stupid, the girl.'

'I'll try,' says Albert. 'So far as a pretty face is concerned, I know my way around, but stupidity, sometimes it's unfathomable.'

'I'll go home, now,' says Cidrolin.

'My chauffeur'll drive you,' says Albert.

'No, thanks,' says Cidrolin. 'I'd rather go by bus.'

'Still got unpleasant memories, eh?'

Cidrolin doesn't answer. He shakes Albert's mitt, makes polite noises to the man in the black cloth cap with the white polka dots, takes the two requisite buses and, when he's back on his barge, opens a tin of paté de foie mousse and spreads it on some bread. He then imbibes three and a half glasses of essence of fennel and, in the end, goes to bed and goes to sleep. He finds himself face to face with a mammoth, a real one.

The Duke coldly sizes up the animal. He says to Mouscaillot:

'I was thinking of an aurochs or a urus, but not of this particular beastie. I didn't think there were any left on my territories. Artillerymen! hey there! to your guns! The objective: the mammoth! Take aim!...'

[81]

The mammoth, having taken a deep breath, charges his aggressors at a slow trot.

'Every creature for himself!' neighs Sthenes, who was toying with some lichen at the foot of a tree.

'He's starting to give orders, now!' says the Duke indulgently.

'Every man for himself!' bleats Mouscaillot.

'Tu quoque fili . . .'

The Duke of Auge goes to bash the page over the earoil, but said page has buggered off, likewise the artillerymen, the hunt and the horses. This desertion doesn't make any impression on him; he unsheathes his braquemard and prepares to have at the wild beast, but the latter ignores the comrade in arms of Jeanne d'Arc and Gilles de Rais. With a powerful foot it drives the culverin into the ground and continues hot-trunk on its way in the pachydermic hope of reducing to mincemeat the vermin it perceives, but the dogs are already in their kennels, the horses in the stables and the artillerymen hard by the drawbridge. The Duke of Auge, therefore, stays where he is, unscathed, panting and nobiliary.

He looks sadly at his piece of ordnance which has been transformed into a root, that makes two he's lost in the same day, they're finally coming rather expensive, these modern inventions. He puts his braquemard back in its scabbard and undertakes to consider, be it ever so little, the historical situation.

It was, for the time being, forest-clad and depopulated. The trees were growing in silence, and the animal kingdom was confining its presence to obscure and mute acts. The Duke of Auge, who usually dedicated very little time to the contemplation of nature, decided to make his way to more inhabited regions; for this purpose he judged it particularly intelligent to go back along the path he had taken to come to this spot and which, in the normal way, ought to lead him to his castle.

He identifies without hesitation the path that seems to him to be appropriate and walks at a good pace for something like an hour. He then realises that it is a Heideggerian path. Much encacked, he turns round and walks at a good pace for something like an hour, hoping to find the clearing where his culverin was reposing, its soul filled with humus and rotting leaves. He comes out in a clearing all right but he can't find any trace of his little cannon in it. Carefully examining the data of the problem, he concludes that: it must be one thing or the other; either it isn't the same clearing or else sciurus communis and tineola biselliella have gobbled up his piece of ordnance. As Buridan had taught him a few lustra earlier, such a dilemma could only lead to famine, and the Duke of Auge feared summary repasts more than anything, and with greater reason those that were inexistent. Utilising a probabilistic method he committed himself to a direction that was no less aleatory than arbitrary and started wandering thus until twilight fell.

'Obviously,' said the Duke out loud, to keep himself company, 'I could have strewn my path with little white stones, but for one thing I didn't have any to hand and for another a fat lot of good that would have done me now that it's going to get dark and even pitch dark.'

Sure enough, it got dark and even pitch dark. The Duke went on obstinately, but either fell over in various thickets or bumped his nose against centuries-old oak trees, uttering howls of rage and swearing in the most unseemly possible fashion, with no respect for the nocturnal beauty of the locality. He was starting to have had a bellyful, but a real bellyful, when he observed, embroidered on the sombre satin of the shadows, a gleam.

'I'll go and see what it is,' said the Duke out loud, to keep himself company. 'Perhaps it's only a large-sized glow-worm, after all, but I'm so hungry I wouldn't mind making a snack of it.'

It was not a glow-worm at all, but a thatched cottage.

[83]

'I must still be treading on my own lands,' murmurs the Duke, feeling reassured, 'and whoever lodges in that cosshe must be one of my serfs. A woodcutter, no doubt. If Sthenes were here he'd be able to tell me his name, he knows everyone, but the sod's run away and I'm lost like a poor little Tom Thumb, that's where you get when you go hunting cannons without taking some sort of a snack with you, and some portulans and the list of your talliables.'

He tries to push open the door (he's on his own lands, isn't he?) but the door resists: the thing's bolted. With the pommel of his sword, he knocks and, at the same time, announces the lie of the land:

'Open up, yokel, it's your Duke!'

He waits, but nothing is modified in the ambient situation and he repeats:

'Open up, yokel, it's your Duke!'

And so on, several times.

The result: still nil.

The Duke, having considered the matter, expresses his thought for his own benefit:

'He's afraid, the poor devil. He must take me for some noctambulant and sylvan spirit. He hasn't my courage: he is of too base extraction, but perhaps he's not insensible to compassion! Let's try a little guile . . .'

Snivelling, he utters a despairing cry:

'I'm hungry!'

Immediately the door is opened *as if by enchantment* and a *radiant apparition* makes its apparition.

The aforesaid apparition consists of a virgin of a conspicuous filth but an impeccable aesthetic. The Duke's *breath is taken away*.

'Your poor Lordship,' says the young person in a *sweetly melodious* voice, 'come in and sit by the fire and share our *humble fare* of mashed chestnuts and acorns.'

'Is that all there is to eat?'

[84]

'Alas yes, my Lord. My papa has gone to town to buy a few ounces of smoked cod, but he isn't back yet and no doubt he won't be back now till dawn.'

This remark starts the Duke off musing: in any case, he doesn't need all night to eat the humble fare, especially if he's got to share it with the *tender child*, who is now watching him with *genuine diffidence*. For his part, he examines her.

'You're just a thought plump,' says the Duke.

She appears not to *get the message*.

'Sit down, sit down, my Lord. Would you like me to put some pepper in the nosh? I possess a sachet that my godmother gave me last Christmas. It comes from Malabar, my pepper, and it's highly authentic, not in any way ersatz.'

'My goodness,' says the Duke, blushing, 'I really can't refuse. Just a very little . . .'

'The whole sachet, my Lord! the whole sachet! It'll fortify you.'

'Do I look as if I'm in need of repair?'

'Your Lordship cuts a magnificent figure, but he must have been subject to some emotion . . .'

'Well er . . . losing a cannon . . . just like that . . .'

'A cannon? have you got a cannon?'

'I even have several,' says the Duke proudly.

The child jumps for joy and claps her hands.

'Oh! You've got cannons? I just love cannons! At least *they're* modern.'

She starts running round the somewhat restricted perimeter of the room, and singing: 'Dansons la Carmagnole, Vive le son, vive le son. . . . Dansons la Carmagnole, vive le son du canon . . .'

'She's charming, this child,' murmurs the Duke of Auge, 'but her ritornello doesn't mean a thing to me.'

And he asks her:

'Who taught you that song, sweetheart?'

'Papa did.'

[85]

'And what does he do, your papa?'

'Why, he's a woodcutter.'

'And to whom does he belong?'

'To the most exalted and powerful seigneur, Joachim Duke of Auge.'

'In other words, to myself. Good, I'll have him hanged.'

'And why will you have my papa hanged, Monsieur the Duke?'

'He teaches you wicked things.'

'What! don't you like the sound of the cannon? But I sang that to please you.'

'It's the Carmagnole that doesn't please me.'

'You aren't a bit nice. I welcome you into our home and then you want to hang my papa. And what about the laws of hospitality, then?'

'I am on my own territory here, my child. Everything here belongs to me: the forest, the wood, the woodcutter, the thatched cottage, the daughter.'

'Not so fast, Monsieur the Duke. If you're still thinking of hanging my papa, I'll spill the nosh into the fire!'

'By my figgins, you'd never do such a thing!'

'Then promise me you won't hurt my papa.'

'I promise, I promise.'

'I don't trust you. You've got a lousy reputation. You'll choke back my acorns, my chestnuts and my sachet of pepper, and then you'll please yourself.'

'Oh no, oh no. I've promised, let's not talk about it any more, and now bring me that peppery delicacy: you're making me water at the mouth.'

'You're just promising because you're hungry. But afterwards . . .'

'What d'you want me to do, other than promise?'

'Well, there's such a thing as a promise in writing, but coming from you it wouldn't be worth much more.'

'A promise in writing! Ha! ha! ha! Have you got a gallimard here, then, and some parchment? This is really too funny!'

'You cruelly mock our illiteracy, Monsieur the Duke.'

'But not the quality of your cooking. Come on, now, bring me this odiferous pepperage. Come on, come on. Chicky, chicky, chicky.'

The Duke had got up discreetly and was all set to pounce on the pan at the risk of burning his fingers, but the little girl is closely watching her suzerain. When he finally takes the plunge, plonk, the chestnuts, the acorns and the peppercorns are precipitated into the fire. Where they are burnt to cinders.

'Another fucking fiasco,' murmurs the Duke, who hasn't even the heart to lambast the little woodcutteress.

He sits down on his stool again and, hunching up his back, he laments:

'I'm hungry, oh la la, I'm hungry, oh la la, how terribly hungry I am.'

He scolds the child:

'That was a stupid thing to do. In the first place, it's always deplorable to waste food, and then I'm not bound by any promise now, and finally, the laws of hospitality, hm, you may well talk about them: what hospitality!'

He looks around him:

'Is there really nothing else to eat here?'

His eye comes to rest:

'Obviously, there's this young person. My friend and comrade at arms, Gilles de Rais, wouldn't have hesitated a single instant, but I've got enough on my plate as it is. The people round about might take it amiss. My future sons-in-law would perhaps not appreciate it. And anyway . . . without pepper . . .'

He sinks into morose meditation which turns to somnolence. He no longer feels terra firma under his feet, he seems to be a bit groggy, the cottage starts going round and round, he's going to be able to lie down on his chaise-longue on deck, but a little girl woke him up.

'Monsieur the Duke, Monsieur the Duke!'

'What what what?'

'Why don't we play a game while we're waiting for the dawn and for papa to come back?'

'What game?'

'A game.'

'What stakes?'

'Papa's life.'

'What a good idea,' exclaimed the Duke, cheering up.

And they played till dawn.

IX

Since he had spent eighteen months in prison, Cidrolin had never been back to any of the gastronomic restaurants he had previously frequented. He was afraid of being recognised. He sometimes bought the Glutton's Weekly, a publication which gave a list of the best places, there were some Cidrolin didn't know, he would have quite liked to try this one or that, but he never made up his mind.

As the interim between Lamélie's, (now Madame Cuveton's) departure and Albert's protégée's arrival, (she had still to be found) left him to take care of himself, and as the results were proving, as had been expected, monotonous and mediocre, he thought he would be well-advised to take advantage of the said interim by trying some particularly well-recommended de-luxe establishment hitherto unknown to him in order for once to have a meal that wasn't a fiasco.

He had barely entered the cavern when he heard himself being interrogated about his intentions, though they were pretty easy to guess. Having objectively and modestly answered that he had come here to have lunch, he was asked whether he had a reserved table. As he had nothing of the sort, he was notified that everything was booked. It only remained for him to withdraw; this he did, examining as he went by some hors-d'oeuvres and sweets which were on show and which looked most inviting.

'Another fucking fiasco,' he murmured as he found himself once more on the pavement.

He was wondering whether he would try another experiment elsewhere when he observed his daughters and his sons-in-law getting out of two cars. The group was complete since it even included the omnibudsman, the man of the name of Cuveton. While Yoland and Lucet went to park their cars no one knew where, the rest entered the de-luxe establishment with some confidence.

'They're doing themselves well,' said Cidrolin under his breath. 'They're celebrating without me.'

'Pardon?' asked the passer-by.

Cidrolin looked at him: it was a different one. Or else the same one whom he didn't recognise.

'Nothing,' he replied. 'I was talking to myself. A habit you get into when you live on your own for a long time.'

'You ought to try and get rid of it,' said the passer-by. 'People think you're asking them for some information, they get ready to give it to you with pleasure; when they discover that it isn't that at all, then they're disappointed.'

'Please do excuse me. As you see, I'm most distressed.'

'What were you saying?'

'What was I saying? Yes, now I come to think of it, what was I saying?'

He looked as if he was trying to think and frowned solemnly,

[89]

as one should in such circumstances. Then he spoke again, in these terms:

'I said: they're celebrating without me.'

'And what did you mean by that?'

'I agree that the expression is ambiguous, and the fact is that I was using it in both meanings: (a) indulging in pastime or festivities, in other words, stuffing their guts, and (b) honouring (something) with ceremonies, the something in this case being a marriage, but I'm not going to bore you with my private life.'

'Why not?' asked the other, engagingly.

'Because I'm not going to,' replied Cidrolin.

'In that case,' said the other, without taking offence, 'I don't want to take up too much of your time . . .'

'That's all right . . .'

Delivered, Cidrolin was spotted by the two sons-in-law who'd finished parking their cars and couldn't pretend they hadn't seen him. They greeted him with patronising good-nature.

'Well, well,' says Yoland. 'so that's the way we abandon our barge, is it?'

'It's true it's a nice day,' says Lucet, 'so we're going for a walk.'

'And what about you two?' says Cidrolin. 'Are we going for a walk too?'

'Um yes, we're going for a walk. Just happened to be passing.'

'Well, pass then. See you one of these days!'

Cidrolin stays where he is. The other two move on a few steps. They turn round and acknowledge his presence once again with a little wave.

Cidrolin reciprocates, but he hasn't budged.

'What do we do?' asks Lucet, 'Do we go in or don't we?'

'If he saw the others go in,' says Yoland, 'we'll look pretty silly.'

'We don't want to miss *that* sort of blow-out, though.'

'Is he still there?'

'Hasn't budged.'

'He obviously saw the others go in. He's just taking the piss out of us.'

'We look like a couple of dopes. Got to do something.'

'Let's ask him too.'

'He'll take it the wrong way.'

'We've got to have lunch, though.'

'I should hope so! Especially as it probably won't be all that lousy! Did you manage to get a look at the place? It's at least a five-star de-luxe joint. We'll really be able to make pigs of ourselves.'

'Well, do we go back?'

'Yes. You explain what's going on.'

'All the dirty work, eh.'

Cidrolin watches them coming back towards him with an innocent air. It's Yoland, then, who says:

'Bit of luck we met you. Lamélie didn't have a party at her wedding so we thought we'd have a good lunch for the occasion. As you happen to be in these parts it'd be only right for you to be one of the party.'

'And who's paying?'

'We're going Dutch.'

'My, my, you are prosperous. You didn't choose the corner caff, eh. What about the omnibudsman, can he stand himself a lunch like this?'

'We warned him. Pah! You don't get married every day.'

'But he didn't get married today, it's a good week isn't it?'

'It's never too late to mend.'

'It's a funny idea, even so. An odd idea.'

'Well, are you coming?' said Lucet impatiently. 'They're waiting for us.'

'Not for me,' said Cidrolin. 'No one's waiting for me.'

'Oh come on, don't sulk!'

'And in any case,' said Cidrolin, 'I haven't booked a table.'

'We have.'

'No,' said Cidrolin. 'I was there just now, there wasn't any room for me.'

'Did you want to have lunch there?'

'Why not?' said Cidrolin.

The two sons-in-law said nothing.

'I wanted to have a good meal,' said Cidrolin. 'I'll have it some other time.'

He takes the bus and, at the corner of the embankment, he buys some bread, but the other local shops are shut. There are still a few tins left on the barge. The fence has again been besmirched by defamatory graffiti.

Cidrolin puts the bread down and goes and gets the paint pot. He applies himself to the task of covering the inscriptions adequately. He's hungry, but he concentrates on his task. Some nomads at a loose end stop and watch him. They watch him in silence. This doesn't worry Cidrolin. He's as used to the nomads as he is to the repainting. He doesn't enter into conversation with them. Contrary to an extremely widespread custom, he doesn't sing either, nor does he whistle under his breath. When he's finished, the nomads walk off.

He puts the paint pot back in its place and then pours himself out a glass of essence of fennel.

'I drink too much,' he murmurs. 'Lamélie isn't here to tell me so any more.'

Then he goes and looks in the store-room to see what tins are left. There's still enough for about a fortnight, if he doesn't exaggerate. Cidrolin doesn't know whether, a fortnight from now, Albert will have found him someone. If Albert hasn't found anything Cidrolin will have to renew his stock; he sees scurvy heaving in sight. For the moment he chooses a tin of fillets of tunny fish in purified ground-nut oil. There's an intelligent way to open the said tin, Cidrolin doesn't need to have recourse to a hammer and chisel as he usually does. Next he cleaves the bread in twain and pours the contents between the two slices which he carefully closes up in order to reconstitute the original aspect of the *baguette*, the only difference being that oil is flowing out of the incisions. When the whole has been consumed, Cidrolin murmurs:

'It wasn't so bad. Only, if you do it too often, there's the scurvy.'

He wipes his hands and mouth on a polyvalent cloth and goes up to see what's happening to his fence. No further inscriptions have been inscribed on it but some fat-head has been leaning against it and got the bloody paint all over his jacket. He addresses Cidrolin:

'Hey, you there, is that your barge? is this your fence? you could at least put up a notice wet paint. That's the least you could do. My jacket, now, it'll have to go to the cleaner's. Are you going to pay the bill?'

'Of course,' replied Cidrolin. 'How much is it?'

'And you think you're funny, what's more! That's the end.'

'You may observe,' said Cidrolin, 'that you've wrecked the coat of paint I'd just put on. I'll have to start all over again and I've got other things to do.'

'What?'

'Have a siesta.'

The future client of one of the numerous existing dry-cleaners looks at Cidrolin thoughtfully, then he goes off.

Cidrolin goes and fetches his paint pot and repairs the damage; then he manufactures a little notice wet paint which he conscientiously places in a very visible position.

Then he settles down on his chaise-longue. He murmurs:

'I forgot to tell Albert that I didn't want a minor.'

He shuts his eyes.

[93]

'I wonder what she'll look like,' he also murmurs.

'We'll see about that later on,' says Lord de Ciry to his two brothers-in-law, Count de Torves and the Vidame de Malplaquet.

'What does it matter!' says Count de Torves. 'Let him remarry, why not, but let's see what compensation he offers us.'

'If he does offer us any,' says Lord de Ciry.

'I'd like to see that,' says Malplaquet, stroking his moustaches.

Mouscaillot leads the way into the dining room, where they are to refresh themselves a mite. Lord de Ciry examines the furniture appreciatively.

'Hm, hm,' he murmurs, 'pure thirteenth Louis style.'

'Monsieur the Duke likes to be absolutely up to date,' says the page who is now entitled to entitle himself Viscount d'Empoigne.

Some boar pâtés and other matutinal delicacies were brought and some essence of fennel was poured into Venetian crystal goblets.

'No expense has been spared,' murmurs Lord de Ciry, and adds, for the benefit of the Vidame, who's using his fingers: 'You must use that fork.'

Because there were forks, and silver ones, at that.

'I'll never get used to them,' says Malplaquet. 'And to begin with I don't think it's hygienic to use these tools. You never know where they've been beforehand, whereas your fingers, you always know where you've been putting them.'

'You have to move with the times,' says Torves, maladroitly manipulating one of the said objects.

'Gentlemen,' says Ciry, 'if you were to go to Court . . .'

'But we don't, ' says Malplaquet.

'Who knows,' says Ciry.

While they are waiting for the Duke they go on munching the boar pâté and other matutinal delicacies, while whiffing up many a wiederkom of claret wine.

'Tell me, Empoigne,' Malplaquet suddenly says in a shrill voice, 'has Auge remembered us?'

[94]

'I know not,' says Empoigne prudently, 'but I think the news is good.'

'I'm boiling with impatience.' says Torves.

'I hear a footstep,' says Ciry.

He heard it in spite of the sounds of mastication and digestion, either starting or finishing. Sure enough the Duke appeared, followed by the Abbé Biroton, the steward and a few flunkeys.

'Oddsbodikins!' exclaims the Duke. 'What d'you think of my beard? I sent for a barber from the town to arrange it for me.'

The sons-in-law vociferate: it's sublime.

The Duke points at Onésiphore. 'Take a good look at him,' he says. 'He's a bishop!'

The sons-in-law vociferate and go to kiss his ring; but the bishop in partibus of Sarcellopolis* hasn't yet been provided with one.

'And now look at me,' adds the Duke. 'You see before you a man who has received from his Majesty three hundred thousand livres to get married on.'

The sons-in-law vociferate, they cry: Long live the Queen, long live Marshal d'Ancre! The Duke laughs with pleasure. He rubs his hands. He grabs up a whole pâté and, without using a fork, devours it.

'And what about us?' the Count de Torves then asks.

'Yes, what about us?' adds the Vidame of Malplaquet.

'What about me?' says Lord de Ciry.

The Duke goes on laughing while devouring his pâté. It's dangerous, to laugh when you're eating like that, thus he nearly chokes himself. They pour him out wiederkom after wiederkom.

'Is he ever going to come to the point?' says Ciry to Malplaquet under his breath.

* Sarcelles, one of the first new housing estates, north of Paris, much criticised for its 1984-like qualities.

'And what if he didn't get anything for us,' murmurs Malplaquet, who's grimishing with anguace.

'I boil, I boil, I boil,' sighs Torves.

The Duke's hunger and thirst are now occluded and his spasms assuaged by the essence of fennel. He has become serious and he's certainly going to start to speak and to enunciate the good news announced by the Viscount d'Empoigne, when it becomes manifest, to the great despair of the sons-in-law, that a new idea is going through his head.

'What about my daughters?' he demands.

They're in the ladies' apartments, naturally.

'Tell them to come here!' he commands, 'I'm not going to make my speech twice.'

The sons-in-law stamp their feet with impatience, they could easily piss with rage, but they have to put up with it. The Duke has some more goodies brought, baby boar fritters, cod liver soufflés, fried pig's trotters. He tells them to serve them some hippocras and hydromel, so as not to overdo the essence of fennel. He enquires nice and politely of his sons-in-law about their respective journeys; gritting their teeth, they answer him. As in any case the subject doesn't interest him he turns to Monseigneur Biroton and reminds him that it is he who is going to give him his amethyst, though the benefice is quite substantial enough for Onésiphore to be able to pay for it himself. Finally he enquires about the location of Sarcellopolis. This ridiculous curiosity makes it quite obvious to the sons-in-law that he isn't thinking about them, and they therefore anticipate that there is nothing good to be divulged. Monseigneur Biroton, who is in total ignorance of the site of his bishopric, and he has no need to know seeing that he'll never have to go there, Monseigneur Biroton starts with a pious lie and replies that Sarcellopolis is in Asia Minor.

'In the hands of the Ottomans, then?'

[96]

'As you say.'

This renders the Duke pensive:

'And what if I were to organise a little crusade to get you back your bishopric?'

The sons-in-law are appalled: they see all Dad's lovely lolly disappearing in the Dardanelles.

Onésiphore is there to calm the Duke:

'A fine, pious gesture, my Lord, a fine gesture, but it is God's will that my bishopric should be in partibus: His will be done.'

'Don't you really want me to? This is an opportunity that isn't likely to happen again.'

'Gramercy, my Lord. Gramercy.'

The sons-in-law have had a narrow escape. They sigh with relief. Lord de Ciry even manages to produce a witticism.

'You're a real Don Quixote,' he says to the Duke, with a subtle smile.

'Eh, what? what's that?'

'Don Quixote? The best foreign book to appear in the year 1614. I read it in César Oudin's translation.'

The Duke looks pityingly at Ciry.

'What a pedant,' he murmurs.

But the other doesn't hear him, for some feminine chirruping is approaching. They become silent as they enter the dining-room and come and curtsey respectfully to their papa. When they'd all sorted themselves out the Duke enumerated all the governorships, benefices and privileges which, by the treaty of Sainte-Menehould, he had just obtained for his sons-in-law and consequently for his daughters.

'Baa, baa,' said Phélise, thus expressing the general satisfaction.

The sons-in-law therefore saw, without bitterness, their father-in-law marry, as his second wife, Russule Péquet, a peasant, the daughter of a woodcutter.

Cidrolin wakes up with a start; he had a feeling someone had

[97]

rung the bell at the gate that opened on to the embankment. He got up to go and look; there was no one there. It was dark, now. He looked to see if there were any new inscriptions but saw none. He went below again to dress as correctly as he could and knew how, locked up everything on board the barge and went off to the bistro on the corner of the embankment and the avenue.

A few couples were still hanging around slobbering over each other; some omnibudsmen were eating sandwiches and drinking half-pints, while commenting on the trivia of the day's work. Cidrolin ordered himself an essence of fennel with still water, acquired a telephone counter and consulted the directory. Having waited seventeen minutes until a couple who were pretending they were leeches in the booth saw fit to vacate it, he established contact with the de-luxe joint that had repelled him that same noon.

'I'd like to book a table. For tonight.'

'For how many?'

'One. Just one.'

He felt the receiver grow cold in his hand, they couldn't have been very pleased at the other end of the line. He shouldn't have said that.

'But I eat enough for four,' Cidrolin added.

The receiver resumed its tepidity. He was asked his name.

'Dicornil. Monsieur Dicornil. D for Duke, I for Joachim, C for Capetian, O for Onésiphore, R for Riphinte, N for N, and the rest accordingly.'

'Dupont. That's right, is it? For Monsieur Dupont.'

'That's right.'

When he entered the de-luxe joint the first thing he noticed was that his telephone call had been quite unnecessary: the restaurant was empty. People used it for their expense-account lunches, but the dining clientele proved to be rather sparse. Nevertheless, a head waiter asked him haughtily whether he had reserved his table. Cidrolin answered yes he had. What name?

'Dupont. Monsieur Dupont.'

'If you would care to come this way, Monsieur Dicornil.'

Cidrolin was expecting to be given a table in a draught or by a sideboard. Nothing of the sort. It was a proper, normal table of decent dimensions covered with crockery and cutlery. Cidrolin was favourably impressed. Handing him a menu of an area of some sixteen hundred square centimetres, the head waiter asked him if he would like an aperitif. Cidrolin opted for essence of fennel.

'Is there any particular brand you prefer, Monsieur?'

'White Horse,' he told the wine waiter.

Then he looked authoritatively at the names of the dishes. The head waiter pointed out the specialities and the plats du jour with the point of his pencil. When Cidrolin had decided to start with fresh gros grain caviar the conversation became extremely friendly. It became frankly cordial when he next envisaged the idea of tackling a salmon koulibiac which would be followed by roast pheasant which would be accompanied by truffles from Périgord. On mature consideration, Cidrolin, who was highly partial to vol-au-vent financière, considered it would be possible for him to insert one in between the koulibiac and the pheasant. After the cheese he would have a soufflé made with twelve liqueurs.

The wine waiter brought the essence of fennel in a bottle which indeed had the White Horse label stuck on to it; he went away again, his mission being to return with a small carafe of Russian vodka, a bottle of 1925 Chablis and a bottle of 1955 Château d'Arcins.

The head waiter had effaced himself in order to leave the field clear for his colleague to operate, but when the latter had returned to his cellars, he leant over towards Cidrolin and, extremely amiably, asked him for his permit.

[99]

'My permit? What permit?'

'Your Social Security permit.'

'What for?'

'Monsieur is joking. Monsieur is certainly aware that, without a Social Security permit, we are not allowed to serve a meal of more than three thousand calories, and yours must be six thousand at the very least.'

Cidrolin had indeed seen some figures on the menu by the side of each dish, but he thought they were the prices.

'Monsieur will not be unaware that a large proportion of the claims on the Social Security consist of cases of indigestion and enteritis. Something had to be done; perhaps you do not subscribe to the essess, Monsieur? And yet, Monsieur, you must be something like a President-Administrator-General.'

He produced a flattering smile.

Cidrolin, as an ex-prisoner, was indeed a subscriber, but he didn't know of this new law. He could see no way out of it. He murmured:

'Another fucking fiasco.'

'Oh no, Monsieur, oh no!' exclaimed the head waiter compassionately, 'You mustn't throw the helve before the hatchet.'

'After,' said Cidrolin.

'After? After?'

The head waiter looked perplexed.

'Throw the helve after the hatchet,' said Cidrolin.

'Are you sure?'

'Certain.'

'When you come to think of it, what does it mean? Where does the expression come from?'

'It's an expression they used in the old days,' said Cidrolin.

'I don't understand it. You say something like that, to throw the helve after the hatchet, and then, if you try and understand what it means exactly, you don't understand any more. Ah, Monsieur, it's terrible when you start to think.'

'Forget it.'

'That's easy to say! Personally, I want to understand. Why after? If you throw the helve, you throw the hatchet with it. Not after it. No, I certainly don't understand.'

'I'll explain. Once upon a time there was a woodcutter . . .'

At this word Cidrolin fell silent, and seemed to be thinking of something else.

X

Sthenes was champing at the bit. The Duke had strongly recommended him to silence, as he travelled with a numerous retinue these days and didn't want any gossip on the subject. He was in any case just as sad about this as was his horse, whose gay prattle he appreciated. Stef was likewise trotting in a state of extreme mutism which, however, was no change from his habitual reserve.

In default of Sthenes the Duke was chatting with the Viscount d'Empoigne. The prospect of these States General filled him with great joy: an excellent reason to go and bum around in the capital city. Young Russule, the new spouse, would also have liked to go and taste the capital pleasures, she had even insisted, and the Duke had found himself obliged to give her a good hiding.

'You were a bit heavy-handed, my Lord,' said the Viscount.

'What's it got to do with you, Cicisbeo? Might you be in love with the Duchess?'

'God preserve me from that, my Lord.'

'You're not very gallant. Personally, I sincerely hope you are, in love, with the Duchess.'

[101]

'In no way, my Lord.'

'Would you be a hypocrite by any chance?'

'I assure you, my Lord . . .'

'All right, all right, but believe me, if I was a bit heavy-handed it was because I couldn't be less so than her father. My dignity was at stake. I judged it fitting that she shouldn't find my clouts gentler than those of a woodcutter . . .'

'Monsieur, monsieur,' said the head waiter gently, 'I'm waiting for the rest.'

'. . . who'd dropped the head of his hatchet down an abyss.'

'Down an abyss?'

'That's how the story goes,' said Cidrolin. 'He couldn't go and look for it there.'

'I should think not,' said the head waiter. 'An abyss . . .'

'So, in despair, the scroglopper . . .'

'I beg your pardon?'

'The woodcutter . . .'

'Was that another old word? Why, Monsieur, do some words fall into desuetude like that? Even I, I've seen some, in my own lifetime, at that, disappear under my very eyes: cinematograph, taximeter, air-raid warden, etcetera.'

'Do you want to know how it ends?'

'I can guess,' replied the head waiter, with a knowing air. 'In despair, the woodcutter, the scroglopper, as you called him, threw himself after it into the abyss. And that's the reason why when you're talking about a chap who's a silly bastard you say he's a helluva silly bastard. The helluva silly bastard threw himself after the hatchet.'

'Now that's an interesting variation,' said Cidrolin calmly. 'In fact, the woodcutter was content to throw the helve. After the hatchet. So that he didn't have anything left. Whereas the helve, at least, could still have been some use to him.'

'It's daft,' said the head waiter. 'What the hell could he do with his helve? Nothing. The difficult thing to find was the cutting part. It's daft, your story. I prefer my version.'

'It may well be daft,' said Cidrolin calmly, 'but in any case, now you know it.'

'I'm much obliged to you. Ah, here's your gros grain extra-status caviar which arrived this very afternoon by supersonic aeroplane; with a nice ice-cold vodka you're going to do yourself proud.'

Cidrolin did in fact do himself proud.

As the restaurant was more or less deserted the head waiter came back from time to time to see if everything was as it should be. The koulibiac was appreciated and the vol-au-vent financière devoured. While waiting for the next course Cidrolin made a little conversation:

'I know some people who came here for lunch; actually it was today.'

'We were very full at lunchtime today,' said the other importantly.

'Six people. Three couples.'

'We had several tables with six people.'

'There were three young women, three sisters. They aren't so enormously like each other, but if you look very carefully you can detect the fact that they're three twins.'

'Triplings? I don't remember noticing. And yet I'm a great physiognomist.'

'The gentlemen, well, there was nothing particularly remarkable about them.'

'Ah, I know, then. Rather vulgar people.'

'You think so?'

'Oh yes, I can guarantee that. They didn't eat . . . like you, Monsieur. They gorged themselves. And they didn't even have their gastronomic permit. They didn't even know what it was: they weren't used to patronising restaurants of over three

[103]

thousand calories. Do you really know these individuals?'

'A little. And what did you do with them when they didn't give you their permit?'

'What could I do, Monsieur? I did what I've been doing with you: I served them.'

The head waiter smiles knowingly, and, while volitant minions were bringing the truffles and pheasant, he continues in these terms:

'I must confess, Monsieur, that this famous gastronomic permit issued by the essess is a pure invention. It doesn't exist. I thought it up all by myself and I amuse myself by diverting the customers with this subtle jest. Some fall for it, and that makes it all the funnier. Of course I saw that you weren't taken in, Monsieur, but those people you say you know a little, they got angry, they were all for smashing the place up. It was so comic.'

'You say you served them in the end.'

'After I'd calmed them down . . . after I'd insinuated that it was a signal favour . . . it was because it was they . . . Well, you see what we hand out to our somewhat simple-minded customers.'

'Yes, I see,' says Cidrolin.

'Yet their tip was parsimonious. People of no substance. Not at all people in your category, Monsieur. And the ladies: almost not what they should be. Were they really triplings? Curious. I didn't guess. And yet I'm a physiognomist.'

The arrival of a couple of unexpected customers relieved Cidrolin of the presence of this joker. He can finish his game and his ascomycetes in peace, treat himself to a few slices of varied cheeses with ̩equanimity, sample the soufflé with the twelve liqueurs in security, and knock back a glass of green chartreuse in perfect quietude. He asks for the bill which he paid. He left a few additional francs so as not to disappoint the head waiter, who bowed very low to him. And when he was out in the street, then he started marvelling:

'It's unbelievable,' he said under his breath, 'the whole lot was perfect.'

'Pardon?' asked the passer-by.

As it was pitch dark, Cidrolin couldn't recognise him.

'Nothing,' he answered. 'I was talking to myself. A habit you...'

'I know, I know,' said the passer-by, slightly irritated. 'I've already advised you to try and get rid of it, that habit.'

'Christmas comes but once a year.'

'It's Christmas for you today, is it? How come?'

'I've had a good dinner.'

'So what?'

'That hasn't happened to me for a long, long time. Either everything was quite simply bad, or else there was always some little thing that went wrong. Here, it was perfect. I was in agony as the meal progressed. I said to myself: it's not possible, it can't go on like this, something's got to go wrong. But no. The pheasant was succulent. The truffles were whole, and properly cleaned. The cheeses were terrific. So then I thought: It's going to be the soufflé - a soufflé made with twelve liqueurs, Monsieur - it's going to be the soufflé that'll go wrong. Not at all: puffed up like a balloon, unctuous, flavorous. Nothing to be said against it. Even the chartreuse was genuine.'

'Pooh,' said the passer-by, 'I can't see that that's any reason for you to be so pleased. You pay a lot of money, that's not very intelligent. Give me the little bistro any day.'

'There are expensive restaurants where you eat like pigs. No, really, I'm most amazed. There's something a bit peculiar about it . . . but I'm not going to bore you with my private life.'

'Why not?'

'Because I'm not going to.'

'In that case,' said the passer-by, without taking offence, 'I don't want to take up too much of your time . . . it's getting late . . .'

'That's all right . . .'

Cidrolin takes his surprise with him into the night. A non-fiasco, he can't get over it. Without having been aware of which way he was going, he finds himself in front of the Ark. He picks up the torch which he is in the habit of parking in the letter box and, in its light, examines the fence and doesn't find any inscriptions.

He'd like to open his mouth to say that he finds all this most peculiar, but he doesn't want to run the risk of the passer-by reappearing. Everything is quiet on the barge, nothing's budged.

Cidrolin drinks one more glass of essence of fennel to help his dinner on its way because after all he finds it a bit heavy. He wonders whether he'll go to bed or whether, for the good of his digestion, he'll take the dinghy and go for a bit of a row. He soon gave up the idea of these hygienic excesses and decided to go to sleep. He had quite some difficulty, but finally managed it. A horse was talking to him.

'May I say a word?' asked Sthenes. 'We're all friends here.'

The Duke did indeed only have by his side Empoigne, riding on Stef. The guide was galloping away a good hundred ells ahead and the rest of the company were following some way behind.

'Speak, my good Demo,' said the Duke affectionately.

'Isn't there going to be a statue to you one day?'

'My goodness,' said the Duke, 'I'd never thought of it.'

'Why not?'

'Indeed,' said the Duke, delighted. 'Why not?'

'An equestrian statue, of course, like the one of good King Henri we saw yesterday.'

'An equestrian statue! You're asking a bit much. I'm not the King of France.'

'Personally,' said Sthenes, 'I just can't imagine it any other way: equestrian.'

'Ha ha, I see! You're the one who wants your statue!'

'Don't I deserve it? A horse like me hasn't been seen since Xanthus. And anyway, Xanthus only spoke through Hera's voice, whereas I don't need anyone to help me know what I want to say.'

'And who is this Xanthus?' asked Mouscaillot.

Sthenes tossed his head to show what small esteem he had for Empoigne's culture.

He deigns to answer, however:

'One of Achilles' horses. The other was called Balius.'

'Sthenes has just re-read all Homer in three days,' said the Duke.

'Good old Balius,' said Empoigne, patting Stef on the neck.

'And will I have a statue to me, too?' asked Stef.

'He deserves one,' said Sthenes, who was a good companion. 'In the Iliad, Balius doesn't talk, only Xanthus talks; now Stef talks, therefore he's entitled to his statue too.'

'They can't make a statue of me riding on two horses at once,' the Duke observed.

'A good sculptor might find a way round it, perhaps,' said Sthenes, who was of an optimistic disposition. 'In any case, let's start with ours. Stef will wait. Won't you, Stef?'

Stef didn't answer and Sthenes didn't pursue the matter any further as the guide had stopped. They could now see the work in progress.

'I am far from displeased with this idea,' said the Duke to Empoigne. 'I had a feeling that there was something missing: to wit, this equestrian statue. As soon as we get back to Paris we'll start looking for a sculptor.'

They caught up with the guide. The retinue came up at a canter.

'Noble seigneurs,' said the cicerone in a crap-talking voice, 'you see before you the sight of Paris that is attracting the largest number of visitors at this moment, after the statue of our good

[107]

King the fourth Henri, of course. The work was begun by order of Her Majesty the Queen Mother.'

'Long live the Queen!' shouted the Duke.

'Long live the Queen!' shouted the rest.

'When it's finished, the aqueduct will be twelve hundred and thirty-one feet long and ninety-four feet high. Its construction has been placed under the supervision of Monsieur Salomon de Brosse . . .'

'Does he makes statues, too?' asked the Duke.

'Not to my knowledge . . . and of the maestro ingeniere fiorentino Tomaso de Francini.'

'Doesn't he, either?' asked the Duke.

'I beg your pardon? I do not understand.'

'I'm asking whether he makes statues as well, or whether he doesn't either. Doesn't he, either?'

'Not to my knowledge.'

'When we get back to Paris you must take me to see one of the most illustrious sculptors in the capital.'

'At your service, my Lord.'

'Unless I send for one from Italy . . .'

The guide, reverting to his subject, suggested that the noble seigneurs dismount and go and watch the work from closer to.

'You go, gentlemen,' said the Duke. 'Personally I've seen quite enough as it is.'

As the others go off he starts looking for a spot that is both agreeable and discreet. On all sides he is surrounded by little meadows and kitchen gardens. The Duke feels drawn to a patch of leeks which seems to him to need manuring. So he just gets nicely settled, when what should happen but the sky clouds over, the wind gets up, the storm breaks, and the rain comes crashing down. The Duke, who has only just had time to accomplish his task, looks around him for some nearby shelter. There is none, but there's a house over there, at the end of a path. The Duke charges off in that direction, he skates in the mud which has immediately materialised, he's soaked through, and what's more he runs like a rickety White Wyandotte. Even so, in the end, he gets there, to shelter, to the house. But the next thing is that in order for this house to be a shelter its door must be opened. Now the door doesn't open. The Duke knocks in vain, nothing happens, and it goes on raining down his neck.

The downpour increases in strength and the Duke is getting a thorough wash; he hasn't been so clean for ages which, however, were he to know it, would not afford him the slightest pleasure. He kicks at the door, shoves at it with his shoulder, and finally the latch and hinges give, the door describes a trajectory of ninety degrees and thus adopts a horizontal position, likewise causing the same thing to happen to the infuriated and soaking wet Duke.

Who picks himself up, cursing. He shakes himself, he finds he's in a sort of cow-shed or stable, unless it's a cellar or attic. The whole place is in semi-darkness, hardly any light comes through the hollowed-out embrasure, the sky is still covered with black clouds. The Duke finally identifies the place: it's a wood-shed, a particularly well-equipped wood-shed. It also contains some coal. The Duke then suggests a programme to himself.

'I'll make a little fire so as to dry my galligaskins, my doublet and my hat.'

The Duke looks for a fireplace, but there isn't one. He notices a door at the far end of the wood-shed, he goes over to it and opens it very gently. At first he doesn't understand what it is he's seeing, until the person leaning over the furnace straightens himself up and then turns round and shouts at him:

'Stand back, rash fool! Your moist presence will contaminate the last operation.'

'Not so fast!' replied the Duke, unmoved, 'I'm not used to being spoken to in such a fashion. I'm going to dry these clothes and I'm going to dry myself.'

'Stand back, I tell you. The ruby tree has been transformed into a green canary, whose beak is already pecking at the nutritial gold.'

'Gold!' exclaimed the Duke. 'Is there gold hereabouts?'

The other, without condescending to answer, leant over the crucible and utters a despairing cry.

'Malediction!' he yells, 'the green canary has been transformed into an egg-shaped leaden hen. I'll have to start everything all over again!'

'Well,' said the Duke lightheartedly, 'you can be starting all over again and I won't have caught a cold.'

'Start again! My Lord, that's twenty-seven years of toil that have just aborted! Twenty-seven years! And the gold was actually just about to appear in this crucible when you burst in in such an unseemly and profane way.'

'All this is highly interesting, but you'll just have to put up with it. I'm going to dry myself.'

He takes off his galligaskins and his doublet and puts them by the furnace; he also exposes himself, having a care not to get roasted. A mist rises from the ensemble.

The other goes on moaning:

'And that moisture, it's going to settle on everything!'

He hastens to put stoppers in various carboys and lute down other vessels. He growls:

'All my essential substances are going to need desiccating again! Years wasted! How can I put it? – ballsed up! And all because of a petty squire who can't find anywhere to shelter.'

'Not so fast,' said the Duke, smiling. 'A petty squire? Do you know whom you are addressing, puffer?'

'Do you know whom *you* are addressing, petty squire?'

'He's stuck on his petty squire. I am the Duke of Auge and I represent the nobility of my province at the States General.'

'Pah. *I* am Timoleo Timolei, the only alchemist in the whole of

Christendom who knows the true recipe for gold, whether potable or not, without counting a thousand other marvels.'

'Which ones?'

'Walking on the ceiling like a fly and on the water like our Lord Jesus Christ, being at the same time here and in New Spain, travelling in the belly of a whale, like the prophet Jonah, riding dolphins like Arion and running faster than Atalanta, going from here to there in a horseless carriage, cleaving the air like the eagle and the swallow. . . .'

'You seem to have a weakness for every sort of means of transport.'

'The thing is that I have treated my subject methodically. Would you like another series? Understanding the language of the bees, speaking the language of the Topinambous without having learnt it, conversing with a person a thousand leagues away, listening to the harmony of the celestial spheres, reading every sort of secret writing without difficulty, knowing by heart the content of a thousand and three works, discoursing pertinently on everything without ever having studied anything.'

'None of that is as good as gold,' said the Duke, who was starting to get dressed again.

'With the powder of projection that was just about to come into being I'd have been able to generate not ounces but pounds – what am I saying! tons, but my Lord Duke's intrusion has wrecked the whole thing. I've another twenty-seven years of distillation in front of me; it's true, though, that this time I shall have the benefit of the experience I've acquired.'

'And how long will you take this time?'

'Um,' said Timoleo Timolei, 'three . . . four years . . .'

'And you can be certain that in three or four years you'll find the philosopher's stone?'

'I can.'

'And the elixir of life?'

'Ditto.'

'Good,' says the Duke, who is ready now. 'Very good, even.'

The rain had stopped. He went out on to the door-step and perceived, a good hundred ells away, his retinue, who were looking for him. He turned back to the alchemist.

'Timoleo Timolei, what would you say to coming and living in my castle and puffing for me? I'll pay all your expenses, I'll protect you from the curiosity of the ecclesiastics, I'll feed you like a prince, and you'll let me benefit from your gold and your elixir. What d'you say to that?'

'To leave Arcueil would greuen me: this needs some consideration.'

'It's all been considered. When the States General are over I'll have your hovel and even your logs moved and I'll take them with us.'

Sthenes, who had seen the Duke, came up at a gentle trot, braked hard in front of his master, and reproached him mildly:

'I can't believe it, my Lord, you were hiding!'

'Oooh,' says the alchemist, suddenly growing pale and starting to stammer, 'a huhuh, an ororse . . . a horse . . . that . . . that . . . tortalks . . .'

'You see,' says the Duke, 'you'll be in good company.'

He throws a leg over Sthenes and disappears at a gallop.

Timoleo Timolei, struck dumb, takes a few steps backwards and, tripping over a log, falls in a faint on a heap of coal.

XI

Cidrolin wakes up in the middle of the night, he has a terrible pain in his belly and a terrible pain in his stomach. He goes up on deck and leans over the water: perhaps he's going to be sick? He must have thought of the price of the meal and that it would be an awful waste to distribute it in such a way; he goes in again and makes his way to the lavatory and relieves himself, hears a plop, one more thing that will drift as far as the next sewage farm, or perhaps even down to the sea.

He goes back to bed again, but he still has a terrible pain in his belly and a terrible pain in his stomach. This is too stupid, when just for once it was perfect. He possesses his soul in patience. Then he doesn't possess his soul in patience any more. He gets up again and dresses, takes a blanket, gets into the dinghy and lets it go; he rows.

A few lorries are still occasionally going by on the boulevard along the embankment; also on the bridge. On the other nearby barges, everyone's asleep. Cidrolin is going down stream, he's not rowing now, except from time to time just to keep on his course. He progresses in silence; when the absence of vehicles allows, he occasionally hears a bubble bursting, a fish coming up to the surface, or the product of some kind of fermentation born at the bottom of the river which has come up to explode within the modest limits of its capabilities between two ripples sown by the wind.

From time to time Cidrolin is overcome by a gust of sleep and his head drops. He alters course and makes his dinghy fast to a stake set by some fishermen. He rolls himself up in the blanket and looks at the sky which is beginning to turn grey. The pains in his belly and stomach have quite gone, but he can't manage to get back to sleep. He stays there with his eyes open. After all it doesn't matter much, he can have a longer siesta after lunch.

The traffic increases both on the bridge and on the boulevard. The first anglers appear. Some ultra-matutinal members of a sports club are going for a practice row. A real barge goes by, the waves come and break along the bank. Cidrolin sees the tree tops going up and down.

[113]

He has untied the dinghy and now he's rowing against the current. It's a bit of an effort and he takes much longer than he did going. Finally he comes alongside and goes on board again after this little excursion. He goes and puts the blanket away, then he walks up and down the deck, rubbing his hands, either because he had got a bit cold or because he wants to show signs of a certain satisfaction. He covers the length of the deck in this fashion a dozen times, then he goes up on to the embankment, paint pot in hand. He looks to see if his gate has again been desecrated with insulting inscriptions, but there are none. Cidrolin seems quite disconcerted, and makes a few absent-minded and gratuitous brush strokes here and there.

A chap who was passing by says to him:

'That's not work, what you're doing.'

'No indeed,' replies Cidrolin, 'it's very precisely a hobby. A gratuitous hobby.'

'It doesn't take much to amuse you.'

'A mere nothing, even. That, for instance.'

And he pointed to the block being built on the other side of the boulevard.

'Now that *is* work.'

'That's just what I was saying.'

Someone on a mobylette braked sharply and hailed them:

'For the greater glory of God,' said he, holding out his hand.

'What d'you mean by that?' asked the passer-by cantankerously.

'All right, all right,' said the other. 'I don't want to start an argument.'

And he went off. He was very correctly dressed, a little like a clergyman.

'That's not work, what he's doing,' said the passer-by. 'The way he goes about it he can't make much of a harvest.'

'Enough to buy petrol for his moped.'

'Because you think that what money he gets he doesn't dedicate to the glory of God?'

'I don't think anything at all,' said Cidrolin. 'He may be collecting for the poor.'

'The poor? Are there any in these parts, even? A rich, well-heeled parish. Is it yours, that barge?'

'It is.'

'Then there's no need to be sorry for you. It wasn't for you that that fellow was collecting.'

'You never know. He may be a crook. Suppose you'd given him something: when you'd gone, he'd have come back and we'd've shared it.'

'I was quite right to be on my guard,' said the passer-by. 'Good-bye, Monsieur.'

Cidrolin watches him as he goes and then, having turned to look in the opposite direction, he saw a feminine silhouette on the horizon. The feminine silhouette on the horizon is complete with suitcase, it's also not moving very rapidly.

'That's for me,' says Cidrolin, under his breath.

He goes down on to the barge again, puts the paint pot away and lies down on his chaise-longue to await developments. The developments occur in the following fashion: having got to the gate that leads to the boulevard, the feminine silhouette complete with suitcase continues on its way.

'What a clot,' says Cidrolin, 'I'll bet she's come from Albert.'

He abandons his chaise-longue and goes up on to the embankment again to see what happens. Sure enough, the feminine silhouette complete with suitcase is making enquiries ten barges further up. It turns round. It's moving towards him, now. It's coming near. It's coming nearer. Here it is. It puts its suitcase down before uttering the words:

'Are you the chap Monsieur Albert was telling me about?'

'What did he say about me that would make it possible for me to identify myself?'

'Don't understand. And anyway, you don't answer a question with a question. Snot done.'

'To whom did Monsieur Albert send you?'

'Another question. Can't you answer mine? My question.'

'What *was* your question?'

'Another one! It's obvious that all you can do is ask questions.'

'Frankly, I don't think that's in my nature.'

'Pooh! You don't know yourself.'

'As you don't know me, either, one wonders who does know me.'

'Monsieur Albert does.'

'Very true.'

'Then you *are* the one that's looking for a bird to brighten up his barge?'

'There you have it.'

'And that's it, the barge?'

'Yes.'

'It's great.'

'Let's not exaggerate.'

'And will we go to Saint-Trop in it, in August?'

'No, it doesn't move.'

'Pity. Oh, but there's a little boat, though. Is it yours, the little boat?'

'Yes.'

'Will we go out in the little boat?'

'Could be.'

'You know, I can row; don't worry, I'll be the one that does the work.'

'That'd be too much for me to ask.'

'Mustn't discourage me when I'm so willing.'

Cidrolin scratched his head.

'Are you of age?'

'Want to see my identity card?'

'I'd like to.'

She was of age. He looked carefully to see whether the date hadn't been altered. It didn't look as if it had. He gave her back her identity card and picked up the suitcase.

'Come on, come and get settled in.'

'Have you had your breakfast?'

He intimated that he hadn't.

'Watch,' he said 'out not to fall on your arse.'

It was a steep slope down the bank.

'And not to fall in the drink.'

They went along the gang-plank over the ooze. The young lady over twenty-one said:

'From a distance it's great, but from close to it's foul.'

'The water looks a bit dirty, but it isn't stagnant. It's not always the same muck you see. Sometimes I give it a shove with a stick and it goes off with the current. This side, even so, it does actually stagnate a bit.'

Then:

'Don't bump your head. Here, this'll be your cabin, it was my daughter's. It isn't big, but on a boat, you know, there's never much room. I'm not talking about liners like you see in the cinema.'

'By the way, have you got the telly here?'

'No.'

'What about my serial, then?'

'What d'you expect me to say?'

'That alters everything.'

'I see your point. Didn't Albert tell you?'

'You're not going to tell me you can't afford to buy yourself a telly?'

'I'm not forcing you to stay. Want me to take your suitcase up again?'

'Don't bother. Just too bad about the serial. Actually, it's pretty lousy. But you know how it is. Habit. It's been going on for sixty-six weeks. Just too bad.'

'I'll leave you. The bathroom's there and the room next to the bathroom's next to it.'

'Okay, okay. I'll be back in five minutes and get your breakfast.'

Cidrolin went up on deck again and stretched himself out on his chaise-longue to await developments, but in no time at all he had closed his eyes.

'Noble spouse,' said Russule, kissing his hand respectfully, 'I have great and joyful news for you: you're going to have a son and heir.'

'Bravo, my dear! That's going to put my sons-in-law in a chafe. But . . . tell me, gracious Russule, how do you know it's going to be a son and heir?'

'The astrologer told me.'

'What astrologer?'

'An astrologer I consulted. And so that he can observe the stars at the moment of parturition I've installed him in the castle. Always providing you give your kind authorisation, of course, noble spouse.'

'The devil,' says the Duke into his beard, 'me that's just brought an alchemist in, there's going to be quite a crowd.'

'Might my decision be displeasing to you?' asked Russule, lowering her eyes.

'Nenni, menni, my dear. Nenni soit qui mal y pense. What do you say to that one, Empoigne? Haven't I come back to our province full of the purest quintessence of court wit? I've come back a pretty wit to my fingertips. Lord de Ciry had better look out: I'll pun him so many puns that even *his* arrogance will finally be expunged. And what about my bishop? Bring me my bishop! I must introduce my alchemist to him. Where's my alchemist? Bring me my alchemist! And what about my son and heir? that's right, my son and heir. Where's my son and heir?'

He pretends to be looking all round him. He pats Russule's belly.

'That's where he is, my son and heir. That's where he's hiding. Charming hiding place. Ah, Russule, you've given me great pleasure, and now I'm going to give you great pleasure, too.'

'I am listening, noble spouse.'

'I'm going to have a statue. And, by my halidom, an equestrian statue. It's going to be erected by the elm tree, opposite the drawbridge. Master Francavilla's done my portrait, and this Master Francavilla is a famous scultor who had something to do with the statue of our good King the fourth Henri which is on the Pont Neuf.'

'How I regret I didn't see it,' says Russule, sighing.

'Have no fear, woman, it won't run away. I'll take you to see it when the next States General meet, and that can't be long, now, for the Queen Mother is in great need of money, hence of taxes.'

'A thousand thanks, noble spouse,' says Russule, curtseying.

'But let's get back to my statue. I shall be on horseback, then, on Sthenes, naturally, and Master Francavilla has likewise done a very faithful portrait of him. Sthenes was highly satisfied with it; when they showed it to him, he neighed. Nay! he even got down on his knees. On knees soit qui mal y pense.'

'Ha, ha,' says Empoigne.

'He didn't really,' says the Duke, 'that's not in his nature.'

He turns to Russule:

'He's going to have his statue, too,' he says, pointing to Mouscaillot. 'A little one. While I was about it. Not for his sake (another gesture), but so that good old Stef shouldn't be jealous.'

'And what about me,' says Russule, lowering her eyes, 'amn't I going to have a statue?'

'Of course you are, woman. I've thought about that. In our chapel, you shall have a magnificent tomb, a far more beautiful

[119]

one than my deceased Elodie had. You'll be seen there carved in stone. Personally I prefer bronze.'

As Russule was curtseying, the Duke said:

'No need to thank me. It's quite natural. Ah, here's the astrologer. Come hither. What's your name?'

'Dupont. At your service, my Lord.'

'And you can read the stars?'

'At your service, my Lord.'

'And you saw I was going to have a son and heir?'

'At your service, my Lord.'

The Duke turned to Russule and said:

'He's a silly dope, your astrologer.'

He resumed his dialogue with Dupont in these terms:

'Did you observe the stars last night?'

'At your service, my Lord.'

'And what did they tell you?'

'Gloriam Dei, my Lord. Gloriam Dei.'

'Is that all?'

'What, my Lord,' exclaimed the astrologer with a fine oratorical gesture, 'don't you think that's already a great deal, the glory of God?'

'For the gloriam Dei I've got my bishop, who is perfectly competent in the matter. I'd rather hear something about your speciality.'

'I have heard the music of the spheres.'

'And what sort of sound was that?'

'Divine, my Lord. Divine.'

The Duke, nauseated, turned to Russule.

'He's a complete idiot.'

He put his hand on the noble lady's belly once more, and resumed his conversation with the astrologer:

'And what's going to come out of here? a filly or a son and heir?'

'A son and heir, my Lord.'

[120]

'Are you absolutely certain?'

'The stars do not lie.'

'But you aren't a star. Now, what man has never lied? It's common, lying, so common that it's one of the sins in the catechism. If Monseigneur Biroton, Bishop in partibus of Sarcellopolis, were here, he'd tell you so at once. Now it's in your interest to lie. You've found board and lodging here and you're putting your feet up at my expense. You thought you'd happened upon a squireen who was as credulous as a woman (gesture in Russule's direction), and you find yourself confronted with a noble seigneur who has just spent six months at court and in the capital city, with someone who has taken the floor at the States General, and from whom they had great difficulty in taking it back again, in short, Dupont, out of my sight!'

Russule throws herself at the Duke's feet, and entreats him thus:

'My noble spouse, me that was so proud at having an astrologer just like Queen Catherine. I was thinking of your prestige . . . of your status . . .'

'But my dear,' replied the Duke, becoming a thought irritated, 'the thing is that I've brought back an alchemist from the capital city, from Arcueil, more precisely. I'm not going to keep a whole host of necromancers. Personally I much prefer the alchemist; when he's found me the philosopher's stone . . .'

'Bunkum!' exclaimed Dupont.

'You,' said the Duke, 'are a false friend. It's very nasty to disparage a colleague's profession. I don't like you.'

Monseigneur Biroton appeared, followed by the Abbé Riphinte. Both were treated to great hugs from the Duke, who immediately puts the bishop into the picture and asks his advice.

'Throw them both out,' says Onésiphore.

'Exaggerating already!' exclaimed the Duke. 'Myself, I want to keep one of them.'

[121]

'So do I,' said Russule.

The chaplain, much perturbed, scratched his head.

'Well,' asks the Duke. 'What do you say? The astrologer? Or the alchemist?'

'The whole business smells of heresy,' says Biroton.

The astrologer turned towards him.

'I'm a good Christian,' said he. 'Haven't you confessed me?'

'That is so,' said the bishop.

The Duke was becoming more and more nauseated.

'What an arse-licker this fellow is. I certainly don't like him at all.'

'He is not lacking in piety,' said Onésiphore, 'and then, after all, it isn't a sin to observe the stars.'

'I think it's even poetic,' murmured Russule.

'And,' added the Abbé Riphinte, 'Master Dupont doesn't in any way profess the heretical doctrine of the Pole, Copernicus. *That*'s a good point.'

'Kopernik soit qui mal y pense,' said the Duke absent-mindedly.

'Ha ha,' said Empoigne.

'The sun goes round the earth,' declaimed the astrologer, 'and he who maintains the contrary is very foolish and very malicious.'

'How wise he is,' remurmured Russule, 'I'm sure to have a son and heir.'

'They're all trying to get round me,' said the Duke, sullenly.

'Alchemy is a most foul pursuit,' went on Onésiphore, who reckoned that the Duchess and her soothsayer had won. 'The fires in its furnaces evoke those of Hell, and the desire for gold is greatly to be condemned. As for the elixir of life, that reminds me that the demon said to our first parents: eritis sicut dei, when he was tempting them to eat the apple, which was also supposed to bring them the gift of long life . . .'

'Hm,' said the Abbé Riphinte.

'. . . and you are aware of everything that followed.'

'Amen,' said Dupont.

'Amen,' repeated likewise Russule, Empoigne and the Abbé Riphinte.

The Duke doesn't say anything. He gives the astronomer a dirty look and begins to get impatient, but he doesn't show too many signs of it yet. Dupont, who thinks it's in the bag, starts perorating:

'O celestial powers, which guide the fortunes of this world, I see you bringing your gifts and your blessings to the sublime heir who will shortly be procreated by the most famous and illustrious Duke of Auge. . . .'

'What!' cries the most famous and illustrious Duke of Auge, 'what . . . will shortly be . . . Then, woman, are you not pregnant?'

'Not yet, noble spouse, but you will attend to that.'

And Russule lowers her eyes modestly, and gets quite pink.

The most famous and illustrious Duke of Auge makes a beeline for Dupont's throat and starts strangling him with his two powerful hands. The astrologer looks as if he's trying to expel his pupils etc. out of his orbits and puts out a pallid tongue, while Joachim is explaining his grievances to him and informing him of his contempt for impostors.

And he shakes him energetically, while progressively tightening his grip. Russule throws herself at his feet and begs his mercy. Onésiphore asks the Abbé Riphinte to bring him what is necessary to administer extreme unction to the victim. Viscount Empoigne takes a firm stand in an attitude of extreme prudence.

'Ah, the drasty gnof!' the Duke keeps repeating, while the other is turning purple.

'Have mercy on him, noble spouse,' shrieks the Duchess, 'have mercy on him!'

'Come come, my Lord,' says Onésiphore, in a mildly reproachful voice, 'a little moderation; I'm not going to have time to administer the last sacraments.'

[123]

Dupont will survive this stern ordeal. The Duke finally lets go of him while he's still alive, and the other rolls over on the ground like cream cheese: people come rushing to sweep him up while the alchemist, who has just come in, bows low to his host.

The Duke manifests his total satisfaction.

XII

Cidrolin opened his eyes; someone was talking gently into his ear. It was Lalix, who was telling him that lunch was ready.

'Well,' she added, 'you've had a hell of a kip. So you've skipped your breakfast, but I couldn't let you sleep all day and I've got a nice meal ready for you.'

Cidrolin looked at her absent-mindedly: this was a recent memory, so he didn't recognise it very well yet.

'I've been having such dreams,' he murmured to himself.

'Mustn't tell them.'

'And why not?' asked Cidrolin, interested.

'It's not done.'

'But why?'

She contented herself with answering:

'Lunch is ready.'

The weather was still quite warm, the table had been taken out on deck. It was laid for one.

'Have you had your lunch?' asked Cidrolin.

'Yes, m'sieu.'

'Next time, you can wait for me, and lay for two.'

'Snice of you. Thank you, M'sieu.'

Cidrolin made for the store-room. Lalix swooped down on him.

'Do you want something?'

'The essence of fennel.'

'Are you going to have an essence of fennel before lunch?'

'I always do.'

'It's bad for your health.'

Cidrolin laughs gently.

'It's true,' Lalix goes on. 'It's very bad for your health.'

'If you want to go and pack your bag,' says Cidrolin, 'I'm not stopping you. I'll even give you a month's wages, if you've blown within the hour.'

'I don't specially want you to waste your money,' says Lalix.

Cidrolin goes and gets the bottle of essence of fennel and pours himself out a quarter of a glass, which he tops up with still water. While he drinks, he vaguely watches a rowing eight in training.

When his glass is empty, Lalix says:

'Can I dish up?'

'Go ahead.'

She brings some butter and a tin of fillets of tunny in pure vegetable oil. She watches Cidrolin eat.

'It gets on my nerves when you watch me like that,' says Cidrolin, 'Sit down and tell me a story.'

'You take me for Scheherazade,' says Lalix.

'Heh heh,' says Cidrolin. 'So we're educated.'

'That doesn't spoil anything. Don't you think?'

'I entirely agree.'

'Ah,' says Lalix, looking pleased.

'You're educated,' says Cidrolin, 'and you've got principles, too: not to drink essence of fennel before lunch, and not to tell your dreams. In point of fact, why shouldn't people tell their dreams?'

'It's bad manners,' says Lalix.

'First time I've heard that,' says Cidrolin.

'People,' Lalix continues, 'they think they're so bloody wonderful, everything they do, everything they are. They make

[125]

out they're so important . . . So if, on top of all that, you had to put up with listening to their dreams, there'd never be an end to it.'

'My dreams are uncommonly interesting,' says Cidrolin.

'That's what they all think. There's nothing to prove it, though, seeing that you can't compare them.'

'Mine,' says Cidrolin, 'if I were to write them down, they'd make a real novel.'

'And don't you think there're enough novels as it is?'

'Don't be afraid,' says Cidrolin. 'I'm not a writing-room worker.'

'Oh, but I'm not afraid of anything.'

'You see,' says Cidrolin, 'when you said that people shouldn't tell their dreams, I thought it was because of psychoanalysis and the psychoanalysts.'

'Because of what?'

'Psychoanalysis. Don't you know what it is?'

'No.'

'And I thought you were educated.'

'You can't know everything,' says Lalix.

'How true.'

And, seeing that he'd finished his fillets of tunny, Cidrolin enquired about what was to follow in these terms:

'What's next?'

'A tin of pâté de foie. Will that do?'

'I don't want to be offensive,' says Cidrolin, 'but I could have done just as well.'

'Monsieur Albert told me that you were a good-natured sort of chap, but you're always moaning.'

'Bah,' says Cidrolin, 'that was just a minor criticism.'

'Let's forget it.'

So she brings the tin of pâté de foie.

'Do I sit down again?' she asks.

[126]

'Of course.'

Cidrolin, melancholically, silently, spreads some pâté de foie on his bread.

'Well,' says Lalix, 'that thing you were talking about just now. About dreams.'

'Psychoanalysis?'

'Sright.'

'And psychoanalysts?'

'Sright.'

'Well er,' says Cidrolin, chewing his sandwidge laboriously, 'they're people who interpret dreams. And it doesn't stop there. They discover the hidden depths of things. Well, of people. And so, very properly, some people are wary of them, they don't want them to discover their hidden depths, and so they stop telling them their dreams.'

'No one's the loser,' says Lalix.

'You surely are anti.'

'Anti what?'

'People telling their dreams.'

'I've already told you: I think it's bad manners, and, as you might say, unsavoury.'

'I'll just have to make the best of it, then.'

He finishes his pâté, absent-mindedly watching a fisherman, over on the other bank, tying his boat up to a stake and getting his gear ready; he's got a dog with him, who's also watching him.

'Do you fish?' Lalix asks Cidrolin.

She could, at a pinch, have put the same question to the geezer opposite, but she'd have had to use a megaphone.

'No,' replied Cidrolin, and not, naturally, the fisherman over on the other side, who couldn't hear, and who in any case would have answered: yes. 'I don't like it. It's cruel.'

'It's idiotic, more than anything else: sitting there like that doing nothing.'

[127]

'And what is there now, to finish off this excellent meal?'

'A bit of cheese, and the remains of a pot of jam.'

'Marvellous,' says Cidrolin.

The fisherman has cast his line; he lights a cigarette and smokes, looking as if his thoughts are miles away. The dog has curled itself up in a ball and is asleep.

'It'll soon be time for my siesta,' Cidrolin observes to himself.

Lalix has brought the conclusion of the excellent meal and has sat down, on her own initiative, this time.

'Well, Scheherazade,' says Cidrolin, masticating the rancid cheese and at the same time anticipating that the jam would be mouldy, 'aren't you going to tell me any stories?'

'Real ones or made-up ones?'

'You want to be careful of made-up ones. They reveal your fundamental nature. Just like dreams. And reveries. Reverie and revelation, they're more or less the same word.'

'What about real ones, then, they reveal your fundamental nature just as much. Don't you think?'

'What if you told me a story about someone else . . .'

'Why should I tell it if it doesn't interest me, and if it does interest me then it's the same as if it was me.'

'Then you don't want to tell me anything?'

'How should I know. You're screwpilating, you know. You aren't a bit like Monsieur Albert described you, a sort of nice quiet old fogey, not at all the sort to get on your wick.'

'Well, there you are, Monsieur Albert, tell me how you met him. Before you do, though, I must inform you that, as I foresaw, the jam was mouldy.'

'You see, you never stop moaning.'

'Another fucking fiasco, I'm used to it.'

'You're not going to start crying over a bit of jam.'

'Well? What about Monsieur Albert?'

'Don't you want a cup of coffee?'

'No, no!' cried Cidrolin, jumping. 'No coffee!'

'You afraid it'd be nauseating, the way I'd make it?'

'What about my siesta? It'd stop me sleeping.'

'You going to have another siesta? You were kipping the whole morning.'

'I'll lie down there, on that chaise-longue and you tell me how you got to know Monsieur Albert.'

'To help you go to bye-byes?'

'If I drop off you can stop, and you can start again some other time.'

'You're not very encouraging.'

'Come on, Scheherazade: the story about Albert.'

'Or right. I'm the only daughter of a father who's a wood-cutter.'

'That sounds familiar, now . . . the daughter of a woodcutter . . .'

'You aren't going to interrupt all the time, are you? If so, I'd much rather you went to sleep.'

Cidrolin didn't deny her immediate satisfaction. The Duke was riding through the forest, silentous and solicit. Sthenes was equally silent, but though the ride was becoming protracted the ducal taciturnity did not seem inclined to evaporate, so he finally opened his lips to ask whether he might speak.

'Speak, my good Demo, speak,' said the Duke, patting his neck affectionately.

'Gramercy,' said Sthenes, with lively satisfaction.

He appeared to be thinking a bit before putting the question he had been itching to ask for quite some time.

'Hm, hm,' said he, 'how's our statue getting on?'

'My goodness,' replied the Duke. 'I've no idea.'

'Isn't it cast yet?'

'I haven't had any news of it for quite some time.'

Sthenes didn't hide his disappointment. He crapped, out of sheer resentment.

[129]

'And,' he went on, 'don't you think that ought to give you some cause for anxiety?'

'At the moment, it worries me not at all.'

'And what about your glory, have you forgotten about it? Have you forgotten about those future generations who will come and contemplate you, bronzed for all eternity, in front of the feudal elm tree? Are you no longer proud to know that the fact of your being statufied will entitle you to have your name in all the histories of art which are not, it is true, numerous in our day but whose number will not cease to grow in the centuries to come? Zounds, I'm prophesying, I do believe!'

Having made this observation, Sthenes breaks into a lively little trot.

'Gently,' says the Duke, 'gently.'

Sthenes starts walking, and at the same time talking, again.

'Do my arguments not convince you?'

'Of course they do, my good Demo, of course they do. I'll send Empoigne to see what's happening to my effigy.'

'Now there's an excellent idea! At the same time he could inquire about Stef's and his.'

'It's a journey that's likely to grieve the Duchess,' says the Duke, with melancholy.

'Why shouldn't she go too? She so longs to visit the capital city.'

'There'd be talk.'

'Add the Abbé Riphinte to the expedition, and cap the lot with Monseigneur Biroton. You'd be rid of them for a month or two.'

'So I would. Having to listen to their admonitions and admonestations every day. And I can count myself lucky, as it is, that they don't denounce me as an atheist or a sorcerer.'

'They have to carry on like that because it's their job; it's only to keep up appearances, but if your alchemist managed to manufacture the elixir of life they wouldn't refuse a wee glass of it.'

'We haven't got so far as the elixir of life yet, we're contenting ourselves for the moment with the powder of projection.'

'And it's going well?'

'I can't see the end of it yet.'

Sthenes was silent for a few moments, before starting to speak again in these terms:

'I'm beginning to wonder, Joachim, whether you were right to bring Master Timoleo Timolei to your castle. Ever since he's been quartered with you and has been heating up his furnaces on your premises, you have become, Joachim, morose and taciturn, and you've now spent practically all those good silver crowns you got from the treaty of Sainte-Menehould. Isn't that so?'

'The fact is that my coffers are empty and I'm shortly going to be reduced to breaking into the piggy-bank of my hypothetical son and heir, which makes me think that I might after all have been better advised to keep the astrologer. He'd've cost me less, and the Duchess'd've been pleased.'

'Pah,' said Sthenes, 'all that crowd's much of a muchness.'

'Would you be a sceptic, my good Demo?'

'If you really really really want to know what I think, well, I don't believe in horoscopes.'

'Nor do I, much.'

'Or in the Philosopher's Stone, either.'

'Ah,' said the Duke 'if anyone other than you had said such a thing to me, I'd've dealt him a back-hander.'

'*I* don't believe in them,' said Sthenes, 'but I'm not stopping *you* believing in them.'

'I should hope not! Ah, if you were to see us, Timoleo and me, in the middle of our athanors and our aludels, our pelicans and our matrasses, our retorts and our alembics, manipulating our salts and our metals, some of them violet, others indigo, some blue, others green, some yellow, others orange-coloured, yet others red, not to speak of the whites and the blacks, watching

[131]

them change from one colour to another, watching solids becoming liquids and liquids becoming solids, watching the palpable becoming impalpable and the impalpable becoming palpable, and I'm only telling you about the most superficial of our operations, then, my good Demo, you'd tell yourself that it's surely not in vain that your master and his alchemist are putting themselves to so very much trouble. The day will come when the angels will reward our labours, and then it won't be in bronze but in solid gold that I'll have my statue cast.'

'Our statue.'

The Duke didn't even hear this correction, and he fell once again into his melancholious mood, from which Sthenes no longer dared extricate him. They went their way another league in silence; then Sthenes decided to turn back, but to go home a different way; the Duke had nothing against it, but was still silent, frowning and gazing into vacancy. He started when, some time later, he heard someone interpellating him; they were crossing a clearing where some woodcutters were working, they were cutting wood to feed Timoleo Timolei's furnaces. As for the interpellation, its author was one of the scrogloppers and consisted in these words:

'Noble seigneur, is my daughter the Duchess well?'

Cidrolin started.

'And what about your brothers and sisters?' he asked.

'I told you I was an only daughter! Did you sleep well?'

'Errr . . . so your father was a woodcutter . . .'

'I've just finished telling you how I met Monsieur Albert and how he came to send me here.'

Cidrolin yawned.

'Wouldn't like to start all over again, would you?' he added.

'Certainly not,' said Lalix. 'You should've listened.'

'Ah well, can't be helped,' said Cidrolin. 'Another time.'

'There won't be any other times: once is enough.'

'I'll just have to make the best of it, then.'

He stretched and stood up. The fisherman was still there, over on the other bank, and the dog curled up in a ball was still asleep in the dinghy.

'They aren't so cruel as all that,' says Cidrolin, 'they never catch any fish.'

Lalix looked at the angler, but made no comment. She had still been sitting down, but now she too stood up.

'I didn't want to spoil your lunch or your siesta for you,' she said, 'but someone's written a whole lot of stuff up on your gate. Horrible things. More than horrible.'

Cidrolin, in silence, went to fetch the paint pot and brush.

'Insults,' said Lalix. 'Abuse.'

Cidrolin went towards the gang-plank.

'Is it you they've got it in for?' asked Lalix.

'Well, yes,' replied Cidrolin.

'What have you done, then?'

'I'll tell you that when you're asleep.'

Cidrolin climbs up the bank. He doesn't even look to see what's written, and starts whitewashing. Lalix goes to wash up. A gang of nomads, coming from the camp, stop to ask Cidrolin something; they know the French for metro. That's what they're asking him. He replies with gestures.

'They're starting to migrate,' said Cidrolin, watching them as they went. 'The Autumn approaches. Mon automne éternel, ô ma saison mentale.'

'Pardon,' asked a passer-by.

'I was quoting,' said Cidrolin.

'From whom?'

'From a poet, of course. Didn't you hear the twelve feet?'

'I wasn't paying much attention. I thought you wanted to ask me something. The time, perhaps.'

'I didn't want anything at all,' said Cidrolin.

[133]

He went back to his painting; the other watched him in silence.

Another group of nomads came up; they knew the French for metro and that's what they said to the passer-by. The latter mimed ignorance.

'Is there a metro around here?' he asked Cidrolin.

Cidrolin showed the nomads the way; they thanked him warmly and went off.

Cidrolin went back to his painting and said under his breath: 'That's what it is all right. They're starting to migrate. The Autumn approaches.'

He went on with his work in silence.

'And what comes next?' asked the passer-by.

'What comes next after what?'

'After the quotation.'

'You're impatient. It hasn't begun yet.'

'Was that yours: "They're starting to migrate. The Autumn approaches"?'

'Entirely mine.'

'And the words you're painting over, whose were they?'

'A passer-by's, I suppose.'

'Are you accusing me?'

'Do you imagine you're the only passer-by?'

Not hearing any answer, Cidrolin glances behind him: the other had turned his back on him and was pretending to look at the building which was nearing completion. Cidrolin makes a few more brush strokes; it's done. He leaves the brush in the paint pot and picks up the paint pot by the handle, a thin, metallic handle that cuts your fingers a bit.

The passer-by has disappeared.

XIII

The village church clock had long since struck five when the Duke of Auge left the castle, accompanied by Pouscaillou, the youngest brother of the Viscount Empoigne, newly in his service. They were both on horseback, the one was riding Sthenes and the other Stef. The Duke didn't say a word, Sthenes didn't put a foot wrong. Stef and Pouscaillou did likewise. As they crossed the burg they met, in the market place, a group of notables who bowed very low to the Duke.

'Well, gentlemen,' said the Duke absent-mindedly, 'do we enjoy good health?'

'Excellent,' replied the bailiff. 'Excellent.'

'And apart from that, is there anything worthy of attention?'

'We,' replied the bailiff, 'are this very minute going to elect our delegates to the States General.'

'Ah, that's right, the States General . . .'

The Duke said no more on that subject.

'We,' went on the bailiff, 'have made a start on our complaints book. Monseigneur Biroton and the Abbé Riphinte are going to join us, and if Monsieur the Duke would deign to grant us his noble assistance we could send to Paris a single book for the three estates of the bailiwick, which would show His Majesty the union of all Frenchmen behind the sacred person of the King.'

'Long live the King!' shouted the notables. 'Long live the King!'

'Long live the King!' Pouscaillou thought fit to yell.

A back-hander from the Duke sent the squire flying into the

dust; he picked himself up and then remounted his horse in a daze. The notables abstained from comment on this incident.

'Well!' said the Duke, a bit more cheerful now, 'work well, gentlemen.'

And he went off at a gallop towards the cemetery. He dismounted and entrusted Sthenes's reins to Pouscaillou, who had followed as best he could.

'You popinjay,' said the Duke, 'who said you could shout "Long live the King"?'

'I did what all the others did,' replied Pouscaillou, snivelling.

'Well then, you must learn . . . But get off your horse, first.'

When this was done, the Duke took him by one ear and, pinching it rather hard, pursued his discourse with these words:

'You must learn, then, dear little page, parrot and popinjay, that you mustn't do what all the others do, but what I do, d'you hear?: What, I, do. Got it?'

'No. Don't understand a word.'

The Duke, changing ears, continued in these terms:

'Now I, what was I doing? Was I shouting "long live the King"? No. Got it now?'

'Yes, indeed, but, isn't it advisable to shout "long live the King" on every possible occasion?'

'Perhaps,' replied the Duke, letting go of the ear, which had become somewhat reddish, and suddenly seeming extremely thoughtful. 'Perhaps,' he repeated after a few moments.

And he went into the cemetery.

When Pouscaillou judged him to be sufficiently far away, he rubbed his ears, grumbling:

'He hurt me, the dirty beast. Just for shouting "long live the King". As if, in the year seventeen hundred and eighty-nine of our very Christian era, you weren't allowed to shout "long live the King" any more. Well, personally I shall go on shouting "long live the King".'

Which in fact he did, but in a fairly low voice.

'You cannot understand, young man,' said Sthenes. 'It's because the Duke doesn't go in for politics.'

'Ah, Lord Jesus,' exclaimed the page, 'a talking horse.'

'You might just as well know straightaway, it'll facilitate our relations. And in any case I'm not the only one, Stef talks too. Don't you, Stef?'

'Yes,' replied Stef concisely.

'But don't tremble like that,' said Sthenes to Pouscaillou. 'Might you be afraid? On the eve of a revolution that is not recommended.

'A revolution? ·sked Pouscaillou, his teeth chattering. 'Wha-what revovolutiontiᴄ.ᴧ?'

'The one that's brewing,' replied Sthenes.

'And he prophesies!' cried Pouscaillou, in a voice as heartrent as heartrending. 'Like Balaam's ass!'

'He isn't a squire,' said Sthenes scornfully, 'he's a seminarist. And what's more, he takes me for a she-ass. He hasn't looked under my belly.'

This jest caused the sober Stef to unbend and the two horses laughed, and then, by chain reaction, guffawed, which completed Pouscaillou's demoralisation, and he rolled over and over on the ground, crying. When he'd got over his attack and emitted a good pint of lachrymal liquid, he got up, still trembling, and saw Sthenes and Stef peacefully, mutely, looking for goodies amongst the pellitory plants. This activity, though it was perfectly orthohippic, completed his terror, and he judged it prudent to seek refuge with his employer. So he went into the cemetery and saw the Duke, at the far end of the path, meditating by a grave; he also saw, just in front of him, two grave-diggers exhuming some bones and making little piles of them. This sight completed the page's nausea; he turned on his heel and, being a good runner, was soon back on the terrace of the castle where a few people were drinking coffee and alcoholic beverages, among others, essence of fennel, while chatting of this and that.

'Well, Pouscaillou,' exclaimed his brother, 'what on earth's the matter with you? Have you abandoned the high and mighty seigneur Joachim, Duke of Auge?'

Laughter. Not from Pouscaillou, though, who, in a tearful voice, expresses his dearest wish:

'I want to go home to Mummy!'

'What is it, Pouscaillou?' says his brother. 'Has the high and mighty seigneur been fumbling with your cod-piece?'

Laughter. Not from Pouscaillou, though, who goes on wailing:

'It's not the Duke! It's not the Duke! It's the horses.'

'As for that, Pouscaillou – you'll never get me to believe that those gees have a weakness for little boys.'

Laughter. Not from Pouscaillou, though, who jumps up and down with emotion.

'They talk! They talk!'

'Isn't he a silly little thing,' says the Duchess, charmed.

'Imbecile,' his furious brother says to him. 'You aren't going to believe that gothic and antiquated legend, are you?'

'One reads of such things in novels of chivalry,' says Monseigneur Biroton with a derisive little laugh. 'During the last crusade, or the one before last, I don't remember exactly . . .'

'The seventh,' says the Abbé Riphinte.

'Isn't he erudite,' exclaimed the Duchess, waving her lorgnette.

'During the seventh crusade,' went on Onésiphore, still in an ironical tone of voice, 'the Duke of Auge's horse terrified the Saracens because he shouted insults at them.'

'How extremely foolish,' says Viscount d'Empoigne. 'Has anyone ever heard a quadruped talk?'

'Yes indeed,' says the Abbé Riphinte. 'There is one: Balaam's ass.'

[138]

'Sthenes prophesies like her,' says Pouscaillou, still scared stiff.

'You aren't very good at your catechism,' the Abbé Riphinte tells him severely. 'Balaam's ass didn't prophesy, she only opened her mouth to protest against the blows her master smote her, because she'd seen the angel of the Lord. It was a miracle.'

'I,' concluded Pouscaillou, 'want to go home to Mummy.'

'You'll stay here,' said his brother. 'That's an order.'

'If Mummy knew there were talking horses here she'd tell me to come home at once.'

'But we're telling you that they don't exist, talking horses,' says the Abbé Riphinte. 'Barring miracles.'

'And miracles are becoming more rare, in this day and age,' added Monseigneur Biroton with a sigh.

'Well, Pouscaillou,' says the Duke, whom they hadn't seen coming, 'is that how you look after the horses? You can go home to your mother.'

Without even a word of thanks, Pouscaillou disappeared.

'He's an idiot, your brother,' said the Duke to Empoigne, pouring himself out a glass of essence of fennel.

He watched the liquid in silence for a few moments and then added:

'One of Timoleo Timolei's recipes. Alas, poor Timoleo. I've been to meditate on his grave again today.'

'Forget that bone-setter, that charlatan,' said Onésiphore. 'These days, who can still believe in the elixir of life and the philosopher's stone?'

'Do you really think the world was created very precisely in the year four thousand and four B.C.?'

'Monsieur the Duke,' retorted the Abbé Riphinte, 'we have good reasons for believing that.'

'Which are?' asked the Duke.

'What a bore you are, Joachim,' said the Duchess. 'Are you going to become a theologian now?'

[139]

'If you have no objection, my little duck,' replied the Duke, filling his empty glass, 'Well, Abbé, what reasons?'

'But the Holy Scriptures, Monsieur the Duke!' said the Abbé Riphinte.

'A good answer, Riphinte,' observed Monseigneur Biroton.

'They're contradictory, your holy scriptures,' said the Duke, 'you only need just to poke your nose into them to find that out. And what about reason – what use do you make of that? In the year four thousand and four B.C., the world had already existed for thousands and thousands of years.'

'Absurd,' exclaimed Onésiphore.

'Joachim,' observed the Duchess, 'has never been very good at astrology. At astronomy, I should have said.'

'At chronology,' added the Abbé Riphinte, correcting her. 'And men,' he asked the Duke ironically, 'did they exist thousands and thousands of years before the creation of Adam?'

'Of course.'

'And what proof of that can you offer, Monsieur the Duke?'

'Aha' said Monseigneur Biroton,' our preadamite has his back to the wall, now.'

'Yes, where's the proof, Joachim?' said the Duchess in her turn.

'You're embarrassing him greatly,' observed Viscount d'Empoigne who had so far not dared take part in the discussion.

'I'm not in the least embarrassed,' retorted the Duke calmly, 'the proof must exist somewhere, it's just a question of finding it.'

'A fine answer,' said the Abbé Riphinte with a snigger. 'Monsieur the Duke will permit us to see it as nothing but a simple evasion.'

'Riphinte,' said Monseigneur Biroton, 'you've taken him down a peg!'

'Joachim,' said the Duchess, 'you will insist on trying to discuss theology with the Abbé, but you're making a mistake. You aren't up to it!'

[140]

'I wouldn't risk it, personally,' added the Viscount, with what was intended to be a knowing air.

'By Gog's nownes!' exclaimed the Duke, sending the table flying with an energetic kick, 'do you take me for milksope?'

Of the Chinese coffee set of the Ming era, only some smithereens were left, and of the bottles and glasses, some other smithereens. The Duke, on his feet, vehemently harangued those present:

'Blackguards! do you think you're just bourgeois, to dare to pasquinade me in this fashion? The church thinks it can do what it likes, these days. I don't know what's stopping me giving these creeping jesuses a good hiding.'

'Joachim!' exclaimed the Duchess, 'you're just a nasty feudal lord.'

'As for you, my little duck, you deserve a good spanking.'

He got hold of her by the wrist. Russule wasn't willing. The Duke takes hold of the other wrist. Russule jumps up and down. The Duke tugs: he drags her over to the little room where the whips are kept.

A lackey picks up the china- and glass-ware. Monseigneur Biroton and the Abbé Riphinte retire, tightlipped. The Duke is still tugging at his good wife who brakes energetically; her heels make sparks on the paving-stones.

Viscount d'Empoigne tried to intervene.

'Monsieur the Duke,' said he, in a voice whiter than a piece of linen, 'with all due respect . . .'

'Who asked you to interfere, Jack Sauce?' yelled the Duke, exasperated.

He let go of the Duchess, who fell on her posterior, and sent the Viscount flying with a powerful slap on the face. The latter, again out of atavism rather than courage, drew his sword. The Duke drew his, and then Empoigne is on the ground, completely dead and stabbed. The Duchess flings herself on the corpse, making a lot of noise. The Duke wipes his sword on Russule's petticoat and replaces the murderous weapon in its scabbard. He examines the situation.

Someone else who had timidly come up was likewise examining the situation.

'You've killed him,' murmured Pouscaillou.

He had his bundle in his hand, because he was going back home to his mummy.

'Is he really dead?' he added.

'If he wasn't yet,' replied the Duke, 'he soon would be: the lady would suffocate him.'

The Duchess didn't stop yelping. She finally declared:

'He's dead! He's dead!'

'There,' said the Duke to Pouscaillou. 'Now you know.'

'Then,' asked Pouscaillou, 'Viscount d'Empoigne, that's me, now?'

'No doubt,' replied the Duke, full of admiration.

'Oh, that's great.'

The Duchess's cries brought back priests and varletry.

'Well,' said Monseigneur Biroton, 'another Happening.'

'It was a duel, if I understand aright,' said the Abbé Riphinte.

'Not the slightest doubt,' said Onésiphore, 'Empoigne still has his sword in his hand.'

'To kill a man in a duel is not a small sin,' said the Abbé Riphinte, 'but it is less serious than not believing in the calendar.'

'Monsieur the Duke,' said the Bishop in partibus of Sarcellopolis, 'you must do penance for this incident and make public apology for your preadamite convictions.'

'As you see,' said the Abbé Riphinte, 'God's justice is more severe than the justice of men, which will absolve you.'

'I haven't much faith in it,' said the Duke of Auge, 'and, all things considered, I prefer to absent myself, perhaps even abroad. I shan't wait for the King's sergeants, nor for the good will of that gentleman. He didn't hesitate to have my excellent friend Donatien put away in the Bastille for a mere peccadillo, the poor fellow. Hm, that rhymes.'

'Indifferently,' observed the Abbé.

The Duke drew his sword, quite decided without further ado to slay the Abbé, who described a prudent trajectory and landed up behind Onésiphore, but the Duke restrained himself and put up his sword.

'You'll have to console Russule,' he said to the two priests. 'Personally I've got a suppressed spank in the palm of my hand. Adieu, gentlemen.'

'What about the States General?' said Monseigneur Biroton. 'Won't you attend them?'

'They're a lot of crap! For the moment I'm more interested in my liberty.'

He turned to Pouscaillou:

'Go and saddle Sthenes and Stef, Viscount, I'm taking you with me. You're going to see something of the world.'

'Oh, gramercy, Monsieur the Duke, but those talking horses . . .

'You'll never get Sthenes to keep quiet.'

'I've got misgivings . . .'

The Duke spun Pouscaillou round, and, with a well-placed kick, sent him straight to the target. After having described a gracious parabolic arc, Pouscaillou, still holding his bundle in his hand, landed at the stable door.

When the Duke came back a few moments later with his luggage, everything was ready. They left immediately.

The terrace was now deserted. The Duchess had disappeared, likewise the late Empoigne. At the foot of the stairs, Monseigneur Biroton and the Abbé Riphinte were waiting for the seigneur of this locality. They bowed very politely to him.

'Have you given the matter due consideration?' asked Monseigneur Biroton. 'You're putting yourself in the wrong.'

'And you won't be able to attend the States General,' added the Abbé Riphinte.

'My friends,' said the Duke, looking extremely gratified, 'you don't understand why I'm leaving.'

'Why?' asked the two priests in chorus.

'I'm going to look for proof.'

'What proof?'

'The proof of your ignorance. And long live the preadamites!'

'Long live the preadamites,' echoed the two horses in chorus, joined only somewhat belatedly by the prudent Pouscaillou.

And they all four went off at a full gallop.

They had a long ride that day and were fagged out when they arrived at the Wild Man at Saint-Genouillat-les-Trous, a big burg situated in the Vésinois, not far from Chamburne-en-Basses-Bouilles.

'By my halidom,' said the Duke, sitting down to table, 'we deserve a good meal. Something to drink and some sausage!'

'Heh heh, my dear,' he added for the benefit of the serving girl, patting her on the rump, 'I've got a suppressed spank in the hollow of my hand.'

'Thanks a lot! I don't want none of it.'

'Heh heh! a Duke's hand . . .'

'A rotten pig's hand,' she retorted, making herself scarce.

'You see,' said the Duke to Pouscaillou merrily, 'she's already a republican. Well, we'll see later on.'

And he started to devour some sausage.

'And now,' he went on, with his mouth full, 'what d'you think of Sthenes? isn't he a cheerful companion?'

'Oh yesh,' said Pouscaillou, I can't think how I could've been so scared the first time. I find it quite natural, now.'

'Natural, nothing's more natural than the natural. Such is the motto of my excellent friend Donatien.'

'Tell me, Monsieur the Duke, preadamites, what are they?'

'Just something to tease good old Onésiphore about. They don't exist. But if they did exist, good old Onésiphore would be in great difficulties.'

'But what are they?'

'Men who are supposed to have lived before Adam.'

'How silly!'

'Anyone might think that was the Abbé Riphinte talking. Don't make me regret having brought you with me.'

'It's very difficult to talk to you, Monsieur the Duke, you say they don't exist and at the same time you don't like it when I say how silly.'

'A thing that doesn't exist isn't necessarily silly, imbecile. Ha ha, chous gras, that's something I'm very fond of.'

'Hands off, old pig,' said the serving girl to the Duke who was trying to combine anatomy and gastronomy. 'Next time I'll upset the whole plateful over your head. And then it'll be a hotchpotch.'

'She's hard to please.'

'How can you allow yourself to be treated like that, Monsieur the Duke?'

'Don't forget I'm travelling incognito, and let's finish off these chous gras.'

They were stuffing themselves in silence when a postilion dressed up as a postilion appeared, ostentatiously manifesting abject terror. He was yelling:

'Incredible but true! There's . . . in the stable there's . . . a talking horse!'

Everyone laughed heartily, first and foremost the Duke; Pouscaillou alone was uneasy, and remained unsmiling.

'You're boozed again,' said the innkeeper, 'aren't you ashamed of coming and spreading alarm and despondency?'

'Leave him alone,' said a traveller to the innkeeper.

And to the postilion:

'And what did he say to you, the horse?'

[145]

'When he saw me coming into the stable he shouted: "Long live the preadamites!"'

'He's mad,' someone shouted.

Everyone laughed heartily, first and foremost the Duke; Pouscaillou alone was getting more and more uneasy, and remained unsmiling.

XIV

For the third time everyone started laughing heartily as the postilion continued the description of his emotions in these terms:

'And the horse added: "you don't believe your ears, do you?"'

Pouscaillou alone, extremely uneasy, remained unsmiling.

'That was true enough,' continued the postilion, 'I didn't believe my ears, so I hopped it and here I am and I'm not likely to go near that stable of the devil again. Hey, innkeeper, give me a pitcher of claret to put my wits back where they belong.'

'I shall do nothing of the sort,' said the innkeeper, 'you've had enough to drink as it is.'

'Zounds, I'm not the least bit drunk. Go and see for yourself!'

'The Lord preserve me! And anyway, which horse is it?'

'It's mine,' said the Duke.

Everyone turned and looked at him.

'And he talks,' he added. 'He can even read. For instance, he's in the middle of reading Young Anacharsis's Travels in Greece, which he much appreciates. Innkeeper, give Monsieur the postilion a pitcher of claret: he is not in the least drunk.'

An approving murmur followed this short discourse, each man saying to his neighbour: what a wit.

'You're looking glum,' said the Duke to Pouscaillou. 'You can see that it doesn't take much to please them, though. You'll see, sooner or later, someone will certainly get around to saying: In France, ridicule is fatal. The postilion's discredited now; but I must admit that Sthenes has been very rash, he can't hold his tongue.'

'Supposing the law starts getting interested?'

'Pah! at the very most, the local curé.'

The servant girl brought a fowl which the two travellers got through with ease, and also the sweets, cheeses and tit-bits that followed. They emptied a few more pitchers before they went to bed and they went to sleep immediately, extremely replete and extremely tired.

Lalix and Cidrolin opened their eyes wide as the lights went on again and left the cinema somewhat dazed.

'We'll have a drink before we go home,' suggested Cidrolin.

Lalix agreed.

'I've got a weakness for cloak and dagger films,' said Cidrolin.

'You think so?' asked Lalix.

'I don't think so, I'm sure I have.'

'I didn't mean that. I meant: do you think it was a cloak and dagger film?'

'Yes, unless I was dreaming.'

'Personally, I thought it was a western. But I think I was asleep too.'

'Shall we go back and see what was on?'

They went back and looked. The posters and photos referred to Spartacus and Frankenstein versus Hercules and Dracula.

'Maybe that's next week's programme,' suggested Lalix.

'We'll never know,' said Cidrolin. 'In any case, you may be against it, but it's as if you'd been telling me a dream.'

'That's annoying.'

'Let's go and have a drink.'

[147]

At the corner of the embankment the bistro was empty; they were putting the tables away. The customers had to be content with the counter, and stand in front of it.

'I don't like that,' said Cidrolin. 'We'll go on back to the Ark.'

'Why's it called the Ark?' asked Lalix.

'No doubt because there aren't any animals living in it,' replied Cidrolin.

'Don't understand.'

'It isn't, indeed, a world-shattering joke. Let's say that that's what it was called when I bought it.'

'Expensive?'

'Half and half.'

'Personally, I like your boat. Really I'm very glad I chucked the music-hall and became a housekeeper. Monsieur Albert gave me some good advice, there.'

'How did he persuade you?'

'With a few kicks. Mm, I must say, he's a good pal of yours, he'd do anything for you.'

'I hope he didn't hurt you too much.'

'We–ell, he didn't exactly have cramp in his foot, but I soon got the point.'

'Then you don't regret the music-hall too much?'

'I've already told you: I like your boat.'

'And what would you have done in the music-hall?'

'I'd have liked to be a chorus girl. I don't dance badly and I've got a good figure; I'd've liked to sing, too, but Monsieur Albert didn't think that was necessary.'

'And did you have some engagements in view?'

'Yes, I was hesitating between Zanzebia and the republic of Capricorn, but all those places, you have to admit, they're pretty far-off countries. I much prefer to stay within a latitude of forty-nine degrees. North, of course.'

'You're well-up in geography.'

'I was preparing myself for all those great journeys. Is it true that your barge never moves?'

'She's quite incapable of moving. She'd have to be towed.'

'A little tug, that shouldn't cost so very much.'

'Even so it's more than I can afford.'

'All right, I didn't say anything.'

They had been walking in silence for some time when a group of grown-up scouts passed them. One stopped and asked them:

'Camping site?'

Cidrolin made the gesture which means straight on.

The other made the gesture which means thank you.

The grown-up boy scouts continued on their way more quickly.

'They're still coming,' said Cidrolin, 'and yet it's already autumn. They'll soon be coming in the depths of winter, tough ones, they'll be snuggling down, nice and warm, in the snow.'

'What do we do when there's snow on the barge?'

'We push it into the water, and it goes plop. Sometimes, even, in the middle of the summer, there's something that looks like snow on the water, but it isn't snow, it's like the lather you get from soap, or like cotton wool, it comes from the car factory up-river, I suppose they wash the jalopies before they fob them off on to the customers. Here we are.'

Cidrolin took the torch from the letter box and inspected the fence.

'There's nothing written on it,' said Lalix. 'Is that what you were looking for?'

'Yes.'

'Because it wasn't the first time?'

'No. Practically every day.'

'Who does it?'

'I don't know. Mind you don't fall on your arse, it's slippery.'

'One night you ought to hide somewhere and keep watch, and

[149]

when the chap turned up you could give him a good going over, and, as a bonus, you'd know who he was.'

'Mind you don't fall in the drink. That's it, we're there.'

'What's the matter with you, where're you going?'

'To get the essence of fennel, a jug of water and two glasses.'

'And what about me? That's my job. Sit down.'

'Right,' said Cidrolin. 'The electricity's on the right.'

'I know.'

Cidrolin sat down. The bulbs on the deck lit up.

'It's getting chilly,' he said to Lalix, when she came back with the essence of fennel, a jug of water and one glass, 'I can't see myself staying out all night.'

'Wrap yourself up. Put on an extra pullover.'

'Aren't you going to have a drink?'

'I can't stand essence of fennel.'

'It's a bit old-fashioned, I agree. Have something else.'

'No thanks. I'm all right.'

She watched him pouring his drink and went on:

'Won't you really have the courage to spend the night out of doors so that you can teach that bastard a lesson?'

'It isn't that I haven't the courage, but I prefer to sleep.'

'And dream.'

'That's it; and dream.'

'If that's the way it is, then *I'll* do it.'

'And you'll teach him a lesson? There may be several of them.'

'Haven't you got a revolver? a rifle?'

'No! No! there aren't any firearms on board.'

Cidrolin, in his emotion, poured himself out another glass of essence of fennel.

'You drink too much,' observed Lalix.

'That's what they all say.'

Lalix went on:

'I'll hide, and when the chap or chaps are busy writing up their

[150]

whatsits, I'll yell boo, and frighten them. I'll even put a sheet over my head. They'll never come back after that. Or he won't come back. What I think, it's just one man. Who could have it in for you like that?'

'I don't know,' said Cidrolin in a distant voice. 'I haven't the slightest idea.'

'Even so, there must be some reason,' said Lalix.

'I hope you don't believe what was written up? I'm not an assassin. Not even a murderer. Nothing. I was innocent. I did two years preventive detention. In the end they admitted I was innocent. I thought it was all finished with. But no, there's this bastard, as you call him, with his graffiti, as I call them; but I quite like house-painting. As I haven't got many hobbies, this gives me one. And then, this way, my fence is the best kept along the whole embankment. I tell you all this, but, really, I never think about it. It doesn't affect me. Much.'

'Aren't you curious to know who on earth he can be, the chap?'

'Not so very.'

'Even so, you ought to go and see.'

Cidrolin looked as if he was thinking hard, then, after a few moments of silence, he finally said:

'You'd prefer me to spend the night out of doors?'

'When you make love on a bunk,' observes Lalix, 'the man has to bump his head.'

'After all, you don't have such bad ideas.'

He got up and went to get a blanket. He also took a bottle of rum, a torch and a broom-handle, the only weapon at his disposal, apart from some dangerous kitchen knives.

Thus equipped, he went to hide, in compliance with Lalix's suggestions.

He shouted to her:

'Put out the deck lights.'

Which she did.

[151]

He knew a suitable place, and settled into it, rolling himself up in his blanket. He drank a mouthful of rum and was soon asleep.

Pouscaillou jumped as Sthenes said in his ear:

'Here's the boss.'

The new Viscount d'Empoigne was reposing in the shade of a nice leafy tree in the company of the two horses who were looking on all sides for delicacies and who were very well able to look after themselves. The Duke had gone off into the wilds some hours before; he made his reappearance leading a mule he'd borrowed from the inn and on which he'd loaded his materials.

'That's a good thing done!' he shouted from afar.

'Have you finished?' asks Pousaillou politely when the Duke had come up.

'It's in the bag. Tomorrow we'll go to Montignac. A boy drew my attention to something interesting over that way. And now let's go back to Plazac.'

He mounted Sthenes; Pouscaillou, Stef, leading the mule borrowed from the inn and on which the Duke had loaded his materials.

Their pace was rapid and Sthenes hardly in a garrulous mood. The Duke finally began to wonder why.

'Well, my good Demo,' said he, 'we aren't very chatty today.'

'To tell you the truth,' said Sthenes, 'I get a bit fed up with being so far away from the castle, and I often wonder when I'm going to turn my footsteps home to my native stable, which to me is a whole province and much more.'

'Alas,' said the Duke, 'you'll have to contain your melancholy in monumental patience. I'm not keen on going and throwing myself into the hands of the constabulary, and I haven't finished my work in this region yet.'

'That's just what I was saying,' sighed Sthenes, 'we shan't be going home tomorrow.'

[152]

'You're suffering very precisely from nostalgia,' said Stef, whom the taciturnity of his companion incited to talkativeness.

'Nostalgia?' said Sthenes, 'now there's a word I don't know.'

'It's of recent invention,' said Stef grandiloquently. 'It comes from nostos and algos, algos which means pain in Greek and nostos which means return home in the same language. It is therefore perfectly applicable to your case.'

'And you,' said Sthenes, 'you've got logorrhoea.'

'Logorrhoea?' said Stef, 'now there's a word I don't know.'

'I can well imagine,' said Sthenes, 'I've just invented it. It comes from logos and . . .'

'I see, I see,' said Stef. 'I've got it.'

'Are you quite sure you've got it?' asked Sthenes.

And the two horses started bickering until they got to the outskirts of Plazac. At the Golden Sun, where the Duke was staying, under the name of Monsieur Hégault, an ecclesiastic was quaffing tankard after tankard while talking politics with the innkeeper. Both were agreed on the necessity of various reforms, but slightly worried about this transformation of the States General into the Constituent Assembly, and about Necker's dismissal.

'Innkeeper,' cried Monsieur Hégault, coming into the room where the two citizens were, 'you'd be better occupied in getting the supper than in nattering about contemporary history. Monsieur,' he added, addressing the ecclesiastic, 'I do not know you.'

And, addressing the innkeeper:

'I'm very thirsty, and I want some chilled wine.'

The moment the innkeeper had disappeared into the cellar, the Duke exclaimed:

'Is this a coincidence, Abbé, or are you spying on me?'

'Monsieur the Duke . . .'

'Monsieur Hégault.'

'Really? Must I . . .'

[153]

'Call me Monsieur Hégault, I tell you.'

'Monsieur Hégault, I bring you good news.'

'I dare say, but that proves that you've discovered my lair. How the devil did you do it?'

'I could answer you with a pious lie.'

'You can spare yourself that.'

'. . . but I will give you the perfectly simple explanation: the young Viscount Empoigne wrote to his mother.'

'Ah, the knave! Ah, the traitor! I'll pull his ears for him all right!'

'You cannot reproach him for his filial love. I ask your indulgence for him, for we have asked that of His Majesty for you.'

'What d'you mean: we?'

'Monseigneur Biroton, who is at the moment sitting in the Constituent Assembly.'

'The Constituent Assembly, what's that?'

'The name the States General have just given themselves. Your presence is requested in Paris. The delegate of the bailiwick of Auge is greatly missed in the ranks of the Nobility, and His Majesty will absolve you – after all, all you did was to avenge your honour – if . . .'

'There's an if?'

'It isn't so terrible: if you will take your place in the Constituent Assembly again.'

'Don't count on me. For the moment, I have other fish to fry.'

'May one know which ones?'

The innkeeper came back with a few pitchers of chilled wine.

'Leave us, innkeeper,' said Monsieur Hégault, 'you can see very well that I'm in the middle of making my confession. Go back to your stoves and prepare us a supper fit for the devil: I'm treating Monsieur the Abbé.'

The innkeeper made himself scarce, but Pouscaillou came in.

He'd finished seeing to the horses and putting the materials away. He exclaimed:

'Monsieur the Abbé!'

He looked highly surprised.

'Come here, knave! traitor!' said Monsieur Hégault. 'So that's the way I'm supposed to have confidence in you, eh? I'll give you what for.'

He got up, to this end.

'But I haven't done anything,' said Pouscaillou, taking a backward step.

'You might have delivered me into the hands of the constabulary.'

'Don't understand. I haven't done anything.'

'You wrote to the Countess d'Empoigne!'

'What of it, Monsieur the Duke! Is it a crime to write to your mummy?'

'And he calls me Monsieur the Duke!'

The pouscailloutian ears were about to fall into the ducal hands when the Abbé Riphinte protested:

'Mercy, Monsieur Hégault. Mercy for this young levite! I must tell you that the Countess was extremely discreet.'

'That's not one of the son's qualities.'

'Let's forget it . . .'

'I won't forget it,' retorted the Duke.

'Let's forget it,' went on the Abbé Riphinte authoritatively, 'and let's get back to our muttons, which in any case are fish.'

'All right,' said Monsieur Hégault to Pouscaillou, 'sit down and have some of this claret wine, but get it into your head that I greatly dislike people having secrets.'

'If that's what writing to my mummy is,' exclaimed Pouscaillou with a noble gesture, 'I won't do it again!'

'We'll see about that later on,' said Monsieur Hégault, then, addressing the Abbé Riphinte: 'What fish?' he asked.

'The ones you have to fry, Monsieur Hégault.'

[155]

'Ah! so far as they're concerned, I've got a great surprise for you up my sleeve! But tell me about my lady Russule.'

The Abbé Riphinte gave him the news of the Duchess, rather bad news, since she had died of consumption a month after Empoigne's murder. After having evoked this sad memory, the Abbé stood up and said a short prayer. The Duke and Pouscaillou concluded: Amen.

Then they supped copiously, and, as they were all three fairly tired, hey presto, to bed.

XV

Cidrolin opened one eye: it wasn't dawn yet. He opened them both: it was still dark. He shivered, which suggested the idea of having a swig of rum, then he looked over towards the embankment: deserted, so far as pedestrians went. Occasionally and rapidly, a car passed on the road. After a certain time, Cidrolin noticed that even if there had been any people on the pavement, it was so dark that he wouldn't have been able to see them. He shivered again, and took another swig at his rum.

He got up quietly and went over to the fence in silence; he switched on his torch suddenly and slashed the darkness with it. There was no one in its beam. He went out and looked to see whether the anonymous coward had written up any insults, but the anonymous coward hadn't come yet, and was perhaps not coming tonight.

'Pity,' he murmured, 'I could have gone to bed.'

He turned round and thought he saw someone walking along the pavement, down by the new block which was finished but as yet had no one living in it. He directed his torch in that direction, but it wasn't strong enough to light up the imagined silhouette. A car's headlamps did better, and Cidrolin was able to see that the silhouette wasn't of any interest to him.

He switched off his torch and took a few steps.

'Hm,' he said under his breath, 'why don't I go and see what the camping camp for campers looks like in the middle of the night . . . almost at dawn . . .'

He waited a bit, but no passers-by appeared. He inspected the horizons, but there really were no passers-by. So he went on his way, and soon arrived at his destination. Calm and silent, the whole of the little community was asleep, some of it in caravans, some in tents, some, perhaps even, in sleeping-bags, not under the stars, because the sky was overcast, but taking pot luck.

The pot soon started to overflow and the rain started to fall, autumnal, chilly and fast.

'Bugger,' said Cidrolin, 'I'm going to get drenched.'

'Come in and shelter, then, Monsieur.'

The night-watchman of the camping camp for campers had just pronounced this civil suggestion.

Cidrolin jumped.

The night-watchman went on:

'I was going for a little nocturnal walk, like you, but with this rain I'm going in. As you were mumbling just now, you're going to get drenched.'

'That's very kind of you,' said Cidrolin, and he followed the night-watchman into his hut.

The watchman lights a night-light and motions to Cidrolin to sit down. He started filling a pipe, while uttering absent-minded remarks such as 'it's already autumn, there aren't many left, soon there'll only be the caravan maniacs and the sleeping-out fanatics left,' then, having managed to transform a portion of his tobacco into embers, he said bluntly:

'I know you, did you realise? Every other week I'm on in the

[157]

daytime. I see you, you come and watch my customers, you watch them as if it was the zoo. I wonder what it is you find so extraordinary to watch. Believe me, they're not so very interesting. And I watch you, too, and I think, because I think, Monsieur, I think: Hm, there's a man who hasn't got much to do in life. When I come here, I see you on your barge, lying on your chaise-longue in the land of nod, and I think, you'll fancy, Monsieur, that I'm trying to insinuate that I never stop thinking, but it's true, though, I certainly think more than the average person, I think: Hm, there's a man who hasn't got much to occupy him in life. Or else you sit at a little table on deck and knock back the essence of fennel, and then I think, you'll fancy I'm exaggerating, but I really must admit it, I was too modest just now, but it's true, though, I never stop thinking, so I think: There's a man who drinks too much.'

'I've often been reproached for that.'

'By your daughter, no doubt. She married an omnibudsman. Is she happy?'

'I don't know, I haven't seen her since. Except from a distance.'

'Aren't you amazed that I know your little family so well?'

'I've got two other daughters.'

'They are not often to be seen.'

'Now and then.'

The assimilation of this fact seemed to make the watchman thoughtful.

Cidrolin went on:

'What about my new housekeeper, what d'you think of her?'

'I've only just had a glimpse of her. From a distance. Then I thought . . .'

The watchman had stopped short.

Cidrolin insisted:

'Don't be afraid. Tell me everything you think.'

The watchman shook his head as if he were exhausted.

[158]

'I thought . . .'

'But what?'

'Ah! Monsieur, if you only knew what a burden it is to think. From what I've seen of your way of life it doesn't look as if you suffer from that torment, but I, Monsieur, and I say it again, I never stop putting my grey matter to work, even when I visit the sanitary quarters. What a life!'

'And do you dream?' asked Cidrolin.

'Never, Monsieur, I couldn't. I have to get some rest.'

'I dream a lot,' said Cidrolin. 'It's very interesting to dream.'

'I don't know. I haven't any ideas on that question.'

'The continuous dream, for instance. You remember a dream and, the next night, you try and go on with it. So that it makes a coherent story.'

'Monsieur, you might as well speak to a brick wall.'

'So that I've lived in the time of Saint Louis . . .'

'Ah, the son of Blanche of Castille . . .'

'. . . of Louis the eleventh . . .'

'. . . the man with the cage . . .'

'. . . of Louis the thirteenth . . .'

'. . . the three musketeers . . .'

'. . . of Louis the sixteenth . . .'

'. . . crack, the guillotine . . .'

'. . . no no, I haven't got any farther than the first days of the Constituent Assembly, yet. If I hadn't undertaken this nocturnal walk I might have been present at the fourteenth of July.'

'Monsieur, I don't understand a word of what you're saying.'

'Wouldn't you like me to tell you my last dream?'

'Pardon me if I excuse myself, but isn't it indecent to tell your dreams?'

'That's what my housekeeper thinks. She thinks too.'

'Oh Monsieur, I don't stop other people, that's if they're capable of it.'

[159]

'Well . . . ? my housekeeper . . . ?'

'Since you insist, Monsieur, I thought, and this thought was a question, I don't know if you're aware of it, Monsieur, but thought can be interrogative, I thought: Where on earth did he fish her up, that person?'

'On the pavement leading from Brittany to Zanzebia or to the Republic of Capricorn.'

'Very far-off countries. If I understand aright . . .'

'You do.'

'That was a good deed you did.'

'It's lasted nearly twenty-four hours.'

'Time will tell.'

The night-watchman shook the ashes out of his pipe on to the floor. He added:

'I didn't invent that expression, but it says what it means all right.'

Cidrolin looked out of the window.

'It isn't raining any more,' he said. 'I'll go home. Thanks for your friendly welcome.'

'Don't mention it,' replied the watchman, filling another pipe. 'Pardon me if I excuse myself, but I need hardly walk back with you.'

'Of course not,' said Cidrolin, who had got up.

Examining the filthy mud as he went out, he said to the watchman:

'Your customers, well, *they* must have got pretty drenched.'

'They like it,' said the night-watchman, putting a light to the tobacco he'd lodged in his pipe made from a briar root from Saint-Claude in the Jura, where the Tacon meets the Bienne, a tributary of the Ain.

'Think so?' said Cidrolin, absent-mindedly.

'I've often thought – and I do hope, Monsieur, that you will realise that I don't use the verb to think lightly – I've often

[160]

thought, as I was saying, that if they didn't like bad weather, whether of one sort or another, storms or dog-days, downpours or siroccos, frosts or heat-waves; if, I say, they didn't like it, they'd go and do their camping in the caves nature seems to have prepared for that activity, since they would find in them a shelter in which, both winter and summer, not to mention the intermediary seasons, spring and autumn, a shelter in which, I would conclude, is maintained an appreciably even temperature, a thing which was wisely taken advantage of by our prehistoric ancestors who, as everyone knows, and you yourself, Monsieur, are not unaware of it either, who, I would add, as my very last word, who, then, made caves their favourite dwellings.'

'Not everybody agrees on that point,' said Cidrolin serenely. 'The experts now claim that prehistoric man was not necessarily a cave-dweller.'

'You are very knowledgeable.'

'Oh, I've read about it in the gazettes.'

'Education! you see what it is, Monsieur, education. You learn something at school, you even go to some trouble, considerable trouble, to learn something at school, and then, twenty years after, or even before, it's not the same any more, things have changed, you don't know anything any longer, so it really wasn't worth while. That's why I prefer thinking to learning.'

'I think I'm going home,' said Cidrolin.

As he shut the door, he added:

'And thanks again!'

Outside, he yawned, and then shivered.

'I've caught my death,' he said under his breath.

The door of the hut opened. The night-watchman called out: 'Pardon?'

'I'm going to make myself some hot toddy,' called Cidrolin.

'You drink too much!' called the watchman.

'Shut your traps!' shouted, in various languages, the would-be troglodytes, some in their caravans, some in their tents, some even in sleeping bags, the latter gently floating on the stagnant pools that had formed.

Cidrolin, with some difficulty, crossed the shittery that separated the watchman's hut from the exit. When he reached the pavement he started walking fairly rapidly, not sufficiently so, though, not to have to suffer yet another shower. When he got back to the Ark he forgot to look and see whether the gate had been contaminated with graffiti. By measuring his length in the mud from time to time he managed to recover the blanket and bottle of rum he'd left in the bush he had been hiding behind, but he abandoned the broom handle.

He was shivering more and more. Having victoriously crossed the gang-plank he swallowed a certain number of varicoloured tablets, interspersed with swigs of rum. He went to bed. Outside the dawn was breaking, grey and mediocre.

On his way back from saying his mass, the Abbé Riphinte found the Duke waiting for him.

'We'll have lunch and leave immediately afterwards,' said the Duke authoritatively.

The Abbé looked at the sun, which was already high on the horizon, the July sun.

'Can't you stand the heat?' said the Duke. 'Don't worry: where I'm taking you, it's cool. Let's eat!'

'What are we going to do for our amusement today?' Sthenes asked Pouscaillou, as the latter rushed past him on his way to lunch.

'We're taking the Abbé out,' replied Pouscaillou, and disappeared into the inn.

'I hope I'm not going to get stuck with him,' said Stef. 'I don't feel like making conversation with him. He's hellish argumentative: all he ever thinks of is putting you in the wrong.'

'You can always drop him off in a ditch,' said Sthenes.

[162]

Stef shut up; likewise Sthenes.

A slapsauce fellow, who doubled as a palefrenier, came and tied up the inn mule near them. She was saddled. As soon as he'd gone, Sthenes said to Stef:

'You see! there's no point in crossing your bridges before you come to them.'

'And how d'you know the mule isn't for Pouscaillou? And I'll get landed with the curé.'

'Oh go on, you're hoof-rending. Just take life as it comes. You can always find something to moan about.'

'Doesn't stop me champing the bit at the idea of being ridden by an ecclesiastic. One has one's honour. That's just the way it is, you know me, I'll never be able to change.'

The mule listened to them in admiration; for her part she only knew a few words of the Limousin dialect and wouldn't have liked to make a fool of herself in the presence of such elegant manipulators of the langue d'oïl. The lunch must have been on the frugal side, because, barely two hours later, the Duke, the page and the Abbé mounted their steeds and hey presto, they're off.

Less than two leagues away they dismounted in the depths of the country. The horses and the mule were entrusted to Empoigne, who went and lay down under a tree.

'We'll have to walk from here,' said the Duke.

'What have you got there?' asked the Abbé.

'A lantern.'

'In broad daylight?'

'Yes, there's a bit of a mystery attached.'

The Abbé was annoyed, and refrained from enquiring as to the eventual use of the rope which the Duke also had with him.

They went through fields, through meadows, through woods, through waste lands, through heaths. The Abbé was muttering under his breath, in no mood to enjoy the natural scene, cursing

Jean-Jacques Rousseau, the nettles and the brambles, stubbing his toes against the stones, which got more numerous every couple of yards. In the end they had to climb up a pretty steep slope and the Abbé Riphinte, out of breath, caught up with the Duke near a crack in a rock.

'And now Abbé,' says the Duke, holding back his laughter with some difficulty, 'you'll see what you'll see.'

'Ah, Monsieur the Duke,' says the Abbé in a subacid voice, 'this is an excursion I find it hard to appreciate.'

'Let's go in,' says the Duke.

The Abbé looks round about him.

'There,' says the Duke, pointing to the crack.

The Duke starts insinuating himself into the rock.

The Abbé turns round, in the direction of his mule and then the Golden Sun Inn, at Plazac.

'Hoy!' the Duke shouts at him, 'come back, will you!'

The Abbé stops. He hears the Duke laugh, very loudly.

'Not scared, are you?' the Duke shouts.

The Abbé turns round again and sees the Duke half-way through the rock. He finds this sight more ridiculous than terrifying. It's his turn to shout:

'Monsieur the Duke, you'd do better to take your place in the States General, rather than play the fool in Périgord.'

The Duke laughs again. The Abbé corrects one particular of his remark:

'In the Constituent Assembly, I meant.'

He turns on his heel again, in the direction of his mule and then the Golden Sun Inn at Plazac; seeing which the Duke wriggles out of his rock, puts down his lantern and runs after the Abbé. He's a bit plumpish, but he has no difficulty in catching him up. He grabs him by the scruff of his neck and the seat of his trousers and brings him back to the point of departure. There they are again by the crack in the rock.

'To do that to an ecclesiastic!' says the Abbé, quite out of breath. 'I shan't forgive you that in a hurry, Monsieur the Duke.'

'No one was watching,' retorted the Duke calmly, 'and I won't tell anyone. Come on, in you go!'

'You're not going to kill me are you?' cries Riphinte.

The Duke starts laughing.

'I hadn't thought of that,' mumbled the Abbé. 'That's what it is. He wants to kill me! He wants to kill me!'

Good-naturedly, the Duke asked him:

'And why the devil should I want to slay you?'

'Why, so that I shan't disclose your hiding-place.'

'Come come, pull yourself together, Riphinte. There's absolutely no question of that. Let's leave all these questions of contemporary history on one side for the moment. Let's forget about them. We're going back into the past, Riphinte, we're even going to talk theology. Follow me!'

The Duke started once again to insinuate himself into the crack.

'Could this be the entrance to Hell?' said the Abbé, scarcely reassured. 'Modern theology is aware, however, that Hell is not intraterrestrial, as our ancestors thought. Newtonian physics has enabled us to reject these somewhat materialistic superstitions. Which doesn't mean to say that Hell doesn't exist, thank God!'

'Finish your sermon: you're simply not with it.'

All that was left outside the rock was one ducal arm; it grabbed Riphinte and pulled him after it. Riphinte disappeared.

'Hold this rope,' said the Duke's voice, 'and just walk. There's nothing to be afraid of.'

'You do have some marvellous . . .'

The Abbé grabbed the rope and follows in the footsteps of the Duke, who holds the lantern in his hand. They advance in silence.

In the dark silence, they advance.

In the silent darkness, they continue to advance.

[165]

As if in a trance, they advance, the rope start to prance, so does the lantern, the silence is enhanced.

It isn't complete silence, because there's the sound of their footsteps, it isn't complete darkness, because there's the little light at the far end of the leader's arm.

They advance in silence.

Suddenly:

'Monsieur the Duke . . .'

'There's nothing to be afraid of, Abbé, you can see perfectly well I'm still here.'

'Monsieur the Duke, don't you think I'm extremely brave?'

'Why Riphinte, are the bowels of the earth really making you vainglorious?'

'A venial sin, when I compare it to the present situation. You may well be leading me to Hell, or to Death, and I do not flinch. Isn't that admirable?'

'Riphinte, it isn't vanity any more, it's pride. A mortal sin, this time. That led you-know-who a long way.'

'If you were to recognise my merits, Monsieur the Duke, I shouldn't have to insist.'

'We'll see about that later on,' retorted Joachim.

This enigmatic phrase kept Riphinte quiet for a few minutes. The Duke advances in silence, the rope prances, the Abbé follows in a trance, the little light also prances, in the end it intrigues the Abbé, who screws up the conversation again:

'Your little lamp is lasting a long time, Monsieur the Duke.'

'A very long time.'

'It almost looks as if its light is cold and perpetual.'

'That's what it is.'

'You're joking, Monsieur the Duke.'

'Not at all.'

'With all due respect, I don't believe it.'

'Look.'

The Duke stopped, turned round, held the lantern under the nose of the Abbé whose face was now the only thing illuminated in the grottoesque gloom. The Abbé Riphinte had thin lips, a large nose, extremely black eyes, very bushy eyebrows and an ovine forehead. He looked extremely carefully and didn't understand a thing. As he didn't like to be nonplussed, he hazards the following hypothesis:

'Some modern invention or other?'

'You're miles adrift.'

'One of Monsieur Lavoisier's inventions? or Monsieur Volta's? or the Abbé Nollet's?'

'I've already told you, you're miles adrift.'

Riphinte was furious at not having solved this enigma and regretted having broached this subject. He made a little grimace, and said:

'A plaything.'

'A plaything!' exclaimed the Duke of Auge, 'but it's quite simply the philosopher's light, which never goes out, the ultimate secret and free gift of Timoleo Timolei.'

'Oh, that fellow . . .'

The Abbé removed his face from the illuminated zone and conveyed it into the shadow; he heard the sound of laughter coming from the Duke, who had turned round and started walking again. The Abbé decided that, in so far as it was possible, he wouldn't open his mouth any more. The laughter finally died away and the murky walk continued.

Even murky walks have an end. The Duke said:

'Here we are.'

And he stopped. The Abbé Riphinte did likewise.

'Where d'you think we are?' asked the Duke.

'In the shadows.'

'And what are we about to see?'

'Not much.'

[167]

The Abbé Riphinte wasn't in a good mood. The Duke took no notice. He resumed his discourse, in these solemn terms, uttered with emphasis:

'In this cave – lived the preadamites.'

Nauseated, the Abbé Riphinte made no comment.

'Don't you believe me?'

Nauseated, the Abbé Riphinte didn't deign to answer.

The Duke held the lantern up to the wall of the cave, and said: 'Look!'

Nauseated, the Abbé Riphinte casts a vague glance.

'Can you see?' asks the Duke.

'Yes,' replies the Abbé, reluctantly.

'And what can you see?'

XVI

Nauseated for good and all, the Abbé Riphinte answered:

'Some children's drawings.'

'Bravo, Abbé! The preadamites had the purity of children, and naturally they drew like children. I didn't make you say it, but you've brought grist to my mill. The people who did these drawings, these paintings – look, there's some colour here – these engravings – look, there are incisions in the rock, here – these people lived before original sin, they were like the children Jesus talks about in the gospels. So it really was the preadamites who did these drawings, which are the proof of their existence. They lived in these caves, and found shelter in them from the upheavals that beset the earth which was then young itself, too.'

The Duke held the lamp up to Riphinte's face and asked him what he had to say to that.

'Monsieur the Duke,' said the Abbé in an ironical tone of voice,
I shall only ask you one single question.'

'Ask your one single question.'

'If the preadamites lived in this cave, what did they do for light?
Did they already possess the philosopher's light, or were they
nyctalopic?'

'They had cats' eyes,' replied the Duke. 'You do nothing but
bring grist to my mill. As they didn't possess the philosopher's
light they could only have had cats' eyes.'

The Abbé, annoyed at having prompted an answer to the
objection he had thought definitive, nevertheless continued:

'And how do you explain the fact that no one has ever said
anything about it, and, in the first place, the Holy Scriptures?'

'I do beg your pardon, Abbé. What about the giants Genesis
talks about, chapter six, verse four? Ha ha! I'm winning all along
the line.'

'Then what you are saying is that thousands and thousands of
years ago some giants with cats' eyes used to amuse themselves
by drawing like children in a cave in Périgord?'

'You jeer, Abbé, but you're discomfited. And in any case,
there isn't only one cave, there are others. I'll show them to you.'

'They must have been big, these caves, to hold giants.'

'Look.'

The Duke held the light up to the vault and the light dis-
appeared into the vertical distance without encountering that
vault. The Duke moved this light round in other directions and
the Abbé Riphinte could perceive that he was in an enormous
chamber which, it seemed to him, was without confines and
without limits.

He became a prey to a sacred shudder.

'Hm?' said the Duke, 'isn't it as beautiful as Saint-Sulpice?
As for these drawings, you dismissed them somewhat rapidly as
children's drawings. Look at this mammoth . . . this aurochs . . .

this horse . . . this reindeer . . . Greuze doesn't paint any better.'

'We must come to an agreement,' said Riphinte. 'Not so long ago you were claiming that your giants were puerile and pure, and now here they are as clever as an academician.'

'If,' said the Duke, 'children are no longer as clever as academicians, it's because of Adam, his rib, his apple and his fall. Before that . . .'

A profound sigh conjured up the marvellous preadamite union of purity and dexterity. The Duke, moving his lantern about, had more to show.

'Look . . . look . . . these little horses running . . . these reindeers grazing . . . these aurochs charging . . . these mammoths that you can almost hear trumpeting.'

'It must be admitted that it is all extremely interesting.'

'Ah!' exclaimed the Duke with satisfaction, 'you're an honest man.'

'After all, why shouldn't there have been some giant painters with cats' eyes, seeing that you grant me Adam and his fall?'

'I'm not granting you anything. It was a pure figure of speech.'

'Monsieur the Duke, I begin to wonder whether you aren't a dishonest man.'

'You've recognised the existence of my preadamites . . .'

'Excuse me, excuse me, I added an if. If you grant me . . .'

'No bargaining! I'm not granting you anything, Abbé, and you've become a preadamite. But in any case I'm going to show you other proofs and other lairs. This way!'

When they were out of the grotto the Abbé rubbed his eyes, then looked at the countryside and said:

'Monsieur the Duke, when I see that sky, those trees, these plants, these stones, and those birds flying, I begin to wonder by what phantasmagoria I have just been hallucinated. I strongly suspect that your lantern is more magical than philosophical. May I examine it?'

[170]

The Duke handed it to him and the Abbé had to admit that he could see nothing magical about it, though perhaps something philosophical.

'En route,' said the Duke, taking back his lantern.

They rejoined Empoigne, the mule and the horses, and from Rouffillac went to Tayac, where they stayed the night after having seen more grottoes. The next day they continued on their way to Montillac. Near there they visited what the Duke described as the Sistine chapel of the preadamites. They went back to Plazac for supper.

There they drank some chilled wine, while waiting for the grub. The Abbé showed all the signs of active thought and, repressing a smile, which made him make a most peculiar grimace, the Duke gloated over his triumph in silence. At the third glass of claret the Abbé Riphinte took the floor and said:

'All this is highly disquieting.'

'And your disquiet hasn't begun yet,' said the Duke of Auge. 'When I announce my discovery to the world, the Church will tremble on its foundations and the Pope will shiver with fear. When the world acknowledges my discovery the Church will collapse and the Pope's nose will be put out of joint for ever.'

'Lord, Lord,' murmured the Abbé Riphinte, 'where are we going?'

The Duke was no doubt about to answer this question when Empoigne made his appearance followed by a horseman on foot but in appropriate costume.

'Monsieur the Duke!' shouted Empoigne, 'Monsieur the . . .'

'Who gave you permission to interrupt me? I wasn't actually speaking, but I was about to start a phrase of the utmost interest for the Abbé Riphinte in particular and for the ecclesiastical world in general.'

'News from Paris, Monsieur the Duke,' continues Empoigne, not even begging pardon.

[171]

Huh! What do I care about news from Paris! The interesting news is going to come from here, now. And from myself.'

'Indeed,' said Empoigne insolently. 'They've taken the Bastille.'

'Who's they?'

'The people of Paris,' replied the horseman on foot but in appropriate costume. 'The prisoners have been liberated and His Majesty has recalled Monsieur Necker. From now on the colours of France are blue, white and red.'

'Bloody awful news,' murmured the Duke. 'No one's going to be interested in my preadamites now.'

'The Church is saved!' cried the Abbé, joining his hands as a sign of gratitude.

These last two speeches seemed greatly to surprise the horseman on foot but in appropriate costume. He said:

'Gentlemen, even though your remarks are obscure, I can see that you are people of quality. Allow me to introduce myself: I am Lord de Ciry.'

'Well, well,' said the Duke, 'you're my son-in-law. I didn't recognise you. We see so little of each other. You're getting a paunch. What about my daughter Pigranelle, has she often had one?'

'She died sterile,' repled Lord de Ciry, with a slightly disgusted air.

'Poor thing,' said the Duke and, turning to the Abbé Riphinte, he added: 'Abbé, you might say some prayers for her, seeing that they're still going to be valid for some time.'

And, coming back to Ciry:

'Actually, why on earth are you here? Were you looking for me?'

'Not in the least. I'm emigrating.'

'Do you take yourself for a swallow?'

'I didn't say: I'm migrating, but: I'm emigrating. I'm leaving France, with its new men, strange faces and other minds. What's just been happening doesn't appeal to me in the slightest and the people of Paris seem to me to be preparing some ferocity against the aristocrats; not to speak of the peasants, who are starting to burn down our castles. By a circuitous route I'm making for Bayonne, where I shall embark for England.'

'Why England?'

'Why not?'

The Duke remained pensive, he finally said:

'After all, Ciry, that's not at all a bad idea of yours. Personally I'm going to Spain, where a very dear friend will welcome me, the Count Altaviva y Altamira.'

'As for me,' said the Abbé, 'I shall return to the good people of Paris who have just served the Church unawares, which certainly proves that there's a miracle there somewhere.'

'What about you,' the Duke asked Pouscaillou, 'are you coming with me?'

'Me? I'm going home to my mummy. I don't want them to burn down her castle.'

'What a booby,' exclaimed the Duke, 'don't you want to see foreign countries, then?'

'Oh yes, Monsieur the Duke.'

'Well then, you see. Ciry, we'll all three leave at dawn, and we'll leave the Abbé to his mob. By the way, have you any news of my excellent friend Donatien? Has he been freed?'

The grub was brought. While chatting about all this and that, they supped copiously and, as all their emotions had tired them, hey presto, to bed.

In the small hours, even though he greatly detested that abject operation, Cidrolin stuck a thermometer up his behind and, having thereafter delicately withdrawn it therefrom, he noted that he had a quartan and violent fever; he wouldn't, in any case, have needed this manoeuvre to discover his state of health because he felt extremely lousy, but as a man of the healing art would doubtless be called, he was afraid that he would reprimand him if he couldn't inform him precisely as to his thermic disequilibrium. Then he waited. After a fairly long time which he estimated as being near enough an hour, Cidrolin needed to pee. Coughing, shivering, boiling, he got up; stumbling, vacillating, staggering, he came out of his cabin. Lalix saw him making for the lav.

'Well!' she called merrily, 'is this when we get up? Your coffee's ready!'

Cidrolin didn't answer.

On his way back, when she once again invited him to partake of his breakfast, he still didn't answer. He resumed possession of his cabin. After something like another hour, there was a knock on his door.

He said to come in, and Lalix executed this order.

'Aren't you feeling well?' she asked.

'Not so specially.'

'It's my fault, you caught cold last night.'

'That's it.'

'Perhaps it rained, even.'

'Cats and dogs.'

'You ought to have come back.'

'I am back.'

'Too late.'

'And I didn't see anyone.'

'I ought to have kept my mouth shut.'

'Don't worry.'

'Are you cross with me?'

'Nope.'

'Well, the thing is, you aren't feeling well?'

'Not so specially.'

'I'll go and get a doctor.'

'Some pills might do. A chemist will give you some good advice.'

She touched his forehead.

[174]

'You've got a hell of a temperature.'

'I even know what it is. 103·8.'

'I'm going for a doctor.'

She disappeared forthwith.

Cidrolin shivers and dozes.

She reappeared forthwith. The doctor asks what his temperature is.

Cidrolin says that it's something in the region of 103·8.

The doctor writes on a bit of paper, then he disappears.

Lalix reappears.

Cidrolin imbibes various medicines.

He shuts his eyes but doesn't dream.

He drinks some hot thingummies.

Through the fog of the decoction, he hears Lalix saying to him:
'You didn't tell Monsieur Albert that it was a nurse you needed.'

She laughs.

Cidrolin manages a pale smile and shuts his eyes.

The Duke of Auge, Lord de Ciry and the Viscount Empoigne, commonly known as Pouscaillou, are nearing Bayonne.

Cidrolin opens his eyes from time to time.

From time to time he absorbs some medicines.

He still feels sort of tepid and flaccid.

In this connection, the thing that most bothers him is going to the lav. He stumbles as he goes. Lalix wants to help him. He refuses. She says:

'Oh, there's no secret about it.'

Cidrolin is momentarily ashamed, then, when he's properly relieved, he thinks no more of it.

After all, this isn't a bad life.

He wonders how Lalix is managing, she's been such a short time on the barge. She seems to be managing all right, so Cidrolin feels reassured and shuts his eyes.

He sometimes goes to sleep.

At Bayonne, the three companions separate. The Duke of Auge and Viscount d'Empoigne, commonly known as Pouscaillou, continue on their way to Spain. Some smugglers will certainly help them cross the frontier.

Cidrolin feels better. A ray of sunlight comes in through the porthole. It's nice to know that there are good doctors and good medicines. Lalix brings him a hot thingummy to drink with some pills; they aren't the last, but may well be the antepenultimate.

Lalix says:

'You're getting better.'

'I think so.'

Cidrolin is cautious in his prognosis.

The month of October is nearly over. Everyone declares:

'It's an exceptional autumn!'

The thermometer, stuck in the shade of the atmosphere, shows a near-summer temperature.

Cidrolin goes and lies down on his chaise-longue in the sun.

Then here they come to ask after his health. Oh, his health is all right, now. They, the girls, look at Lalix curiously. They aren't rude to her. They also look at their father curiously.

'There's some more writing on your gate,' says Lucet.

'Why d'you have to worry him,' says Sigismonde.

'Would you like me to go and clean it off?' suggests Yoland.

'You'll muck up your nice new suit,' says Bertrande.

'No thanks,' says Cidrolin, 'I'll see to it.'

Lalix has gone to fetch something to refresh the gullets of these ladies and gentlemen.

Bertrande says to Cidrolin:

'You ought to buy her a telly. She'll get bored stiff all alone with you. Specially in the evenings.'

'How can you know?' says Lucet to Bertrande.

'You're barmy,' says Sigismonde to Lucet.

'He may not be wrong,' says Yoland to Sigismonde.

'Can't you leave Dad alone?' says Bertrande to the three others, and to Cidrolin: 'Believe me, buy her a telly.'

Lalix comes back with the refreshments and then discreetly withdraws.

Bertrande is appreciative:

'She's a nice little thing.'

'She's got class,' says Lucet.

'Silly dope,' says Yoland, 'as if you'd know it when you saw it.'

'You've hit the jackpot,' says Sigismonde to Cidrolin.

'Now our minds are at rest,' says Bertrande, 'we can take ourselves off.'

They still stay some time longer, to finish the refreshments. They come back to the telly. Bertrande insists:

'Do buy her one. It'll pass the time for you, too.'

'It's even educational,' says Yoland.

They don't leave so soon as all that because they've started talking about the telly.

The next day it's Lamélie who comes to visit.

'Bertrande told me you were ill. It looks to me as if you're all right again. Who looked after you?'

With a slight nod, Cidrolin indicates Lalix, who's scrubbing down the deck.

'She's a nice little thing,' says Lamélie, 'You didn't do badly.'

Cidrolin composes his physiognomy to indicate: yes, maybe. Next he uses three words to ask:

'How about you?'

'You mean: what's happening to me, marriage and all that?'

'Yes.'

'Boubou and I . . .'

'Who?'

'My husband. He had a week off. We went away.'

'Where to?'

'Périgord. Not because of the truffles, but for something much

[177]

deeper: the prehistoric holes. We visited the lot. Lascaux, Rouffignac, les Eyzies, Font-de-Gaume and all the rest. They didn't half know how to draw, the paleolithic people. Their horses, their mammoths, well . . . terrific!' (gesture).

'Fakes.'

'What d'you mean?'

'They're all fakes.'

'Oh! if they were real fakes we'd know about it.'

'*I* know about it.'

'How do you know?'

'Aha.'

'You dreamed it?'

'An eighteenth-century chap painted all that.'

'Why should he paint all that?'

'To annoy the priests.'

'You're joking, Dad. You're dreaming. You'd do better to buy a telly, it would teach you something.'

'I know.'

'Now my mind's at rest, I'll be off.'

From the embankment Lamélie waves, not to say goodbye but to show that there's something on the gate. Lalix has seen her; she leaves the deck swab and picks up the brush and paint pot.

Cidrolin stretches out on his chaise-longue. He watches Lalix climbing up the bank. He shuts his eyes.

He is riding by the side of his excellent friend, Count Altaviva y Altamira. Empoigne follows. Some rapacious and royalist smugglers have, for a golden consideration, got them over the frontier.

'You were right to emigrate, Joachim,' says the Count in that excellent French that every cultivated European spoke at the time. 'Just think, if I may say so, of that night of the fourth of August, the French aristocrats never stop acting like bloody idiots.'

[178]

'I don't deny it,' says the Duke.

'While you're waiting for this agitation to blow over, how will you spend your time, Joachim, now that you are in Spain? It is an austere country and, apart from the bullfights, I can scarcely think of any distractions for you, Joachim.'

'I shall paint.'

'That is, in fact, an agreeable amusement. I've never considered it myself. And how did that idea occur to you?'

'In a dream.'

'Do you really mean in a dream?'

'I really do mean: in a dream. And in this dream, Phélise, the youngest of my daughters, the one who's an imbecile, came back from Rome and told me she'd seen the Sistine chapel and I said to myself: "I'm a painter too".'

'And what do you paint, Joachim? Bodegones? flowers? battles?'

'Caves.'

'With the temptation of St Anthony?'

'No! I paint on the walls of grottoes.'

'But Joachim, who will ever see your works?'

'The prehistorians.'

'That's a French word I don't know. What does it mean?'

'I'll explain later. Tell me, don't you by any chance know of some place of the sort where I could practise my art?'

'I have precisely that on my property,' replied Count Altaviva y Altamira.

XVII

Cidrolin, now well again, once more took charge of the painting.

He applied the last brush stroke, then took a couple of backward steps so as to have the necessary perspective in which to examine his work. He derived some satisfaction from this examination, and it was then that he heard someone calling him. He turned round. A car towing a caravan had drawn up by the pavement; slightly further back, double-parked, another car towing a horse-box had stopped. According to their number plates the whole lot came from the provinces. The driver of the first car stuck out his head and asked:

'The camping camp for campers, if you please.'

'Very simple. Straight on, five hundred yards further up.'

Cidrolin added:

'You know, at this time of year it's probably closed.'

'I'll go and see just the same. Thank you.'

He put his head back into his carapace and let in the clutch. Before he drove off he called to Cidrolin:

'I'm a painter, too!'

Cidrolin watched him drive off, followed by the horse-box. He waited a quarter of an hour, then twenty minutes, to see if by any chance, having found the camping camp for campers closed, the caravan wasn't going to turn round. After an hour, not seeing anything coming, Cidrolin made his way down the bank again and went and put the paint pot and brush away. Lalix was peeling potatoes. Cidrolin asks:

'We going to have chips?'

'No, gratin dauphinois.'

'I'd rather have chips.'

''Ts going to be gratin dauphinois.'

'Right,' said Cidrolin.

He added:

'I'm going for a walk. I'm just going as far as the camping camp for campers. Some more people have arrived.'

'That must be interesting.'

'Can't we really have chips?'

'What a tyrant. We'll have chips.'

'Some a bit soft and the rest like little sticks.'

'And for me,' says Lalix, 'some half-way between.'

'Perhaps it'd be possible to have half gratin dauphinois and half chips, some one way, some another, and some half way between.'

Lalix doesn't answer.

'Right,' says Cidrolin. 'I'll go and see what's happening up the road.'

The camping camp for campers is more or less deserted, but there is still a vague activity about the place. Cidrolin doesn't see what he was looking for but he discovers it a hundred yards further on. The two cars and their trailers have stopped by the pavement; two men and two women have got out on to the pavement and are discussing matters. Cidrolin walks towards them, he passes in front of the little group, the driver of the first car doesn't recognise him. Cidrolin walks on some fifty more yards and then retraces his steps. When he's on a level with the group he says to the man who'd questioned him:

'It's there (gesture), you know. It looks as if it's still open.'

'Monsieur,' says the other, 'I'm not asking your advice.'

'You were, earlier on,' retorts Cidrolin, 'and I hadn't finished giving it to you.'

[181]

With these words, Cidrolin continues on his way.

'Monsieur,' someone calls him.

He stops. The other goes up to him. He says:

'The idiots, they don't want us because of the horses. Why shouldn't my horses go camping, too?'

Cidrolin doesn't answer.

The other says:

'Don't you think so?'

Cidrolin says:

'We haven't been introduced.'

'Nor we have.'

The caravaner holds out his hand and says:

'Auge.'

'Cidrolin,' says Cidrolin.

They shake hands. Auge adds:

'As you see, I don't stand on ceremony. If you're a house painter, I'm a Duke.'

'I'm not a house painter,' says Cidrolin, 'I'm a ship-owner. I own a barge and a dinghy.'

'I didn't mean to offend you,' says the Duke. 'There are no stupid professions. As I informed you just now, I've been a painter, too, which may seem odd for a Duke, a Duke who's been on crusades. I was even a specialist in mural painting. Something rather in your line, if you like.'

'I do like,' says Cidrolin.

'Here, I'll introduce you to my daughter. Phélise, this is Monsieur Cidrolin.'

'Baa, baa,' says Phélise.

'And this is my trainer and friend, Empoigne. Viscount d'Empoigne.'

'Cidrolin,' says Cidrolin.

'And his mamma.'

'Hallo,' says the Countess d'Empoigne.

[182]

'I'll introduce you to the horses another time,' says the Duke. 'Good, now the ice is broken and we've got to know one another, not intimately, but even so quite well enough to establish contact on the social level, a contact that is obviously fairly superficial, but, who knows? which may yet be profitable and fruitful for the one as for the others in we don't really yet know which domain, and in any case you may perhaps be able, Monsieur Cidrolin, you who seem to belong to the neighbourhood, to tell us of some other place, not too far from the city centre, where my horses, my daughter, Empoigne, his mamma and I may combine the joys of camping with the pleasures of the capital.'

The Duke made an imperious gesture to stop Cidrolin answering at once.

'In fact,' he went on, 'I may be well-born but I am none the less a provincial, as can be seen from my number plate. I'm a squireen, a gentleman farmer, even, and I prefer the open air to the bathrooms with lavatories of urban hotels.'

'That's an opinion that has a lot to be said for it,' said Cidrolin. 'As to the desiderata that you mentioned a few moments ago, I don't see how to satisfy them. There *are* some stables in the district, though, you could board your horses out there.'

'Never,' said the Duke.

'How have you managed before, then?'

'There hasn't been any before. I'm making my camping début.'

'It isn't very encouraging.'

'Monsieur Cidrolin whom I still don't know very well, don't try and demoralise me. In any case, don't worry, I'm not demoralisable.'

'Then you'll agree that your camping début is not very encouraging.'

'Monsieur Cidrolin whom I still don't know very well, are you by any chance a sophist like the Abbé Riphinte?'

[183]

'The Abbé Riphinte,' said Cidrolin, frowning, 'the Abbé Riphinte . . . that's a name that rings a bell . . .'

'The gazettes have made his name famous,' said the Duke. 'He's spent half his time underground.'

'Ah, I've got it,' said Cidrolin, 'the famous prehistorian.'

'My former chaplain,' said the Duke.

'Goodness,' said Cidrolin, 'can you afford a chaplain?'

'Certainly,' said the Duke. 'I gave him the sack, on account of atheism. Atheism on my side, of course. Even though he himself . . . well . . . let's come back to the present situation. Look here, Monsieur Cidrolin, where can I disport myself in nature within a stone's throw of the city centre?'

'I can't quite see it,' said Cidrolin. 'Campers aren't allowed in the squares yet.'

'Ah,' said the Duke, 'where are the days when every inn had its stable? Hotels these days don't even have garages.'

'Some of them do,' said Cidrolin.

'I wasn't wrong,' said the Duke. 'You are a sophist like the Abbé Riphinte.'

Cidrolin didn't react to this piece of impertinence and asks, if it wasn't being too inquisitive, why the Duke cluttered himself up with the two horses. Wouldn't they be better off in some pasture in Normandy or Berry?

'They like the town,' said the Duke. 'Now and then they feel the urge to resume contact with city life. They haven't seen the capital for a long, long time . . . they can't wait to set hoof in the new districts and admire the sights, those that are worthy of admiration, at least.'

'None of that seems very simple to me,' said Cidrolin.

'I'll make it simple,' said the Duke. 'And seeing that you are unable, Monsieur Cidrolin, notwithstanding your obvious good will, to tell me of a camping camp for horse-campers, we'll continue on our way and install ourselves somewhere in those groves I perceive on the horizon.'

'It's a public thoroughfare,' said Cidrolin. 'Mind you don't get fined.'

'Don't give a damn,' said the Duke. 'Adieu, Monsieur. Come on, you.'

The Duke gets into the driver's seat of the first car; Empoigne sits next to him. The Countess drives the second car; Phélise sits next to her. They all drive off. Cidrolin catches a glimpse of the horses' heads. They look like horses.

He goes home slowly. When he gets to his gate he looks absent-mindedly at the building which is in its final stages; they're still working on the roof and on the cellar. From the other side of the road, someone waves to Cidrolin, who cleverly crosses the aforementioned road without getting himself knocked down or even run into by a car.

'You'll be able to give me some information,' says Cidrolin.

'I should think so,' says the watchman, 'but you must be surprised to see me here. They've offered me the concierge's lodge. I came over to see whether I like it.'

'And do you like it?'

'I think so. You've got me as a neighbour.'

'Here's what I wanted to ask you.'

'I'm listening,' says the watchman.

'There are some people who've been turned away from your camping ground.'

'It's shutting in a few days.'

'It's not that. They didn't want them because they had two horses.'

'Gipsies?'

'Not at all. A Duke, a Countess, a Viscount and a simple-minded young lady.'

'And two horses.'

[185]

'And two horses. In a horse-box. You don't know another camping ground for them by any chance? Not too far from the centre, because the two horses haven't seen the capital for a long, long time and they can't wait to set hoof in the new districts and admire the sights, those that are worthy of admiration, at least.'

'Is it a dream?' asked the watchman.

'So you think . . .' said Cidrolin.

'Ah, Monsieur,' interrupted the watchman, smiling, 'I see that you're aware of my besetting sin. Well yes! I do think. When I get up, I think. When I go to bed, I think. In between the two, I never stop. So just think how . . . you see, I even attribute my little mania to other people . . . just think how I need to rest after a whole day devoted to the malaxation of the grey matter of my brain. So I let it rest then, I sleep, I don't dream. As for your horses in their horse-box that want to visit the capital, I should think, seeing that you ask my advice, I should rather think that you've been dreaming.'

'Then you don't know of a camping ground where they'd be welcome?'

'You dreamed . . .'

'Not too far from the centre . . .'

'You were dreaming.'

'Them, the Duke, the cars and all the rest.'

'You're dreaming.'

'Here they are,' said Cidrolin.

The Duke braked. The watchman paled, took a couple of steps backwards and disappeared.

'He doesn't appreciate experimental method.' said Cidrolin under his breath.

'Pardon?' said a passer-by.

'You were right!' shouted the Duke.

'Another time,' said Cidrolin to the passer-by, who vanished.

Cidrolin went up to the car door.

[186]

'They're full of the constabulary, those groves,' said the Duke. 'I'm disgusted.'

He put his head out and looked at the new block.

'Is that where you live?' he asked.

'No, opposite, on a barge. Would you like to come and have a drink?'

'Well, er . . .'

'You've got a place to park there, take advantage of it . . . And come and try my essence of fennel.'

'Hm! I won't say no.'

The caravan went and parked a bit further on. Cidrolin crossed the road with prudence and skill and waited for his guests by his gate.

They went down the bank, Cidrolin leading the way and repeating several times:

'Mind you don't fall.'

When they were going along the gang-plank over the sludge he changed his tune:

'Mind you don't end up in the river.'

The Countess said:

'From a distance it's charming, but from close to it's foul.'

'The water looks a bit dirty,' said Cidrolin, 'but it isn't stagnant. You never smell the same muck twice. I get a stick and give it a shove, it drifts off, with the current. Between the barge and the bank it does obviously stagnate and you do sometimes smell the same.'

'The same what?' asked the Duke.

'Muck,' replied Cidrolin.

Then:

'Don't bump your head. This is the cabin, the living-room, if you prefer.'

'It's nice,' said the Countess.

Cidrolin called:

[187]

'Lalix.'

A person whose sex was probably feminine made its apparition, dressed in pirate's trousers and a blue and white horizontally striped jersey; wearing a middy's cap, he had a deck-swab in his hand.

'Hallo,' said the Countess.

The others didn't say anything to him, except Cidrolin, who asked her to come back fairly quickly with a small carafe of still water and the bottle of essence of fennel.

'What brand?' asked the Duke.

'White Horse,' replied Cidrolin.

When Lalix had disappeared, the Duke made the following comment on his question:

'Naturally I'd prefer the one I distil from the fennel that grows on my property according to the recipe that Timoleo Timolei . . .'

'That's a name that rings a bell,' murmured Cidrolin.

'A famous alchemist. Famous to the people who knew him, at least. He's rarely mentioned in the biographical dictionaries.'

'Did you know him?'

'Extremely well. I worked under him. I was his assistant, even though I am a Duke. As you see, I don't stand on ceremony when it's necessary.'

'Did you discover the philosopher's stone? the elixir of life?'

'Do you want me to be frank?' asked the Duke.

'I do,' replied Cidrolin.

'We didn't discover anything of the sort,' replied the Duke.

'Only essence of fennel?' asked Cidrolin.

'We'll still give yours a try,' said the Countess.

'Baa, baa,' said Phélise.

Lalix skilfully brought an enormous and heavily-laden tray.

Having served them, she sat down, a glass in her hand. Cidrolin said to the rest:

'May I introduce my fiancée.'

And to Lalix:

'The Duke of Auge . . . Viscount d'Empoigne . . . Madame er . . .'

'Countess d'Empoigne,' said the Countess d'Empoigne.

'And Mademoiselle . . .'

'Madame . . .' said the Duke. 'Madame de Malplaquet.'

'Hallo,' said Lalix.

'Baa, baa,' said Phélise.

'Well,' the Duke resumed, 'it isn't so bad, your essence of fennel.'

'Not at all to be despised,' said Empoigne.

'Not so foul,' said his mamma.

Phélise didn't have to express her appreciation because she drank nothing but water.

'We ought to give the horses something to drink,' said the Duke.

'I'll go,' said Empoigne.

'You'll find a bucket on deck, on the port side,' said Lalix.

'Sthenes and Stef must be wondering what's happened to us,' said the Duke.

'Do you always tell them what you're going to do?' asked Cidrolin.

'They prefer me to,' replied the Duke.

'Are they a circus?' Lalix asked Cidrolin.

'I don't know,' Cidrolin answered Lalix. 'At the very least they're campers. They didn't want them at the camping ground because of the horses.'

'On principle,' asked Lalix, 'or because there's something special about them?'

'They're fine animals,' said the Duke.

'What are we going to do now we've had a drink?' asked the Countess. 'Emigrate?'

The Duke didn't answer and looked round about him absent-mindedly; then, in a colourless voice he said:

'It must be big, a barge.'

[189]

XVIII

Joachim d'Auge awoke in an excellent mood; he had slept soundly and dreamlessly. As soon as he thought he was presentable he went up on deck, none of the other passengers on the barge was up yet. He went and had a pee in the river and his heart rejoiced at the merry sound of the jet as it broke on the surface of the water. On the other bank various anglers were taking up their positions. Some matutinal devotees went by, plying their oars. The Duke turned round; Sthenes and Stef were browsing on the rare delicacies growing at the top of the bank. On the embankment cars were going by thick and fast with a monotonous cooing sound.

The Duke set foot on land and went up to the horses.

'Well, my handsome Sthenes, what d'you think of it here?'

'You'd have to be a goat to be completely satisfied.'

'You'll get used to it. It'll give you some exercise.'

'Are we staying here long?'

'I don't know,' said the Duke. 'We may well have arrived.'

'Stef and I would have preferred to stay somewhere on the level.'

'A real, flat meadow,' said Stef.

'And then,' added Sthenes, 'there isn't much to eat.'

'Pouscaillou's going to bring you some hay soon.'

'When? He takes his time, Pouscaillou. You ought to go and kick him out of bed.'

'Patience, patience, my dearest Sthenes. Let innocents sleep.'

'Very well,' said Sthenes, 'What about you, what d'you think of it on board this motionless craft?'

'I've always dreamed of living on a barge,' replied the Duke. 'I'm not at all displeased.'

'I'm glad you like it,' said Sthenes. 'If there were only a bit more hay and oats . . .'

'Patience, patience my good Sthénes.'

Lalix appeared on deck.

'Coffee? Tea? Chocolate? Meat extract?' she called to the Duke.

The Duke rushed back.

'Some nice black coffee,' he replied, 'with some nicely buttered toast, some nice English jam, some nicely fried fried eggs and some nicely grilled andouillette.'

Zounds, navigation gives you an appetite!

Lalix disappeared without comment.

Empoigne appeared on deck.

'The horses are waiting,' the Duke told him instanter. 'I hope there's still some hay and oats left in the horse-box.'

'If there isn't,' said Empoigne, rubbing his eyes, 'I'll go and get some from the supermarket. Has Monsieur the Duke slept well?'

'Marvellously. I must admit that I'm not displeased with our landing-place.'

'What about my breakfast? Where and when am I going to be entitled to it?'

'Just give Sthenes and Stef something to eat. There must be enough left to keep them happy for a bit.'

Pouscaillou disappears in the direction of the horse-box.

Madame d'Empoigne appears on deck.

'Did you sleep well, little sister?' asks the Duke.

'Hallo,' replies the Countess.

Phélise appears. She kisses her papa.

'Baa, baa,' she says.

Lalix calls:

'Grub's up.'

They head for the cabin. They sit down merrily. Empoigne soon manages to join the gang. On the table the nice hot coffee is steaming merrily. There's toast, non-toast, jam and little dishes of butter.

'There aren't any fried eggs,' observes the Duke.

'There aren't any fried eggs,' declares Lalix.

'There isn't any andouillette,' observes the Duke.

'There isn't any andouillette,' declares Lalix.

'All right, all right,' says the Duke airily.

He's already got through seven pieces of toast, including the fatty or sugary substances he had accumulated thereon.

'Isn't Monsieur Cidrolin up yet?' asked the Duke.

'Here he is,' replies Cidrolin, sitting down at the table.

'I slept extremely well,' says the Duke. 'I'm much obliged to you for your hospitality, even though it is andouilletteless.'

'We'll see to that,' says Cidrolin, 'won't we Lalix?'

'There aren't any andouillettes,' declares Lalix, 'or fried eggs.'

'And how are the horses?' asks Cidrolin.

'They find the ground rather sloping,' replies the Duke, 'They haven't got the caprine temperament.'

Even though no one has invited him to do so, Pouscaillou starts to speak in these terms:

'Apropos . . .'

'Apropos of what?' asks the Duke.

'Apropos of the horses. When I was bringing the hay from the horse-box I saw that someone had written some rude remarks on Monsieur Cidrolin's gate.'

'About me?' asked the Duke, frowning.

'Take no notice,' said Cidrolin. 'They're for me.'

'Has someone got a grudge against you?' asked the Duke.

'It's quite likely. Ever since I've been here someone has practised writing graffiti on the gate and fence. I paint over them. Then he does it again.'

'You don't know who it is?'

'I haven't the slightest idea.'

'And you've never tried to catch him?'

'I did keep watch, one night. I got an aberrant viral bronchosis, that's all I caught.'

'Empoigne!' says the Duke in a solemn voice. 'There's an exploit for us cavaliers: we'll rid our host, Monsieur Cidrolin, of his graffitomaniac.'

'Really,' says Cidrolin. 'You are too kind . . .'

'We'll take him in flagrante,' continues the Duke, 'and we'll hang him from a tree on the boulevard.'

'The thing is . . .' says Cidrolin. 'The thing is . . . we'd get into trouble.'

'But why?'

'Into trouble with the police.'

'What!' exclaimed the Duke. 'Haven't you the right to dispense high and low justice? And are you not master after God on board your own barge?'

'Yes, but the tree on the boulevard isn't on my barge.'

'Then we'll throw the delinquent into the drink. Carefully bound.'

'I'm afraid that too . . .'

'Well then, we'll content ourselves with cutting off his ears.'

'No . . . no . . .'

'Then just a few kicks up the arse.'

'That's it . . . if you must . . .'

'Monsieur Cidrolin, don't count on me for kicks up the arse. Never would I wear out the sole of my boots on the behind of a graffitomaniac. I should lose caste.'

'Monsieur the Duke, Monsieur Empoigne, I am most touched by your proposition, but after all, I've got by like that so far and

I can go on. It's an item on my budget: a pot of paint a month and, no doubt, a brush every year. And then it gives me something to do: otherwise, what would I paint?'

'I know of a few more caves,' said the Duke in a dreamy voice. But let's leave them . . .'

Suddenly he banged the table violently with his fist and shouted:

'What about it, Empoigne! are we going to allow ourselves to get soft? No indeed! In spite of everything Monsieur Cidrolin says, tonight we shall capture the graffitomaniac, and time will show!'

'Empoigne's honour! we'll capture him!'

'Capture him!' cries Madame d'Empoigne.

'Baa, baa,' says Phélise.

All of which makes a lot of noise.

'In the meantime,' says Cidrolin, I'll just go and put in a bit of painting.'

He goes out, followed by Lalix. Lalix asks:

'When're they going?'

'Nothing's been arranged.'

'So tomorrow morning, do I give them some andouillette and fried eggs?'

Cidrolin picks up the paint pot and the brush.

'If it isn't too complicated,' replies Cidrolin. 'We must show we're seigneurial.'

Cidrolin sets foot on the gang-plank.

'If we're engaged,' says Lalix, 'shouldn't we call each other tu?'

'Calling each other vous sounds more seigneurial.'

Lalix goes back to her chores. Cidrolin passes Sthenes and Stef. He looks them in the eyes.'

'Don't they look intelligent,' he says under his breath. 'The only thing they can't do is talk.'

'There's nothing we can't do,' says Sthenes. 'Shit,' he adds, stamping his right hoof, 'Joachim did particularly advise me not to open my mouth.'

Cidrolin finds himself on the pavement. He's spilt a bit of paint on the way.

'Strange,' he says under his breath, 'it really is strange.'

'Pardon?'

That's a passer-by, stopping to question Cidrolin.

'Strange. I simply said: it really is strange.'

'And *what* really is strange?'

Cidrolin starts touching up the gate.

'That'd be telling,' he replies.

'Monsieur,' exclaims the passer-by furiously, 'one just doesn't arouse people's curiosity like that: you get them interested and then you shut up. No, Monsieur, it's not done!'

He walks off, flourishing his arms.

Cidrolin makes no comment.

Then he hears someone calling him. It's the concierge of the not quite unfinished, not quite finished building. He's standing in front of his door, on the pavement opposite. Cidrolin returns his greeting and goes on with his work.

Then his guests make their apparition. They discuss what they're going to do. Empoigne has to buy some hay and oats at the snob supermarket, the Duke is going to visit the Palace of Alchemy, the ladies are going to see the collections. That's for the morning. They'll lunch in town in a de-luxe establishment. The afternoon will be devoted to the examination of various sights; a performance at the cinema is likewise anticipated. Dinner in a de-luxe establishment; not the same as the lunchtime one. They won't be very late back and after that they'll capture the graffitomaniac.

'What about the horses?' asks Cidrolin. 'Aren't they going out too?'

'Tomorrow,' replies the Duke. 'Tomorrow. When we've captured your man.'

[195]

'What's that got to do with it?' asked Cidrolin.

'Nothing,' replies the Duke.

He assumes an anxious look.

'It's true,' he murmurs. 'Poor Sthenes, poor Stef. They'd like to admire the beauties of the capital city as well. Could I be becoming an egoist? Monsieur Cidrolin, I should blush for shame. You're a kind-hearted man, Monsieur Cidrolin. You're right, I won't leave two friends kicking their heels while I go and enjoy myself. Empoigne, we'll ride to the supermarket, you women take your car. Empoigne, go and get Sthenes and Stef.'

Mission accomplished, Sthenes and Stef look sullen.

'My dear Demo,' says the Duke.

Sthenes sulks.

'Come come, my dear Demo,' says the Duke. 'I wasn't forgetting you. We just wanted a few words with Monsieur Cidrolin. There was never any question of leaving you here and of your not coming to admire the beauties of the capital city with us. Was there, Monsieur Cidrolin?'

From a study of Cidrolin's face it's easy to infer the horn-wracking situation in which he finds himself; can one lie to a horse? can one give the lie to a guest?

Cidrolin finds an elegant solution. He says to the Duke:

'You talk to him as if he could understand man's language. Has that ever been known, a talking horse? In dreams, perhaps. Or in mythology.'

The Duke didn't think it an elegant solution. He said:

'What the hell's it got to do with you, the way I talk to him? All I'm asking you for is the truth! To wit, that I wasn't forgetting you, my dear Demo.'

'Monsieur d'Auge,' said Cidrolin, 'listen, in that case, to these enthymemes, not to say these sorites. If this horse understands human language, then he's extremely intelligent. If he's intelligent, he's already guessed what's happened. On the other hand, if he's intelligent, he's good, and, if he's good, he will make allowances for a simple oversight on your part and it will not be allowed to cloud your friendship.'

And turning to Sthenes, Cidrolin added:

'Isn't that so, Sthenes?'

Sthenes smiled, a little sadly, and tossed his head.

'Good old Demo,' says the Duke.

He gets into the saddle, so does Empoigne, and they're off, the women in the car too, after having detached the trailer; it was Phélise who took it upon herself to detach the trailer. Cidrolin goes on painting his gate. The concierge has disappeared.

Then it's Lalix, going shopping.

'That's what I do, then, yes? I buy some andouillette?'

'We'll be seigneurial,' replies Cidrolin.

Lalix goes shopping. Cidrolin finishes his painting.

When he's put the pot and brush away he goes and lies down in the cabin, while he's waiting for lunch. There's andouillette for lunch. After lunch he goes into his own cabin to have a siesta. It's three thirty-two when he says to Lalix:

'I've had a practically dreamless siesta. Just a little one, not very interesting. Shall I tell it to you?'

'No,' replies Lalix.

'It's a very little one.'

'All the more reason. And anyway I'm going to the hairdresser's.'

She won't be back until dinner time. Cidrolin went to see what was going on at the camping camp for campers and was able to ascertain that this time it's definitely shut. He went home. As night was falling he took a pole and started the muck that had accumulated in the canal between the barge and the bank on its way to the central current. Then he waited for dinner.

There was andouillette for dinner.

After, Lalix lights a cigarette and goes and gets a pack of cards enveloped in a green baize cloth pinched from a bistro. She starts playing patience, her right eye half shut because of the smoke rising from the stub that she won't let go of. She puts out the stub. The game doesn't come out. Lalix lights another cigarette and starts another patience. Cidrolin watches her operations in silence. The second game doesn't come out. A fresh start, and so on. The fag-ends accumulate. It's soon eleven-seven. At eleven-seven the guests come home and settle down in the cabin. Lalix finishes her game of patience before she brings the syrup of fennel.

'We must regain our strength for the capture of the graffito-maniac,' says the Duke gaily.

'Do you really feel you have to . . .' says Cidrolin.

'Ttt, ttt,' goes the Duke. 'No fuss. We'll have an interval, and then we'll mount guard.'

'I'll come with you.'

'No, no. Empoigne and I will manage this task on our own.'

'So long,' says the Countess.

She means by that that she's going to bed.

'Baa, baa,' says Phélise.

She means by that that she's going to bed.

In fact, they go to bed.

'Was everything all right?' Cidrolin asks the Duke of Auge, who doesn't seem very keen on starting his sentry-go.

'What everything?'

'Your trip round the capital.'

'Sthenes and Stef are delighted.'

'And you yourself? And Monsieur d'Empoigne?'

'There were some awkward moments, the capital has changed a lot.'

'Is it a long time since you were here?'

'More than a century,' replies the Duke calmly.

Empoigne gives a little cough.

'I mean: a very long time,' the Duke corrects himself. 'The traffic, for instance: we had some trouble with the traffic. Sthenes and Stef weren't used to it at all. The constables gave us out heaps of little prospectuses for which I haven't any use.'

He pulled them out of his pocket and tears them into little pieces.

'It was when we were visiting your great tower, that everything nearly went wrong,' went on the Duke. 'Sthenes wanted to go up to the third floor, he had to be content with the first. And even getting him up to the first was quite a business. Luckily there were some people there playing with a cinematographic apparatus, it was thanks to them we managed it; the moment the cinematograph came into it everything became possible, but even so Sthenes had to be content with the first floor.'

'What about the other one?' asked Cidrolin.

'The other what?'

'The other horse.'

'Stef? He didn't want to go up. He felt giddy.'

'It's probably about time you started your watch,' said Lalix.

'Just one more little drop of essence of fennel and then we'll go at once,' said the Duke conciliatorily.

'How was the restaurant?' asked Cidrolin.

'So-so,' replied the Duke. 'They serve you just enough to feed a sick bird and their menu doesn't list any of the dishes I was so fond of formerly and heretofore, nightingale pâté with saffron, chestnut tart made with meadow-mouse fat, cold jellied bear with sunflower seeds, the whole washed down with basinsful of alcohol.'

The Duke finished his glass, then uttered this remark:

'I've just realised why I like essence of fennel. It's because there isn't any other word that rhymes with it. With fennel.'

'Ahem,' said Lalix.

'Except kennel, of course,' said the Duke, frowning.

'Are you a poet, too?' Cidrolin hastened to ask him.

'We-ell,' said the Duke, 'I do occasionally turn my hand to the odd bit of doggerel . . .'

[199]

'Certainly the first *I've* heard of it,' said Empoigne.

After having thus emerged from his respectful mutism he went flying over to the other side of the cabin, knocking some glasses over. While he's picking himself up and rubbing that part of his head comprised between the ear and the back of the neck, the Duke finishes his sentence for Cidrolin's benefit:

'. . . but I'm primarily a painter. Like you.'

Then he exclaims:

'Yes but, now I come to think of it: if, in one way or another we stop the graffitor doing it any more, what will you have to paint? You'll feel quite stupid and idle.'

'I'll think of something,' says Cidrolin. 'I'll think of something.'

'Well! Since the die is cast, andiamo, as Timoleo Timolei used to say. Empoigne, you interrupted me, but I forgive you. Follow me and we'll show Monsieur Cidrolin what we're capable of. Chao! – again as Timoleo Timolei used to say.'

They go out.

'Are you going to wait for them?' asks Lalix.

'It would be politer,' says Cidrolin.

Lalix puts out her cigarette, gathers the cards up into a pack which she wraps in the green baize cloth. She gets up and says:

'Who are they really, these people?'

Cidrolin shrugs his shoulders. He says:

'It's none of our business.'

Lalix says:

'That's not an answer. Or rather, yes it is; it is our business.'

Cidrolin says:

'I sometimes have the impression that I've already seen them in my dreams.'

'That doesn't make things any better.'

'Oh, it's only an impression.'

'I won't press the point. Personally, dreams . . .'

On her way out of the door, Lalix says:

'Then you're going to stay here and wait for them?'

' 'llhave to,' replies Cidrolin.

Lalix has gone.

Cidrolin spreads out the cloth again and picks up the pack of cards. He starts a game of patience.

Lalix reappears.

'What about the horses?' she says.

'What of them, the horses . . ?'

'It's peculiar, all this business about their horses.'

'Even more peculiar than you think, Lalix. One of the two horses talks. I heard him.'

'And what did he say?'

'He started by swearing, but I didn't wait to listen to him.'

'And it wasn't in a dream?'

'Oh, in dreams, talking horses are two a penny.'

Lalix sits down again. She says:

'I'll stay with you a bit longer.'

She picks up the cards and asks:

'Shall we play?'

'That's a good idea,' says Cidrolin calmly.

And they played till dawn.

XIX

At dawn, outside, there was a sudden hullabaloo.

'They've caught the chap,' said Lalix.

Cidrolin said nothing.

The hullabaloo increased and was reinforced by insults, abuse, and probable oaths.

'Trouble's brewing,' said Lalix.

The racket came nearer; finally the door opened. A man was projected on to the table, thus clearing it of cards, cloth, glasses, bottle and ashtray. This done, the Duke and Empoigne carefully shut the door behind them. The man regained his balance, but immediately sat down, being constrained and forced to do so by his two trappers.

'There we are,' said the Duke with satisfaction. 'Good work.'

'I protest,' yelled the trapped man. 'It's abduction! adult-napping! To the rescue! help! There's been a mistake! a ghastly mistake. I was trying to catch them unawares, the people who desecrate your fence, but these individuals grabbed me instead! Maybe they're the culprits!'

'Oh, the wicked slanderer!' exclaimed the Duke, and he clips him one.

'Caveat! Infamy! Repetition of an offence! A major infraction! Listen to me, Monsieur, *you* know me . . .'

Cidrolin said to the Duke and his stable-boy-viscount-acolyte:

'Do sit down, please, we'll listen to what Monsieur has to say. I do in fact know him.'

Next he addresses the concierge ex-night watchman of the camping camp for campers:

'Monsieur, I do in fact know you by sight, but I don't know your name.'

'Louis - Antoine - Benoît - Albert - Léopold - Antoine - Nestor - Charles-Émile La Balance.'

'That's pretty long,' said Cidrolin.

'Why Antoine twice?' asked the Duke.

'Once after my father and once after my grandfather. As for its length, it's usually abbreviated to La Balance (repeated).'

'You wouldn't have another, shorter, one, would you?' asks Cidrolin.

'I'm usually called Labal.'

'Well, Monsieur Labal,' Cidrolin began.

'Drop the Labal, that'll make it even shorter.'

'Well, Monsieur . . .'

'What right have you to interrogate me, Monsieur Cidrolin?'

'Clip him one,' says the Duke under his breath.

'I haven't any right to,' says Cidrolin, 'and you have the right not to answer.'

'He'll take advantage of it,' remarks the Duke, aside.

'Right,' says Labal, 'In that case I'll tell you my story.'

'Aha, a story,' says the Duke, off.

'It will be short and illuminating.'

'Labal took a breath, got into gear and uttered these words:

'The name I bear, gentlemen, has decreed a singular fate for me. The balance, as you are not unaware, is the symbol of justice, and all my life I have done my utmost to make it reign on earth, so far as my feeble capabilities would allow, of course. If society gave me this predestinatory name, nature for her part provided me with peculiarly active grey matter and, from my earliest youth, I perceived that official justice was nothing but an empty word and I promised myself that by my personal efforts I would make recompense for the failings of the regular courts of justice. So I liquidated three or four hundred people who seemed to me to have been insufficiently punished; if this figure astonishes you, I must admit that I only interest myself in serious cases and I know of only one rectification for erroneous judgments – the death penalty. You may rest assured, though, that I only act after having thought at length about the case I am concerned with. Therein, gentlemen, lies the difference between me and ordinary judges: I think. A heavy burden, gentlemen, though, a burden whose weighty presence you may perhaps not have to bear, but I will not linger on this subject: I spoke of it the other evening with Monsieur Cidrolin. Be that as it may, having become, for reasons that do not concern you and which it would take too long to explain to you, having become, I say, a night watchman at the camping camp for campers, and returning home with the dawn, I happened to observe that rude remarks were frequently written on the fence belonging to a piece of land in front of the barge on which you are at present, I myself being there much against my will. The reiteration of the procedure made me think, and you will see that when I say think I am not using the word lightly, made me think, I say, that the author of these inscriptions was perhaps a similar kind of arbitrator to myself, and, in a word, a competitor. This displeased me. If everyone started taking the law into his own hands there would be no end to it; I alone have the necessary qualifications. I held a little enquiry, then, and learnt of your afflictions, Monsieur Cidrolin, and of the grave injustice of which you were the victim. An innocent man suffering two years' preventive detention! The persecution of which you were the victim seemed to me all the more bitter. Wishing to unmask the swine who was pursuing you with his unjustified obloquy, I got myself engaged as concierge in the building that has been put up on the other side of the embankment. I keep watch every night, but I hadn't discovered anything. Just now I noticed two suspicious silhouettes. They were two, I was only one. I nevertheless proceeded courageously to the scene of their doubtless felonious activities. It was the first setback of my career, since here I am in your hands. As for my innocence in the matter of the graffiti, it seems to me amply proved by the fact that I am not and was not the bearer of any means whatsoever of writing, painting or engraving.'

He fell silent, and they then heard the Duke of Auge calmly snoring for, from the very beginning of this rodomontade, he had fallen asleep.

Cidrolin scratched his head. He turned to Empoigne, saw that he was only dozing, and asked him whether it was true that their capture was not the bearer of any instrument for writing, painting or engraving.

[204]

Empoigne, barely opening his eyes, replied:

'The man has told the truth.'

'Then the accused is innocent,' concluded Cidrolin.

'That's easily said.'

'Does Mademoiselle not agree?' asked Labal insolently.

'No,' replied Lalix. 'Everything you've been saying proves by *a* plus *b* that it's you that's the dope-eyed judge, the no-good judex, daddy's monte-cristo, granny's zorro, the mouldy robin hood, the spiteful dauber, the insulter of walls, the maniac of desecration, in short, the established, anticidrolinic buggerer-upper.'

'Mademoiselle,' said Labal calmly, 'allow me to tell you that you reason like a sludge, you don't see any further than the end of your nose and you use your grey matter arse-upwards. Reflect for a moment; I won't use the word think, which might well frighten you, I simply ask you to reflect. Not like a mirror, of course, which would be the most superficial way, even though I am not unaware that young ladies are more accustomed to . . .'

'Are you going to let him go on?' said Lalix to Cidrolin. 'If I were you I'd push his face in. If the Duke weren't asleep he'd have shut this nit up a long time ago.'

'But he *is* asleep,' said Labal. 'I resume: reflect, Mademoiselle. Would I have told you my life-history, exemplary though it be, if I were the person responsible for this persecution? It's absurd! Get it into your head, Mademoiselle, that I am a hundred per cent cidrolinophilic.'

Lalix doesn't answer.

'Monsieur Labal,' says Cidrolin, 'I'm sure you'll excuse my guests; they thought they were acting for the best.'

'I'll be magnificent and generous,' says Labal, 'I'll let bygones be bygones.'

'Huh, we'll see,' says Lalix.

'Hallo,' says the Countess, coming into the cabin.

'Baa, baa,' says Phélise.

'Have I your permission to retire?' says Labal.

He scrams.

'Isn't breakfast ready?' asks Empoigne's mamma.

She asks this in a very friendly way, though. There's nothing for Lalix to take offence at. She adds:

'Who was that gentleman? The one they wanted to catch?'

'There was a mistake,' says Cidrolin.

The Countess abstained from all comment so as not to disturb the repose of her son, who had also gone to sleep, but they all opened their eyes wide when the smell of the grilled andouillettes that Lalix brings in penetrates their nostrils.

'What a pleasant awakening,' exclaimed the Duke. 'What a succulent apparition! A noble recompense for such cavaliers as we! What about our villain? I think I can assume, Monsieur Cidrolin, that, notwithstanding your fine words, you have tossed him into the river, weighted with a few slugs of lead?'

'No,' said Cidrolin, 'I let him go.'

'Catch me,' said the indignant Duke, 'committing a good action again!'

'It was a bad one,' said Cidrolin calmly. 'That man had nothing to do with the insulting inscriptions.'

'Cidrolin let himself be taken for a sucker' said Lalix.

'I don't doubt it,' said the Duke, 'but after all, what do I care. I'll leave you to your painting, Monsieur! I'll leave you to your painting!'

And yet Cidrolin didn't have to repaint the fence the whole of that day and, as the previous day, the whole of that day he didn't see his guests. They didn't come back until after dinner. Cidrolin played cards with Lalix. Lalix smoked while she played cards.

The Duke and Empoigne sat down beside them and helped themselves to some essence of fennel. The Countess and Phélise had gone straight to their cabins.

'Was everything all right?' asked Cidrolin politely.

'And with you?' asked the Duke with gusto. 'The daubery?'

'Today, nothing to report.'

'Well, *we*'ve been going in for architecture. To please Mamma (gesture), we visited all the curé's haunts in the capital, and there's no shortage of them.'

'Are you by any chance anticlerical, Monsieur the Duke?' asked Cidrolin.

'Vehemently! But don't give me that Monsieur the Duke stuff. Now that we know each other, just call me Joachim.'

'And why should I call you Joachim?'

'Because that's my first name.'

'It's mine too,' said Cidrolin. 'I can't see myself using my name when I'm talking to some other fellow.'

'Some other fellow yourself,' retorted the Duke good-naturedly. 'Since we're both Joachims, call me Olinde, then, that's my second first name.'

'It's mine too.'

'I've got five more: Anastase Cré . . .'

'. . . pinien Hon . . .'

'. . . orat Irénée Mé . . .'

'. . . déric.'

'In that case,' exclaimed the Duke, who was in an extraordinarily good mood, 'let's go back to our point of departure; you call me Jo and I'll call you Cid.'

'I'd prefer Cidrolin,' said Cidrolin.

'Cidrolin it shall be, since Cidrolin is what you wish, but in that case I shall call you tu.'

'I've nothing against it.'

'And you must call me tu, too,' added the Duke, downing a bloody great dollop of essence of fennel.

'All right, I'll call vous tu.'

'Well, Cidrolin,' the Duke resumed, in lofty tones, 'I didn't think much of toi this morning when the dawn fell on the evasion of our captive. Fat lot of use, I said to myself, it was me getting my posterior frozen for a whole night to do my host a favour when the said host then goes and behaves like a sensitive and vacillating vestal virgin; but as Sthenes observed, after all, you know more about this business than I do and you must have had good reasons for releasing the fellow, whose looks I still don't care for. If I were you I wouldn't want to have him as a neighbour. Whereupon, good night.'

On this abrupt conclusion he got up, as also did Empoigne, but Lalix intervened:

'Who's the Monsieur Sthenes who made that observation about him?' (gesture in Cidrolin's direction).

'He isn't a monsieur, he's a horse,' replied Joachim.

'And he makes observations?'

'Apropos,' continued Joachim, taking no notice of this question, '*I*'ve made an observation, too. I've discovered that with their treble, the French have become alchemists.'

Neither Lalix nor Cidrolin turned a hair; Empoigne even less.

'Yes,' concluded the Duke, 'they're all hoping to make gold out of horses. This time, good night!'

He disappeared, but reappeared immediately.

'You must have thought my remark odd. But you will agree that it's only natural for horse-play to interest me.'

He disappeared once more and they heard his laugh fading and becoming extinguished.

'Stay with us a bit longer,' Lalix said to Empoigne, who was delaying his own disappearance.

'I can't. I have to help the Duke take his boots off.'

'He doesn't wear boots.'

'He wears moral ones.'

'Do your horses wear boots too?'

'Moral ones? Certainly.'

A long yelping sound was heard.

'You hear him?' said Empoigne. 'He's going to tell me off.'

He made haste to disappear.

'Whereupon,' said Lalix, 'I'll go and take my moral boots off, too.'

'I'll stay up a bit longer,' said Cidrolin.

Alone, he plays a game of patience. Then he puts out the lights.

For minutes on end all that can be heard is the noctambulant cars swish-shinding along the boulevard.

Then there are shrieks, yells, and maybe oaths. The cabin door opens, and there is light. Labal projects into the room the man he has just caught unawares, covering the fence with outrageous graffiti. The man sits down, gets his breath back and helps himself to a glass of essence of fennel. Lalix comes rushing in, she's got up, she's put on a dressing-gown. As for the other passengers on the barge, they are sleeping soundly. They have always slept soundly since they have stopped, or almost stopped, dreaming.

Lalix, having rushed in, sees Cidrolin helping himself to a glass of essence of fennel. Labal has sat down, he looks very serious and says nothing.

Lalix doesn't know what question to ask.

Cidrolin drinks his glass of essence of fennel; he says to the concierge:

'I hope you didn't catch cold while you were waiting for me. You're entitled to a glass of essence of fennel.'

He says to Lalix, with a feeble smile:

'Monsieur is a splendid sleuth.'

Lalix sits down.

'What I'm wondering,' says Labal, 'is what you're going to do now. I'm well aware that it's none of my business, but, since I am largely responsible for the recent events, you will understand why I can ask myself such a question, and even ask you the same question.'

As Cidrolin doesn't answer, Labal continued:

'After all, you could carry on as before.'

He adds:

'Don't worry, I won't be watching. Now that my mission is accomplished I'm going to resign my concierge's job and leave the district for new adventures.'

He turns to Lalix and concludes:

'I don't wish Monsieur Cidrolin any harm, but after yesterday's little incident it was only natural that I should have wanted to get my complete and utter innocence established. Monsieur Cidrolin can further consider himself lucky that I didn't liquidate him for having taken the mickey out of everyone and myself the way he did. Thank you for the essence of fennel, I never touch it. Have I your permission to beat it?'

'You're even invited to,' says Lalix.

He goes out, carefully shutting the cabin door behind him.

'I'm going back to bed,' says Lalix.

'That's right,' says Cidrolin. 'Have a good night-end.'

Lalix goes out, carefully shutting the cabin door behind her. When, at break of day, the Duke comes in to see whether, by any chance, breakfast might not be under way, he finds Cidrolin sitting dozing in front of his glass.

'Hallo there!' called the Duke. 'Already up or not in bed yet? Is the fiancée still asleep? Is there still some andouillette in the frigidaire? Looks as if it's going to rain.'

Empoigne appears.

'You go and get the breakfast,' the Duke says to him. 'I'm starving.'

'What about the horses, Monsieur the Duke?'

'Oh yes, of course.'

Empoigne goes to see to the horses. The Duke sits down opposite Cidrolin.

'I'll have to wait till the fiancée gets up, then. What am I going to drink until then? All the same, not essence of fennel. At this hour. All the more so as it isn't really up to much, even though it *is* White Horse. It can't touch the stuff I make according to the recipe of my alchemist, Timoleo Timolei. There's something called horse-fennel, too, did you know? I wonder whether Timoleo Timolei . . . I ought to have asked him in the old days . . . formerly . . . heretofore . . .'

He yawned.

' 'Sdeath, Cid, you're not very chatty this morning!'

'There's something I have to tell vous.'

'Don't we call each other tu any more?'

'. . . to tell toi.'

'I'm listening.'

'The concierge opposite has collared the chap who was maculating the fence.'

'The real one?'

'The real one.'

The Duke laughed very loud and long before saying:

'So he nabbed you?'

'Well, yes.'

'What does it matter?'

'It might well.'

'All the same, he can't stop you painting and repainting if you feel like it.'

'It isn't him I'm worrying about.'

'She isn't going to get up at all this morning, then,' says the Duke.

'I don't know,' says Cidrolin.

'If that's the way it is,' says the Duke, 'I'll go and exercise the horses, and we'll have breakfast in town. At the Crooked Siren, for instance. You can tell the skirts to come and meet us there.'

'Without fail,' says Cidrolin.

The Duke went out, absent-mindedly banging the cabin door behind him.

XX

Cidrolin tidied the cabin up a bit and then went out on deck. The Countess and Phélise turned up in the hope of consuming some andouillette; in accordance with the Duke's instructions they were invited to wend their way to the Crooked Siren, and therefore obeyed. They had already been gone sixteen minutes when Lalix appeared. She had her suitcase in her hand.

'Adieu,' she said.

She put her suitcase down and held out her hand to Cidrolin.

The latter must have concluded from this that she was leaving, and then felt the need to put this discovery into words, for he said:

'Are you leaving?'

'As you see.'

'Have you any real reason for leaving?'

'I don't like nuts.'

'To whom are you referring?'

'I'd got fond of you. I thought you were being persecuted.'

She started to cry.

'There, there,' said Cidrolin. 'Are you angry with me?'

'Yesh,' she answered, sniffing, 'You were making a fool of me.'

'I wasn't making a fool of anybody. I'd simply found myself an occupation. Something to do in life, no more.'

'Must be bonkers to do such things.'

'It was much better than going to the bistro.'

'And then you drink too much.'

'Am I ever drunk?'

'You must be soused with essence of fennel when you go and scrawl up all that stuff. Insulting yourself! Why not show your behind, while you're about it?'

'That's not at all my style,' said Cidrolin. 'And then, I think you're confusing things there.'

'What am I confusing with what? You aren't going to start quibbling, are you?'

She started crying again.

'There, there,' said Cidrolin. 'I shall be very unhappy if I've made you sad.'

'A fine time to say that.'

She dabbed at the humidity running down her cheeks, and then blew her nose energetically.

'I'm off,' she added.

She picked up her suitcase.

'What are you going to do?' asked Cidrolin. 'Go back and see Monsieur Albert? look for work? go home?'

'What's it got to do with you, seeing I'm going out of your life?'

What she'd just said made her sob so much that she had to put her suitcase down again.

'Since it makes you cry so much,' said Cidrolin, 'don't go out of it.'

'If that's all you can find to say to me . . .'

She choked back her sobs, picked up her suitcase again, said adieu, and went off with a decided step. Cidrolin watched her walk up the bank and push open the gate in the fence. She disappeared.

At the bistro on the corner by the bridge she stopped and had a coffee. On the terrace, various couples were pretending they were leeches and palpating each other before they went to work. This spectacle incited Lalix to let fall a few more tears, which she discreetly wipes away. Inside the café some alchemists are preparing their trebles, with punches and pencils. Amongst them was the administrator of justice. Lalix hurriedly drank her coffee and left.

At the station where she had met Monsieur Albert she put her suitcase in the left luggage office and went and had another coffee to consider, be it ever so little, her present situation. She was sitting on the terrace of a brasserie, a big one with lots of customers and lots of waiters and even a few head waiters. On the pavement lots of passers-by were passing by; on the road lots of cars were also passing by. There was a paper seller who was shouting very loudly, and there was a lady-alchemist who was ringing a little bell to try and sell some lottery tickets.

Lalix stayed there, stupefied, dazed, for a good hour, that's to say about an hour and four minutes; then suddenly, she's paying, taking a bus, getting out, and going into the Bar Biture, a bar that takes pains to look as if it looks like every other bar. She sits down. The room is empty: neither customers nor boss. An open trap-door seems to signify that the latter is busy in his cellar, but doing what? Taking advantage of her solitude, Lalix cries quietly.

Suddenly a black and white checked cloth cap appears at floor level, it's semi-short, semi-long. Lalix dabs at her peepers and her conk with an already totally moist handkerchief, while the concisely above-described headgear slowly rises above ground. A head follows, then the rest, from the shoulders down to the sole of the slippers, slippers which are semi-short, semi-long, in black and white checked cloth. When the whole ensemble has shut the trap door, it pivots thirty-seven degrees, which is responsible for its then noticing a young thing who is vaguely looking in a mirror at the reflection of a reproduction of the Dying Hercules by Samuel Finley Breese Morse.

'What d'you want?' asks the boss. 'We don't serve unaccompanied ladies here. What d'you think we are?'

'I'm waiting for Monsieur Albert,' replies Lalix in a submissive voice.

[214]

'Albert, what Monsieur Albert? You think I know all my customers by name?'

He glances around him in a circular direction to indicate the vastitude of the question, a vastitude which is to be inferred from the established fact of the ambient desert. Lalix insists:

'You know very well who I mean. Monsieur Albert, you know, Monsieur Albert. I don't mean him any harm. I've got to talk to him. I'm going to wait for him.'

Onésiphore raises his cap a bit and scratches his sinciput so energetically that his maxillaries finally start moving and, through their gap, allow the following words to pass:

'Well, Monsieur Albert, if that's the one you're looking for, he's in the nick.'

'Snot true!'

'Do I look like a liar?'

He puts his headgear back on his head with a threatening air.

'Just my luck,' murmurs Lalix.

'If that's what you're looking for, you'll be able to find hundreds and thousands of Monsieur Alberts.'

'I trusted him.'

She's just about to start crying once again. Onésiphore forestalls her.

'Blow,' says he, 'blow.' You won't see him again for a long, long time, your Monsieur Albert. Not for a long time. So go on, blow . . . blow . . .'

With a tragic air, Lalix gets up and goes out, shutting the door carefully behind her while the boss collapses in tears behind his counter.

Lalix goes on her way, a way which isn't a way, since it doesn't lead anywhere, we're not in a forest, though, but Lalix is just walking blindly, any minute now she'll be gone with the wind, because there *is* some wind, we're in November, it's even raining, and Lalix goes on her way, in the rain, but in the end it's cats and dogsing a bit too much, so Lalix shelters under a porch and drops of water – rain, or tears – trickle down her face.

'Well well,' says the Countess, 'you've certainly got soused.'

'Baa, baa,' says Phélise.

Lalix looks at them in a daze.

'Summing wrong?' says the Countess. 'You're looking at us as if you've just been sold some beans that won't cook. Hey! Hey! do you recognise us?'

'Good morning, Madame,' says Lalix, somewhat neutrally.

'Hallo,' says the Countess.

'Baa, baa,' says Phélise.

'We decided to shelter,' says the Countess. 'The moment it lets up a bit we'll make a dash for the car, it's over there (gesture) on the corner. Want to come with us? We're meeting Jojo and Pousspousse for lunch. Want to have lunch with us? We're going to a *super*-luxury place, it doesn't want just three stars to describe it, it'd need a whole constellation, in other words, we aren't likely to turn our noses up at the nosh, znt that right, Phélise?'

'Baa, baa,' replies Phélise, showing the top of a slobbery tongue.

'Tisn't raining so hard, now,' says the Countess. 'Shall we go?'

'No thank you, Madame,' murmurs Lalix.

'Oh, come on, don't make such a fuss.'

She lugs Lalix along with her and Phélise trots behind.

'But if you stay and have lunch with us, who's going to get him his grub?' asks the Duke, when they've all met at the super-luxury constellation.

'I'm never going to get it for him again,' says Lalix. 'Not me. Never again. I'm going. It's all over between us.'

She starts sobbing in a lamentable fashion.

'Ah no, no and no!' protests the Duke, 'you're not going to spoil our luncheon for us!'

'Tell us what's going on,' murmured Pouscaillou bravely.

'I don't like loonies,' said Lalix through her tears.

'To whom are you referring?' asked the Duke.

'Cidrolin,' replied Lalix, snivelling. 'He's the one that . . .'

'We know, we know,' said the Duke with some irritation. 'And then what?'

'It isn't normal,' said Lalix.

This answer made the Duke smile, and he continued the dialogue in these terms:

'Have you got a soft spot for him?'

'I did have.'

'You love him, huh.'

'Yesh, I did love him.'

'And was that normal?'

Lalix was surprised, and said nothing.

The Duke continued:

'And I'm willing to bet you still love him.'

Lalix didn't answer.

'Isn't that so?'

'Yes.'

'What about that, then, is that normal?'

Lalix didn't rejoin.

'You see,' said the Duke. 'Nothing's normal.'

He added:

'Come on, now! You'll go back to your Cidrolin again after luncheon. Promise?'

Lalix murmured:

'Yesh.'

The Duke turned to the Countess and said:

'You see. It isn't any more difficult than that.'

He clapped his hands and said in a loud voice:

'And we'll start with some andouille, waiter, after which we'll have some andouillette, waiter, and we'll finish with douillettes. That's what you call a properly composed meal. And a fig for your caviar, and other muscovitamins! And champagne!'

They regaled themselves, therefore, with andouille, andouillettes and douillettes, but Lalix couldn't wait to get back to the barge. After the coffee she discreetly withdrew, while the Duke was standing himself a ninth bottle of champagne.

The two horses were tied up outside, to a no-parking sign. Various passers-by who noticed them were momentarily transformed into sightseers, thereafter resuming their own character. A small group of the constabulary were having a vague discussion. The whole was not of sufficient dimensions to constitute a crowd. Lalix didn't hang around, for she hardly knew Sthenes and Stef. Having stood herself a taxi she had herself dropped at the corner caff to buy cigarettes. A few couples there were conscientiously pretending to be leeches while some alchemists were waiting for a little apparatus to inform them of the merits of their distillations.

Lalix left the cigarette counter and started walking along the embankment-boulevard and from a distance noticed a large crowd. As she got nearer she could make out police buses and fire engines.

'Hell,' said she, under her breath. 'Now what can have happened?'

'A block of flats they were building has collapsed,' replied a passer-by who was coming from the opposite direction. 'There was nobody living in it, naturally, as it was still being built. There was only the concierge. They're pulling him out of the debris. Are you interested in what I'm saying?'

'Moderately,' replied Lalix.

'You're very hard to please,' retorted the passer-by, and he goes on his way, nauseated.

The boulevard is closed.

'I live there,' says Lalix. 'On the barge.'

They let her through.

She looks for Cidrolin. There's no Cidrolin on the barge. She sits down in the cabin, lights a cigarette, spreads out the green baize cloth and starts a game of patience. As for Cidrolin, he's on the embankment amongst the sightseers. Other people are working: they're clearing the road, they're trying to get the concierge out from the debris, they're filming it for the news and the telly. As it's beginning to get dark some soldiers bring up some searchlights. It's all really fabulous, but the searchlights aren't going to be necessary. They finally extract something from beneath the debris, La Balance's corpse in a very bad state. They cause it to disappear as discreetly as they do rapidly. The road is cleared, the cars start going by again, the sightseers go and look elsewhere, the passers-by once more pass by: but there aren't many of them, they're nocturnal now. And the constabulary, the firemen and the soldiers disappear into the night.

Cidrolin, by the gate in the fence, sees all this newsinbrief activity gradually fading away. Turning round he noticed the lights were on on board the barge.

'Goodness,' he said, under his breath, 'can my guests be back?'

No passer-by answered him.

He went down the bank, crossed the gang-plank and went into the cabin. Lalix stubbed out her fag-end in an already full ashtray and smiled at him.

'Is it coming out, this game?' asked Cidrolin, sitting down opposite her.

Lalix didn't answer; she turned up a new card, then another, and suddenly she tapped her forehead with the tips of her fingers and exclaimed:

'My suitcase! I've left my suitcase in the cloakroom!'

'I'll go and get it for you. Which station?'

'Don't bother, I'll go tomorrow.'

'Just as you like.'

After a little silence, Lalix went on:

'There *have* been some goings-on, while I've been away.'

[219]

'Oh, not so very many. The block opposite fell on the concierge's head.'

'And what happened to Judex?'

'He's dead.'

'And you? Your painting?'

'I'm out of work.'

'Even so, there *have* been some goings-on while I've been away.'

After a little silence, Cidrolin went on:

'Poor chap.'

'Who?'

'The concierge.'

'Why poor chap? A spiteful bugger and a murderer.'

'He's still dead.'

'Obviously there's nothing to laugh about, but we'll get on quite all right without him. It wasn't any of our doing.'

She took a cigarette and lit it. She added:

'Unless . . .'

After a little silence she went on:

'It couldn't have been so terribly badly built, that block. It can't have collapsed all by itself. Can it?'

After a little silence, Cidrolin answered:

'I'm a painter, I'm not an architect.'

He smiled gravely, and concluded:

'No, really: it wasn't any of our doing.'

Lalix stubbed out the cigarette she'd only just begun, and said:

'I'll go and get the dinner.'

'There's still some andouillette in the frigidaire,' said Cidrolin, 'but I wasn't feeling strong enough to go and buy bread. Would you like me to go now?'

'Not worth it. We'll do without.'

Lalix gets up and puts the cards and cloth away; when she's at the door, Cidrolin suggests:

[220]

'After dinner, shall we go to the movies?'

When they came back they found the horses on the deck of the barge and their guests in the cabin. Cidrolin goes to see what's happening to them.

'There's been a slight hitch,' exclaimed the Duke, with gusto. 'The horse-box got atomised in the holocaust! An enormous parpen fell on it. You couldn't put Sthenes and Stef up in the hold, could you?'

'We could arrange that,' said Cidrolin.

'That's not the end of it, though,' continued the Duke, with equal gusto, 'A few quarry-stones have also wrecked my car: you could even call it completely and totally unusable. And as Ma Empoigne's car broke down this afternoon, I'm just wondering how we're going to get back home.'

'Is that what you were going to do?' asked Cidrolin.

'As for them,' added the Duke, ignoring this question, 'they've smashed up their bike.'

'A motorised tandem,' said the Abbé Riphinte.

Counting carefully, Cidrolin perceived that from four, his guests had become six.

'An excellent vehicle,' said Monseigneur Biroton.

'They don't come any better,' said the Abbé Riphinte.

'An Italian make,' said Monseigneur Biroton.

'We bought it at Trent,' said the Abbé Riphinte.

'Yes,' said the Duke. 'They're just back from the Council.'

'In which we upheld various theses on the monotheism of the prehistoric peoples,' said Monseigneur Biroton.

'Of which their wall paintings are obvious proof,' said the Abbé Riphinte.

'What about your fiancée?' the Duke asked Cidrolin, interrupting the ecclesiastics. 'Isn't she here?'

'Oh yes,' said Cidrolin. 'She was tired. She's gone to bed.'

'I understand,' said the Duke. 'Emotion.'

[221]

'That's it,' said Cidrolin, and then hastened to add: 'I'll go and see to your animals.'

And he went out.

Having cleared the opening to the hold, he took up the position of the standing thinker and held it for so long that he finally heard a voice saying to him:

'All you have to do is find a plank that's wide enough, then we can slide down.'

Cidrolin turned round; the two horses were looking at him, but nobody else.

'What about getting up again?' he asked. 'How'll you manage?'

'Ah, for that you'll need a block and pulley and a belly-band,' replied Sthenes. 'And a certain amount of force, whose unit of measure will ever after bear my name, which in this respect will be a thousand times superior to that of Newton.'

'Once you're inside, you've got a good chance of staying there.'

'You'll manage. For the moment we have no wish to spend the night out of doors, especially if it starts raining. Have we, Stef?'

As Cidrolin didn't move, Sthenes continued in these terms:

'It's getting late. If you really look you're sure to find one, a plank that's wide enough. The one you use for a gangway, for instance.'

Cidrolin did as Sthenes told him.

And when the horses were under cover, he went to bed.

XXI

When Cidrolin went out on deck the next morning, he saw the Duke cutting the mooring ropes with a pair of kitchen scissors, while Empoigne and the ecclesiastics, with the aid of poles, were with some difficulty pushing the barge away from the bank.

'May one ask what you're doing?' said Cidrolin politely.

'I'm going home,' said the Duke.

As Cidrolin was getting ready to ask a few supplementary questions the Duke said to him, with authority:

'We'll talk about it later on.'

Cidrolin, scratching his head, went to the galley where he found Lalix grilling some andouillettes.

'Well,' said she, 'are we going for a trip?'

'Seems so.'

They said no more to each other. Cidrolin, next, went into the cabin. There he found several ladies or young ladies silently waiting for breakfast. Going back on deck he perceived that his guests hadn't stopped multiplying. The Duke was giving orders, addressing the newcomers. The last cable had been severed and the barge was moving away from the bank. Cidrolin turned round and went once more to the galley. The others took no notice of him. He took Lalix by the arm and led her out on deck.

The barge was gently moving upstream. The Duke was at the helm and looked as if he was taking great pleasure in this occupation. He saw Cidrolin and Lalix getting into the dinghy and letting it go; they were soon back at the bank and had disappeared.

That was when it started to rain. It rained for days and days.

There was so much fog that it was impossible to tell whether the barge was moving forwards, backwards or stopping still. It finally ran aground on the summit of a keep. The passengers stepped ashore on it, Sthenes and Stef not without some difficulty; poor things, they were extremely thin and extremely tired. The water had receded to its usual beds and receptacles and the sun was already high in the horizon when the Duke woke up the next morning. He went over to the battlements to consider, be it ever so little, the historical situation. A layer of mud still covered the earth, but he could already see, blossoming here and there, some little blue flowers.

AFTERWORD

When asked which of his works was his favorite, Raymond Queneau told Bettina Knapp: *"The Blue Flowers or The Sunday of Life. I don't really know why."* Queneau's readers may not know why *The Blue Flowers* is also one of their favorites. One reason for the particular pleasure derived from the novel is Queneau's humorous play with language and history. Another is the multiplicity of readings the text makes possible, readings which evoke questions about history and the unconscious, origins and ends, time and space, the subject and language, literary codes and their decoding. Before looking more closely at some of the elements that make this novel special, the context of the novel's appearance should be mentioned.

Published in France in 1965 by Gallimard, the book was admirably translated two years later by Barbara Wright. The novel did not create the brouhaha that Queneau's deliberately popular *Zazie in the Metro* did. Robbe-Grillet, Michel Butor and other New Novelists dominated the literary scene in 1965. And Queneau, who was associated with the surrealists more closely than with any other literary movement, was given scant attention by critics who nevertheless delighted in his fictional game-play and in the "jocoserious" tone of his work. Yet neither play nor tone are gratuitous, for both serve to liberate readers from certain narrow perspectives in which they tend to view Art—as a serious communication in which the enlightened writer dispenses his superior wisdom to passive receptors according to sacrosanct conventions. Queneau, on the contrary, and with the reader's participation, undermines those conventions while revealing what they are. The violation of the traditional identification of the reader with a believable character in the fiction is an example. Queneau uses a number of devices to accomplish this. In *The Blue Flowers* he introduces talking horses, taking the notion of the incredible character a step beyond the presence of Laverdure, the parrot in *Zazie*. This draws attention to the fact that a novel is essentially an imaginative, verbal construct; the author can attribute the function of a character to whomever or whatever he chooses to call one. The human protagonists are equally unconventional. Neither their biography nor their psychology is of great importance in the text, as Queneau's own summary of the novel in *French Novelists Speak Out* reveals:

> In *The Blue Flowers*, I focus on a person who goes back in time—and one who merges from some past era. In other words, modern and ancient. My historical character lived in the thirteenth century and reappears every one hundred and seventy-five years until he meets the other protagonist and becomes his contemporary. There is an old Chinese saying in this connection: "I dream that I am a butterfly and pray there is a butterfly dreaming he is me." The same can be said of the characters in my novel—those who live in the past dream of those who live in the modern era—and those who live in the modern era dream of those who live in the past.

Because each protagonist dreams the actions of the other, we wonder whether they are one character or two. Are they alter egos? Are they two aspects of the same psyche? One critic proposes a Freudian model: he identifies The Duke of Auge, the historical character, with the ego while associating Cidrolin, the modern one, with the id. But the stories of Auge and Cidrolin can also be interpreted according to other systems of oppositions: the conscious and the unconscious, or time and space, for example. Auge, although a fictional character, appears in the context of Queneau's narrative of "historical" moments. Situated in the past,

Auge dreams of the future even as he reappears every one hundred and seventy-five years. Auge does not evolve in the seven hundred years of his odyssey, but his historical situation and his language do. In that sense, Auge can be seen to represent time. The Cidrolin narrative, on the other hand, emphasizes his place of residence, a stationary barge called L'Arche. Indications of distance and direction, points of departure and destination evoke spatial associations with the Cidrolin narrative line. This is reinforced by the absence of temporal progression. Time is even reversed as Cidrolin's situation stagnates. At the beginning of the novel, Cidrolin explains that it is a fine autumn day (p. 29); towards the end of the novel autumn is said to be approaching (p. 134). Just as in dreams, then, the events in this spatial narrative are temporally indeterminate.

Queneau also situates dreams in the context of the philosophical tradition of dream or illusion and reality. The epigraph he chose for the novel, "He heard a dream for a dream," is taken from Plato's *Theatetus*. In it the two main sources of human error are defined: the relativity of knowledge, which depends on the background and point of view of the knower, and dream or illusion, which may be experienced as real. But what is reality in a novel? In Queneau's narrative that question is even more striking since each character is the dream of the other. Perhaps we are to understand that dreams are the true reality? Queneau's reference to the Chinese adage, "I dream that I am a butterfly and pray there is a butterfly dreaming he is me," when read in connection with *The Blue Flowers,* suggests that the dreamer captures an essential part of his own identity in his dream. The butterfly represents the dreamer to himself. It reveals his being and his desires with a freedom that is not possible in waking life where repressions and others' expectations hold us in their web.

The variety of interpretations the text makes possible is not only a function of the identity of the protagonists and the themes of the novel; it is also a function of its form. Composed of two narrative lines, it is the relationship between the lines that captivates us. Initially distant, the historical line eventually meets the spatial or modern one as Auge enters the twentieth century. The novel concludes with a timeless myth. Auge and his entourage arrive, board Cidrolin's Ark, and depart through the flooding rains to a new Mt. Ararat, a shore abloom with blue flowers.

The phrase "blue flowers" which gives the novel its title is a ready-made expression in French. When attributed to a person, it can suggest outdated notions regarding love, manners, or ideals, whether they be ideals or purity or decorum. Or the noun can refer to a specific moment, when knighthood was in flower, when the ideals of chivalry were in effect. This gives a double meaning to Auge's exclamation: "Here, the mud is made from our flowers," to which Demosthenes, Auge's talking horse, adds: ". . . our blue flowers, I know" (p. 8). Auge gives vent to his nostalgia for less degraded times. His desire for purity is ultimately fulfilled by a transformation of the Noah myth. At the end of the novel the blue flowers reemerge from beneath the deluge; the flowers are now a symbol of hope and regeneration. The title also evokes a number of associated meanings. Flowers are the ancient figure for rhetoric, suggesting the bouquet of tropes, even the decorative use of "flowery" prose—to which Auge is occasionally given. As for the adjective, "blue," it is used in connection with literature to indicate tall tales or popular literature, elements of which are found in *The Blue Flowers*. Finally the title calls to mind specific texts, such as Novalis's, *Heinrich von Ofterdingen*. The hero of Novalis's fiction seeks the blue flower of poetry. Reading Queneau's work in the light of the German romantic text allows us to grasp the evolution of the novel as a genre.

It should be added that while Queneau's title has a number of connotations, the expression "blue flowers" is still a ready-made one in French. It is not original with Queneau and this may be seen as revealing his attitude toward literary language: that literature is not composed of a special language but is merely one of the "uses" to which ordinary language can be put. The title engages us to examine the linguistic codes that each of us adapts for our own unique purpose.

The Blue Flowers invites us to read it as a model novel. By model I do not just mean that it is worthy of imitation or that it is representative of the genre, but that it makes us think about how novels are composed and how they work. It is not only the novel itself that suggests such a reading, but also the introduction to Queneau's *Une Histoire modèle*—which might be translated as *A Model (Hi)story*—for it plays with the double meaning of the word in French: history and story. Begun during the Nazi occupation of France and completed in 1966, Queneau claims he published this essay on history using a mathematical model to shed light on *The Blue Flowers*. He does not explain, however, how his "historical" treatise illuminates his fiction. Certainly we can see the connection with the historical component of his fiction, but that is not all. In *A Model (Hi)story,* Queneau explains the common origin of all narrative: man's misfortune. Historical and fictional narratives are said to share not only a common source but a similar structure; originating in a disequilibrium, a tension that provokes the narrative, they end when a new equilibrium is attained, for as Queneau asserts, happiness has no history. What Queneau describes, then, is the minimal plot of any story. And his historical essay tells us how narratives originate, how they are constructed, and what pleasure they procure for us. Reading about the misfortune of others provides us a momentary respite from our history, from the limitations and contingencies of our lives, our time, our space. That is especially true when the author's style is amusing. Queneau's puns, his play with different registers of language from the most noble to slang, his surprising associations

[231]

engage the reader to play as well and to enjoy the novel at a number of different levels. In these and other ways, we can read *The Blue Flowers* as an extraordinarily rich model of narrative.

Vivian Kogan
Dartmouth College
Hanover, NH

New Directions Paperbooks—A Partial Listing

For complete listing request complete catalog from
New Directions, 80 Eighth Avenue, New York 10011   † Bilingual